The Frisco Falcon

Jack Murray

The Frisco Falcon

THE FOURTH KIT ASTON MYSTERY

Jack Murray

Jack Murray

Books by Jack Murray

Kit Aston Series
The Affair of the Christmas Card Killer
The Chess Board Murders
The Phantom
The Frisco Falcon
The Medium Murders
The Bluebeard Club
The Tangier Tajine
The Empire Theatre Murders
The French Diplomat Affair (novella)
Haymaker's Last Fight (novelette)

Agatha Aston Series
Black-Eyed Nick
The Witchfinder General Murders
The Christmas Murder Mystery

DI Jellicoe Series
A Time to Kill
The Bus Stop
Trio
Dolce Vita Murders

Danny Shaw / Manfred Brehme WW2 Series
The Shadow of War
Crusader
El Alamein

The Frisco Falcon

ISBN: 9798510651232
Imprint: Independently published

Jack Murray

For Monica, Lavinia, Anne and our angel baby, Edward

The Frisco Falcon

Prologue

Constantinople, June 1920

'By Gad, sir, that is a magnificent weapon. No, don't tell me. I must have my fun, sir. Let me guess. It looks like a crossbow.'

It was a harpoon gun.

It was also pointed at the man's rather large chest.

'Yes, that must be it. A cross bow. Invented in China, I believe but used if I'm not mistaken, in the crusades.'

As he said this, the fat man paused for a moment and looked at the dark-skinned features of the sailor in front of him. Mentioning the crusades was, in hindsight, unwise. The fat man smiled nervously hoping that his slip up had gone unnoticed. He was a man approaching his seventies from the angle of a life lived fully, immoderately, and without regret. Well, for the most part anyway. Yes, a full life accompanied, invariably, by an even fuller stomach.

He had long since given up caring about his weight. At an early age he knew his destiny was not that of the sportsman. Fine food and fine wine were his sports and he played them with unmatched skill and no little enthusiasm. His florid

1

features and the kittenish purr of his voice bespoke a man who had known the good things the world can offer. The hard glint in his grey eyes suggested something else. He stepped back from the point of the harpoon. This was not a big step, however, as he was backed into the wooden cabin wall.

His small eyes narrowed, swollen into mere slits by his pink puffy cheeks. He was smiling. 'You are a close-mouthed man, sir. I see that. Good. I distrust men who enjoy their own eloquence more than the rest of the world. By Gad, sir, I must confess I like you. You are a man. I can see that.'

The fat man was, unusually, speaking the truth. The person holding the harpoon gun was, unquestionably, a man. More than that, he was an angry man. This was an unwelcome combination in the circumstances.

'Yes, you are a man, but I wonder if you are someone open to business opportunities?' The fat man chuckled but the attempt at humour was undermined somewhat by the beads of sweat queuing up along his forehead to drip down over his eyes.

Was there a change in the inscrutable features of the man before him? Just a moment of doubt? A relaxation of his grip on the harpoon gun? The shadow across his face made it difficult to decide. The only clue to the man's intentions was the hatred in his eyes.

The two men looked at one another. Outside it was night; a distant ship's horn blew. It was a grand sound that echoed through the darkness. A tug responded. A pathetic toot by comparison. The boat rocked very gently. The waters of the Bosphorus lapped lazily against the side. It was almost hypnotic. The sound. The rocking. Lights from the shore filtered through the porthole lighting one side of the fat man's *face. It was a small cabin, barely room for the two men. The door behind the man with the harpoon swung to and fro, swishing persistently at the rocking of the boat*

The fat man attempted an ameliorating smile. He continued chatting to the other man.

'*I like a man who is firm sir, yes I do. I like firmness of purpose matched by minimalism of expression. This is the very definition of character, sir, and I can see you are just such a man. Yes, by Gad you are. Now, why don't you lower that weapon, and let me tell you what I have in mind? It's an astonishing story but more than that, it has a promise of a rather happy ending for any man with a strong sense of business, who can judge other men. A man, such as yourself, in other words. You have, for too long, been undervalued by a succession of employers. Employers? No, never, sir. These men were users. For years they have exploited your good nature.*'

The man facing him touched the scar that ran down half his face. It had been gained in a knife fight. He had forgotten which one. It was one of many scars, both physical and mental. The touching of the scar was momentary. His hand returned to the trigger. It did not go unnoticed by the fat man, however.

'*Yes, a battle scar, no doubt where, once again you had to risk your very life in pursuit of another man's dream; I say "enough". The time has come for you to make a stand and demand recompense for your true worth. Gad sir, this is your lucky night. Your time has come. Believe me,*' *said the fat man in a deliberate voice, the smile fading dangerously from his face,* '*your time has come at last.*'

Jack Murray

1

Troon Golf Club, June 1920

The golf ball rolled slowly towards the hole, wiped its feet at the entrance, then toppled forward like a drunk trying to pick a coin off the bar floor. There was no celebratory cheer despite the fact it was a birdie. Instead, the golfer walked forward briskly and whisked the ball from the hole. Another golfer stepped up and addressed his ball.

The putter drew back slowly and then after a short pause, he released the head. It clipped against the ball, propelling it forward. It rocketed past the hole like a cannonball.

'Blast,' said the man. Then he stood erect, attempted a smile and walked forward, hand outstretched.

'Well done, Gloria. Two up. I didn't make use of the shots you were giving me here.'

Gloria Mansfield nodded curtly. She turned and walked over to her caddy, handing him the putter.

'Well done, miss,' said Hamish Anderson with a grin wider than the Irish Sea. He would earn a little extra reward thanks to his mistress's victory. He liked caddying for Miss Mansfield. She was generous with her tips when she won, and she usually won. The two golfers left the green quickly, followed by their caddies. There was a smell of salt in the air. And defeat. Humiliating, overwhelming defeat. By a woman, no less. But what a woman!

The wind was at their backs, coming off the sea. Soon it would be damn near unplayable. Miss Mansfield looked up at the sky and shivered involuntarily. She headed directly to the changing room.

*

Inside the clubhouse, Aldric 'Spunky' Stevens watched all that had taken place through a military telescope he had neglected to hand back when he returned from France.

'Yes, old chap, she certainly has good form,' said Spunky, nodding sagely.

'She's single figures now,' said Reggie Pilbream, a young man of twenty-four, and that was probably just his IQ. He was a slightly built, pallid boy with short dark hair and a laugh that often ended in an unfortunate snort, the impact of which he was wholly oblivious to, but not the legion of women who had, sadly, tended to avoid romantic entanglement with him.

'I don't doubt it,' replied Spunky admiringly, his telescope travelling down the well-made body of the young woman. By no means slender, she was unquestionably a sporty young lady, whose outline matched her handicap of eight.

'I mean how on earth will I ever get a look in?' cried Reggie. 'A fella off twenty-six shouldn't really have any chance when the love of his life plays off seven or eight. She's hot stuff.'

'Certainly is,' agreed Spunky, puffing on his pipe contentedly, eyes glued to the approaching vision. At nineteen, Gloria Mansfield was attracting many admiring glances from the men at the club. This was less to do with her ability to draw a mashie onto the centre of the fairway in the midst of a stiff nor 'wester than the presence of big blue eyes, surrounded by bubbling blonde curls and a healthy bank balance.

'I say, Spunky, dash it all, we're talking about the lady who's stolen my heart. She's not some sort of...'

'Understood old chap, but I think you need to open your mind to the rather singular reality that the young lady who has, as you say, stolen your heart, is rather easy on the eye. If you don't believe me then take a look at the pride of lions circling the prey on the practice green.'

'I see what you mean,' said Reggie, looking out the window. He collapsed to the seat, and drained Spunky's gin and tonic before his face took on a melancholic frown that would have been tragic had it not been so funny, at least to Spunky's one good eye.

'What's a chap to do?' he asked plaintively.

'It's the age-old question, from Socrates down to...'

'Wasn't Socrates a bit..?'

'Well yes, a bit, but it doesn't mean he didn't put his noggin to the mystery of goddesses or some such topic. Anyway, give me the skinny on this filly's form.'

Reggie looked up. He was a little put out at the somewhat frivolous attitude of his friend. He was, also, too miserable to give his old friend a piece of his mind which, he would have been honest enough to admit, was not of the first rank.

'Gloria Mansfield, the angel, is from the Berkshire Mansfields. I think she's a cousin of Tuppy Thomas. Anyway, this divine creature plays at Sunningdale apparently, and could be a starter in the British Women's Amateur soon. Plays off eight but she's been round Troon in scratch apparently. You see, Spunky, it's no use.'

'Well, I presume there's more to her than just golf,' pointed out Spunky patiently.

'Well, she's with that beastly boy. It's her young brother, George. Beelzebub if you ask me. Whiney little character.'

Spunky turned to Reggie. This was interesting. Brat kid brothers offered promising avenues of strategy for a man such as Spunky.

'Go on, tell me more about the little monster.'

'Of course, she dotes on him. Perhaps her only fault. Anyway, I've the little terror off scaring wild wolves and crocodiles while Gloria is playing golf.'

'Adventurous little sod then?'

'Rather,' said Reggie, emphasising both syllables.

Spunky sipped at his gin and tonic and gave the matter some thought. Despite the appearance of being a fatheaded ass, Spunky was, in fact, a highly valued member of British Intelligence. Such a role was not lightly bestowed nor was the Service likely to employ anyone with a deficiency of intellect unless, of course, it was accompanied by a soundness of breeding.

Owing to the loss of his eye during the War, Spunky's remit was mostly backroom where he applied a surprisingly mathematical mind to understanding economic pressure points in potential enemies of the empire. These days that seemed to encompass the rest of the map not coloured red.

A plan began to grow which, to Spunky's mind, was as devilish as it seemed logical. That it was, in all likelihood, devoid of any sign of good judgement was entirely another matter, and, in this case, someone else's problem. To be precise: Reggie's.

Spunky leaned forward causing Reggie to lean forward also. Taking another sip from his glass, he began to outline his plan. What he had in mind was strategically sound but posed some executional challenges.

'We need to imprison the boy, raise the alarm that he has been kidnapped and then, low and behold, Reginald St John Pilbream saves the day, rescues the boy and watches Miss Mansfield collapse gratefully into his strong arms.

Reggie glanced down dubiously at his arms. Never the most athletic of chaps, the prospect of a young woman, even one as attractive as Miss Mansfield, requiring physical support from him struck Reggie as overloaded, both figuratively and literally, with risk. It was with some trepidation that Reggie raised a finger to interject a couple of perfectly sound points around the plan being as illegal as it was immoral.

Anticipating such bellyaching, Spunky waved away any hint of complaint by reminding Reggie of what seemed to him the key fact to consider.

'You can't win the fair maiden's heart on the golf course. Not off twenty-six anyway. A flanking attack, mark my words, will carry the day.'

The soundness of this principle was unquestionable. Reggie's complaint was less about the underlying strategy than about the practicality of carrying it out. Realising that Spunky would not listen to sense, at least from him, Reggie tried his own flanking thrust.

'Shouldn't we wait until Kit arrives? He's a chap with a sound grasp of things. I'm sure he can think of something.'

Spunky shook his head and looked at his friend with patient affection.

'Reggie, old chap, when you look at Kit what, and follow my logic here, do you think a young woman might see?'

'Well,' acknowledged Reggie, a little uncomfortably, 'He's a good chap.'

'You miss my meaning. Let me elaborate. Kit is rich, correct?'

'Yes, he's certainly minted.'

'One has to admit, sadly I might add, he's not ever going to be mistaken for the back end of a horse.'

'No, I suppose he's rather good-looking too,' said Reggie glumly.

'Showed up well in the war.'

'A bally hero,' said Reggie almost on the point of tears.

Spunky realised he was pushing this idea way beyond the limits of Reggie's self-esteem. He quickly brought the train of thought to a juddering halt.

'Point is,' said Spunky with exaggerated patience, 'what does Kit know about trying to woo a young woman? My word they're falling over themselves to marry the damn fool.'

'You mean Gloria will fall in love with him, don't you?'

This was proving more of an uphill battle than Spunky had bargained for. There were times when his dear friend displayed all the imagination and daring of a hunting hedgehog. On the point of trying an alternative angle of attack he saw his friend's face register first surprise and then delight.

Entering the bar was a tall man, walking with a slight limp. The man smiled and waved over at Spunky and Reggie.

'Hello, Kit,' said Spunky with something less than his usual enthusiasm. 'We weren't expecting you until around dinner time.'

'Caught an earlier train,' explained Kit arriving at their table which instigated a round of vigorous handshaking.

'I say, Kit,' said Reggie, relief soldered into every syllable. 'You're just in time.'

'Oh, just in time for what?' asked Kit with a smile.

Kit sat silently staring at a faraway object through the window. Finally, he turned to Spunky and said, 'Yes, I can see how the plan might work.'

'You can?' exclaimed Spunky in genuine shock. This was close to a first for one of his schemes; they invariably crumbled under the onslaught of cold reality, which usually coincided with Kit's first exposure to them.

'Yes, certainly,' reassured Kit. 'Tell me, is that the little blighter over there?'

The other two men turned from facing Kit to look out the window. They saw a small boy of around ten or less, and a black Labrador. The boy was swinging a club and deliberately missing the ball. However, the poor dog, in expectation of chasing said ball, was tearing off in search of the phantom projectile before returning dejectedly to the source of his persecution, ever hopeful that the next strike would be the one.

'Charming little fellow as you can see,' said Spunky sourly.

'Indeed, and if I may ask, who are the other runners and riders in the field?'

'Sorry?' said Reggie completely confused.

'One other chap,' said Spunky taking over again. 'Name of Hugo Fowles. Bleater of the first rank. Fowles by name and__.'

Kit nodded. Their paths had crossed before. Spunky's assessment was surprisingly moderate. Reggie added a few other less-than-admirable qualities besides and soon a picture emerged of a man who not only didn't deserve to best Kit's friend in a duel of the heart but more pertinently, did not deserve the fair hand of the maiden who could drive a ball in excess of two hundred yards. Straight.

The Frisco Falcon

The rival soon arrived at the bar accompanied by Gloria Mansfield. He glanced swiftly over in Reggie's direction. A sly smile and a knowing wink. This was met with a round of "I Say's" *sotto voce*, at the table where the three men had been so happily discussing his downfall. The wink added another level of resolve to the participants in the plan.

Kit rose immediately to say hello to Fowles. Spunky and Reggie watched as the two men greeted one another like long lost buddies from a forgotten war. Kit's arrival gave Fowles the chance to fluff himself up even more. He introduced Kit to Miss Mansfield. Much to Reggie's chagrin, it was abundantly clear that the young lady was very taken with the new arrival. So much so that at one point, Reggie was beginning to doubt the good intentions of his friend.

However, a few moments later he saw Kit pointing out the window in the direction of the putting green. This resulted in a hasty exit by Gloria Mansfield. Clearly Kit had squealed on the young tyke forcing his big sister to rescue the unfortunate canine dupe.

Spunky and Reggie watched Kit chat amiably with Fowles before collecting a round of G&T's and returning to the table. A few moments later, Fowles left the bar with a steely steadfastness set firmly in his eye.

Reggie looked up expectantly at Kit, but the great man shook his head and checked to see if Fowles had gone. Outside the window an amusing scene was developing. Gloria had arrived and was giving young George a severe ticking off that stopped just short of physical violence. Kit raised his eyebrow at Spunky, who had turned to him with a grin.

Gloria Mansfield then departed the scene carrying the poor dog who was breathing rather heavily by this stage having run several miles on the fruitless quests staged by the vile boy. The Labrador in question was as grateful for the lift as the viewing gallery in the clubhouse was impressed by the ease with which the young woman picked him up and transported him away from psychological harm.

'Two hundred yards off the tee,' said Spunky by way of explanation to Kit.

*

An hour later the cry went up, or perhaps more of a gasp. Where is George? Gloria, already on her third G&T, had suddenly realised she hadn't seen the little beggar for a while. After sending a young caddie off in search of the evil sprite, she was persuaded to have a final snifter before dinner.

The young caddie returned empty handed. This cued a few humorous comments from Hugo Fowles designed to calm the now slightly concerned object of his affection with a "what a good-natured devil the child was" comment whilst, at the same time, emphasising his good-man-in-crisis credentials. This seemed to be working after a fashion.

A little more time passed before Reggie arrived, looking somewhat bedraggled.

'Good lord, Pilbream,' said Fowles, wanting to highlight his love rival's appearance, 'You look like you've been dragged through a hedge backwards, old chap.'

Reggie's next comment started the panic and, inadvertently, ended with the heart of the fair maiden finding its hero.

'I've been looking for George. I can't find him anywhere.'

Gloria Mansfield's eyes widened as fear set in. She looked at the jovial countenance of the frontrunner, now sipping his fifth G&T. Fowles lowered the glass from his lips as he realised the impression, he was giving lacked some, if not all, of the man-of-action credentials that were needed in the developing crisis. However, he had an ace up his sleeve.

'Leave this to me. I will organise a search party,' he announced decisively. He pointed to the young caddie and ordered him to round up the remaining staff. With that, he set his G&T down, looked Gloria Mansfield in the eye and declared, 'I will find him.'

Reggie looked on, powerless in the face of such authority mixed with resolve, and a slice of lemon. He trooped sadly over to Spunky and Kit. He sat down dejectedly and put his hands over his face.

'It's over. I shall have to stand aside,' said Reggie, nobly acknowledging the likely success of his rival.

'What happened?' asked Spunky, completely confused.

'I went to find the evil little beggar to do as you suggested, y'know, to hide him away from kidnappers by locking him up somewhere, fake a massive bout of fisticuffs before rescuing said imp and winning the hand of my one true love. But fate has dealt me a pair of twos.'

'I see,' said Spunky, who plainly didn't.

'Are we to assume you couldn't find the child, hence you were not able to play out the scene you planned?' interjected Kit.

'Right on the money, old bean.'

Kit stood up and suggested they join the search party. In fact, he specified they look somewhere in the area of the tractor shed.

'It's where I would put a monstrous little so and so if I was of a mind to get him out of the way for an hour or two. I suggest you make haste there, Reggie. We'll follow behind.'

Jack Murray

There comes a time in a man's life when the truth of it being darkest before dawn becomes, well, true. A light that had gone out in Reggie Pilbream's eyes suddenly flickered again. Hope once more grew in the mind and, more importantly, the heart of that stout archaeologist. Before you could say Nefertiti, Reggie was out of the bar, a steely glint in his eye, which did not go unnoticed by Miss Mansfield, who had drained the rest of her drink and was preparing to join the search party. She called out to him as he passed, but Reggie was a man not to be held back.

Spunky eyed Kit wryly as they ambled out of the bar towards the early evening air. It was a beautiful evening. The sky was a purple-blue and seagulls played above, singing the joy of summer, perhaps.

'You don't seem in such a rush; old chap. Makes me wonder if this plan hasn't been adapted slightly from its original design.'

Kit looked at Spunky and replied, 'I'm not rushing because I don't want the stump to chaff my leg too much.'

'I see,' said Spunky. And this time he did.

*

Spunky's plan worked brilliantly.

The boy was found, and the hero duly sat beside his betrothed. Gloria Mansfield was a picture of perfect contentment. She had found her Lancelot, her Tristan, her Harry Vardon. Her life was almost complete, although the British Women's Amateur title would certainly put a ribbon on it. She glanced down at George. Children would have to wait a little.

Spunky looked at Reggie, with a smile redolent in affection mixed with no little relief. The young man was in heaven as he sipped a G&T. He looked across at his former rival, Hugo Fowles. A stab of sympathy pierced his triumphant heart. He gazed upon a face that could not have looked any more dejected than if he'd had a young child beside him continually poking him in the chest which, coincidentally, he did.

Such was dinner that night in the clubhouse at Troon. Spunky turned to Kit, removed a cigar from his mouth and said in a low voice, 'Well, bloodhound, I have to hand it to you. Some people work by the ordnance survey map of life, but not you. No, you don't just see the map, you see the whole damn milky way. In short you are a marvel.'

'Really, Spunky, your plan was flawless.'

'No Kit, you, sir, are a marvel. It needed your genius to unlock its real treasures.'

The two men looked across at Hugo Fowles again. His face was set in a rictus grin as the pie-faced sprite had now taken to punching his right arm. The simple solution, of course, would have been to swipe the evil imp with his other hand. However, it was currently holding the hand of his fiancée, Gloria Mansfield.

'You put that bleater up to imprisoning the child, didn't you? How did you do it?'

'I merely adapted your brilliant idea,' replied Kit. 'It seemed to me right from the off that the match was a mistake. It occurred to me that Fowles was better-suited for the young lady.' They glanced across the table at Fowles. He had just received a little peck on the cheek from the future Mrs Fowles, which seemed to put him in better fettle. So much so in fact, he accidentally clipped young George on the back of the head. He apologised profusely of course, but his heart didn't seem in it.

Kit, meanwhile, continued, 'I suggested to Fowles that the child had an active imagination and a message that sent him to the barn on some pretext of foreign spies might unlock an opportunity to, so to speak, get the frog-faced excrescence out of his poor sister's hair for a while longer. This would give him time to seal her fate and then act the hero to find him, should he choose to bother.'

'I'm sure he wishes he'd left hell alone.'

Reggie leaned over to his two friends, 'A near miss, methinks.'

'A near miss indeed,' agreed Spunky.

'I think I shall exit stage left tomorrow morning bright and early in case anyone has a change of heart.'

'Where will you go?' asked Kit.

'Off to Malta actually,' responded Reggie, lighting a celebratory cigar. 'A bunch of us are looking for some lost treasures of the Knights of St John.'

'Well, I think that merits a toast,' said Spunky, for whom any occasion merited such a cheerful response.

The three friends clinked glasses to the success of this venture and perhaps of the episode just passed.

2

Turnberry Golf Club, June 1920

Ailsa Craig is a volcanic plug to an extinct volcano, midway between the north of Ireland and Scotland. It looks as though God, in a moment of absent-mindedness, started to build a mountain, lost interest and accidentally swept it away like crumbs off the table as he observed fresh scones arriving. From there it fell into the Irish Sea. It forms a spectacular view along the Ayrshire coastline and can be used by golfers to line up putts, as Spunky Stevens found himself doing on the first hole at Turnberry.

He turned to his caddy, Hamish Anderson, and said, 'I hope you're right.' He took aim, drew his putter back and moments later his ball nestled comfortably in the hole like a schoolboy in bed at midday during the summer holidays.

Spunky nodded to Hamish and gave a steely look of determination towards his opponent, Kit Aston. 'Hamish is an absolute wonder; I tell you Kit. You're not going to have it all your own way this year.'

Kit laughed agreeably, as memories of their golfing holiday in Scotland came back. Three days, three courses and three fairly comfortable victories against his old friend.

'I don't doubt it. You seemed off your game last year. Missing your Mademoiselle Mantoux, perhaps?' suggested Kit.

Spunky's eye softened for a moment as he recalled the attractive features and welcoming figure of Angela Malcolm, a girlfriend for barely a week or three who turned out to be a French spy named Angelique Mantoux.

Jack Murray

'Ahh,' he said wistfully, 'Yes, I still miss her y'know. My word Kit, the things she could do with a stick of celery and a bottle of gin.' Kit stood up from his putt, slightly shocked by the implication of Spunky's reminiscences. Blissfully unaware of Kit's discomfort, Spunky continued on contemplatively, 'Never had a better martini, I can tell you.'

'What did she use the celery for?' asked Kit, now genuinely curious.

'To stir it. I don't know what it did to the gin but my word, afterwards...'

'Thanks, Spunky,' said Kit returning to his putt, not wishing to hear more about the demise of the celery stick. He promptly missed the putt.

'My hole,' said Spunky cheerfully.

The two friends carried on for another seven holes, the quality of golf deteriorating with the worsening conditions and details of Spunky's latest conquests. One of the perils of links golf is the impact of wind coming off the sea. Spunky, aided and abetted by Hamish, managed to keep Kit at bay.

Overhead a dark black cloud asserted itself over the grey clouds that had been obscuring the sun for most of the afternoon. A dangerous crosswind was making life difficult for the two men.

Spunky stepped up to the ninth tee, somewhat nervously one might add. The ninth at Turnberry is one of the thirty-two wonders of the world. A hole that clings to the curves of the coastline like a wet swimsuit on an "It" girl. Robert the Bruce's castle, or what remained of it, lay behind the green.

To reach the green in such a wind, it was necessary to aim the ball to the left of the lighthouse just behind the green. This meant aiming out to sea. Somewhere in the direction of Newfoundland, observed Spunky grimly.

'Taking your life in my hands here, old boy,' said Spunky. As if to emphasise this point, a wave splashed noisily onto the sea wall just to the left of the tee box.

Staring like a hunter at his target, which from Kit's angle looked like a herring in the middle of the steel grey sea, Spunky looked down again at his ball. A waggle of his mashie, a rapid upswing and he sent the ball forward towards the sea. 'C'mon, old girl,' said Spunky, hoping the wind would bring the golf ball in towards the hole.

It hooked dramatically away from the green and probably beamed an innocent fish going about his lawful business.

'What poisonous luck,' said Spunky miserably. 'Best of luck, old chum. Playing a bit long methinks.'

This was an understatement. The only way of getting a ball onto the green in this wind, thought Kit, was by walking two hundred yards and dropping it there from your pocket.

With something approaching dread, Kit stepped up to the tee. He didn't waste any time with practice swings such was his certainty of disaster. Instead of aiming to the right, he aimed directly at the green.

The ball set off good and true. Then the wind caught the ball in its grip. Momentum was lost, and the ball dropped listlessly onto the rocks. This acted as a signal to the golfing gods to make life even more difficult. The clouds opened up.

*

'Best decision, no question,' said Spunky, before taking a sip of his G&T. As if to amplify the point, a gust of wind blew rain across the window of Turnberry hotel's bar, overlooking the golf course. It splattered the window like the last pheasant at a shoot.

'Sorry, Spunky, but my leg isn't at its best in this weather. Hurts damnably,' replied Kit. He was sitting in a tartan-covered armchair, a newspaper nestling on his knee and a gin in his left hand.

'Anything of interest?' asked Spunky, indicating the paper.

'No, it's been a quiet month or two. Mary's hopes were so high after the Phantom affair but now we have the...'

'Crushing reality of life with Aston,' interjected Spunky with a grin. 'Tell her, the offer still stands if she ever fancies...'

'Studying tables about widget outputs in Minsk,' suggested Kit, one eyebrow raised.

'Exactly, she'll be in heaven.'

'I see there was a robbery of the Sultan's blue sapphire; not our chap by any chance?'

'No, definitely not. We had him in the Italian embassy that night.'

'Oh?' It was a question.

'Nothing of interest, just wanted to find out more about this D'Annunzio chap.'

The two men returned to a companionable silence. Spunky looked down the hill at the course and then over the sea towards Ailsa Craig. If anything, the weather was worsening. Summer rain had arrived with the inevitability of the first grey hair on a middle-aged man. The only sound in the hotel bar was that of newspaper pages being turned by Kit and rain rat, tat, tatting on the large window.

Spunky turned to Kit after a while and asked, 'By the by, what's this about you going to America soon?'

'Yes, Algy's getting married. Did you meet him?'

'No, don't think so. He's your cousin, isn't he?'

'I suppose he is,' said Kit enigmatically before continuing, 'Good fellow. Came over in seventeen with the Americans. I wasn't around then obviously, but he saw some action around eighteen at Belleau Wood. Came through it well enough. He came to visit me when we'd finished; stayed for a week and then he returned to America in early nineteen. It was round about the time we were in Paris. I think we just missed him, in fact. Aunt Agatha is coming obviously.'

'What about your father and Edmund?' asked Spunky.

'No, I can't see that happening,' said Kit sadly. 'He and Uncle Alastair still don't speak.'

'*Plus ça change*,' replied Spunky but did not add anything more to this.

'Mary's coming too,' said Kit.

Spunky lifted his monocle off and looked at Kit in surprise. 'Really? Her Aunt Emily sanctioned her going to San Francisco with a rake like you.'

'Aunt Agatha's coming, remember?'

'Ah armed guard, patrol dog and minefield, all in one five-foot aunt.'

'Yes, that would certainly describe Aunt Agatha.'

They lapsed into silence to admire the shocking weather outside. Spunky lifted his telescope and put it to his good eye. 'Still some hardy individuals out there,' he noted.

'A murder in Yorkshire, I see,' replied Kit from somewhere behind his newspaper.'

'Using a mashie from fifty yards of the green, must be a hellish breeze.'

'It says here that it was predicted by a medium. They're calling it the "medium murder", apparently. How ghoulish.'

These profound reflections on the kismet of life were interrupted by the arrival of tea and a platter of sandwiches. The silver tea pot shone like, well, silver, and the platter, also silver, was on three tiers. The top two tiers contained sandwiches on a paper doily and the bottom, some scones. Spunky poured the tea and added a dash of milk to both cups.

'You don't do the milk first?' asked Kit, sardonically.

'Of course not, silly way to do it,' replied Spunky taking sip. He continued, 'Say what you will about the Picts being an uncivilised bunch of barbarians...'

'I don't think I ever said anything of the sort,' pointed out Kit.

'But they do make a rather good cup of tea,' replied Spunky, ignoring Kit. 'When does Mary return from organising weddings?'

'Soon, I hope,' said Kit looking up from the paper. 'No offence, but I miss her horribly.'

'None taken, completely understandable. 'So, Esther will get hitched in September and you'll be...'

'St Valentine's Day next year,' replied Kit wistfully. A promise of another life. He couldn't wait and said as much. Spunky's eyebrows arched almost off his forehead. Kit burst out laughing. His face reddened slightly. Spunky saw his opportunity and went in for the kill.

'I shall be amazed if the citadel isn't breached by enemy forces before then,' said Spunky.

Kit nodded thoughtfully, 'I shall hold off her advances as best I can, old man.'

The Frisco Falcon

3

San Francisco, June 1920

A smug grin grew on the features of Alastair Aston. He began to nod slowly, then he began to chuckle and then, oddly, his head began to shake. His features suggested that it was all too easy; any fool could have guessed it. A mere trifle for a man such as he.

The he in question was in his mid-sixties. Light reflected off his bald head courtesy of the bed lamp. He had a friendly face that always suggested, however kindly, that he did not take you seriously and nor should you.

He turned a page of the book, '*The Case of the Broadway Virgin*'. Another page turned, his head nodding slowly. 'Of course, it has to be,' said Alastair with an almost smug it-was-obvious-from-the-start certainty. A casual observer would not have failed to detect a note of triumph in the voice. He turned to the final page.

If Marcus Aurelius had not coined the phrase about counting chickens before they hatch, then he missed a trick. One moment Alastair Aston was sipping from the vessel of victory, the certainty of his Holmesian powers of deduction about to be confirmed when all of a sudden nemesis tapped him on the shoulder and stuck its tongue out. Triumph turned to shock, then dismay. He snapped the book shut.

'Must be getting old.'

He turned to the bed lamp and switched it off unhappily.

*

Eight hours later he was awoken by the curtains of his bedroom being opened violently. Light flooded into the room blinding Alastair's semi-conscious. He blinked and tried to hide his eyes from the light with his hands.

'What on earth?'

'Time to get up,' said Ella-Mae, his housekeeper. She was a diminutive, dark-skinned woman of indeterminate age save for the streaks of grey in her hair. Ella-Mae's mood was a constant sourly-sunny. Housekeeper to the Astons this last twenty-five years, she ruled the home with an iron rod dipped in acid.

'Oh, it's you,' said Alastair, from halfway under the sheet. 'Haven't I fired you yet?'

'Every day.'

'Yet here you are,' he said wearily, covering his eyes from the bright sunlight, 'as welcome as a hangover but without the bonus of a wonderful night had.'

'What on earth are you reading?' asked Ella-Mae, staring at the battered paperback on his bedside table. She picked it up and stared at a picture of beautiful young lady in a state of undress in front of a man in a suit holding a pistol.

'Ah, a very deep and penetrative work on the human condition. It would go over your head,' said Alastair dismissively.

'I'm five feet tall,' pointed out his housekeeper, 'everything goes over my head.' She stooped down to retrieve some clothing off the floor and walked towards the bedroom door. 'I'm going,' she said on the way out.

'Don't come back,' shouted Alastair before adding in a quieter tone, 'Did you bring my tea?'

'In front of you as usual,' came the reply.

'Ah yes.'

25

'You're welcome,' replied Ella-Mae from the corridor. She was knocking on another door.

Alastair made a face at her before squinting angrily at the sunlight. To be fair, he was the first to admit that he wasn't at his best in the mornings. As much by instinct as anything else, he looked to the side of the bed. The space beside him was empty. He glanced up at a photograph of a young couple on the wall. His heart sank. Again.

With some effort he hauled himself out of bed. He slipped his feet into the slippers Ella-Mae had perfectly placed on the floor beneath the bed. Another glance at the photograph before his thoughts were interrupted by Ella-Mae shouting at his son. Another day had begun.

*

Alastair sat alone at his breakfast. The breakfast room was comfortably large, decorated in the English style. There were two paintings on the wall: a Winslow Homer watercolour of a fisherman and a portrait by Eakins of an attractive dark-haired woman of around forty. There was a sideboard with an array of breakfast food on silver platters. Ella-Mae had made bacon, eggs and a peculiarly American delicacy he had acquired a taste for, grits. Any embarrassment regarding his submission to American culinary predilections had long since subsided.

As he refilled his teacup, the door to the breakfast room opened. A tall, friendly-looking man with straw-coloured hair and dark eyes entered. He wore a tweed jacket and a bow tie. The tie was yellow with black polka dots. The black matched his eyes, the yellow his hair.

Alastair regarded him and the tie with undisguised distaste. Having made great theatre out of looking his son up and down, he said sardonically, 'Well Algernon, delighted you could join me; it's a beautiful evening.'

'Very funny dad, it's eleven in the morning.'

'Really, I rarely see you out of bed before nightfall.'

The two men breakfasted in silence. Alastair read the morning paper while Algernon read the back and front pages of the same paper. After a few minutes Alastair became aware of this.

'I do wish you'd get your own paper, Algernon. It's somewhat disconcerting trying to read about the issues of the day with you shifting your head to see the baseball news.'

'Sorry, pops.'

Alastair rolled his eyes. Nearly thirty years or so of living in America, twenty-eight years since the birth of Algernon, he still held out resolutely against the degradation of his mother tongue by the colonials. It was a lonely battle, but duty required that he fight to the last man which, strictly speaking, he was.

'Do you have something against the English language?'

Algy laughed breezily, 'Pops, you're the tops.' With that he rose quickly and exited the room before Alastair gave full vent to his ire. He watched the door close.

'I declare, the boy's getting worse,' said Alastair to himself. More by instinct than any particular noise he looked up, startled, to see that Ella-Mae had arrived in the room. He drew the newspaper up against his chest defensively as if fearful his housekeeper would stab him. This wasn't necessarily out of the question. It had been on the cards for years. Decades even.

'I do wish you wouldn't do that. You'll give me a heart attack one day.'

'I've been working on that for twenty years and you're still here,' replied Ella-Mae picking up the plates and cups from the table, not bothering to look at the master of the house.

Alastair made great show of returning to his newspaper, ignoring his diminutive housekeeper. When she'd left the room he said, 'I really must put a bell around her neck.'

4

There were barely three people in the bar. One man sat alone looking at a pair of empty glasses. He was in his twenties but seemed older. A slim moustache reluctantly decorated his top lip. One of the other men in the bar came up close to him to order. The seated man turned around; the stench of alcohol, or worse, almost made him gag. There was something sad about a bar with no women, thought the man at the bar. We civilise one another, he realised.

'Hey Joe, another one over here.' It was a Chinese guy. The accent was pure American. Second-generation, thought the other man in the bar still capable of thought.

The seated man wasn't sure of many things in life, but he was pretty certain the barman wasn't called Joe. A glass of bourbon sailed down the bar, western style. This raised a smile in the man and not just because the other man returned to his seat. The smell of bourbon seemed to stand up and walk with him.

'Good trick,' he said to the barman. 'Do you want to try again with me?'

Seconds later a glass of bourbon cruised towards the seated man, arriving within half an arm. The man reached and took the glass in his hand. He stared at it for a moment and then downed the liquor in one gulp. Removing his wallet, he slapped a dollar down on the bar top. Saluting the barman, he got up from the stool and made his way to the exit, breakfast finished.

Van Ness traffic had died down but rather than take a cab he decided to walk to the office a few blocks away. Then he glanced up at the sun and changed his mind. He hailed a cab.

'870 Market Street.'

Ten minutes later, the cab pulled up outside a not-so-flatiron style grey-brick building. The James Flood building rose twelve stories from the street. To one side was a cable car turntable, to the other was Powell Station. The man walked in through a large set of wooden doors into an ornate, white-marbled lobby. The doorman smiled as he entered.

'Hello, Pete,' said the man to the doorman.

The man took the elevator a few floors before exiting and walking along the corridor. He stopped outside room 314. The sign on the door read: Pinkerton National Detective Agency.

He walked through the door past a few citizens, through a low wooden swing door to an office in the back. The head of the agency spied him and motioned with his hand, which was clutching a thin file, to follow him.

The man walked towards the haze of cigarette smoke that permanently hung around his boss. Phil Geauque was a man nearer forty than thirty but looked older. They called him 'the old man', behind his back. His hair was thinning, and he could have done with losing a pound or two. There was no mistaking the hard glint of his eyes. No one in the building messed with him.

He looked at the man and sniffed. Shaking his head, he said, 'I have something for you that'll keep you away from drink for a day or three.' He handed the man the file he had been holding. The two men looked at each other, waiting for something.

'What do you want me to do, read it to you as well?'

The Frisco Falcon

'Thought you were going to be nice to me.'

'That was last week. New week, kid. Crack this I'll be nice to you again. Maybe.'

'You're a sweetie,' said the man and turned to walk out of the office.

'Hey, Hammett,' shouted Geauque.

Hammett turned around. 'Yes?' asked the Pinkerton man.

'Lay off the booze; and stop making your reports like literature. I don't have the time.'

There was nothing in that for him, so he shrugged and went back through the small outer reception area. It was filling up. Usually older men or older women, their fearful eyes full of the betrayal or uncertainty or the forlorn hope they were wrong.

Hammett made his way downstairs, tired of waiting for an elevator that never seemed to come. He went through a different exit onto Ellis Street. Outside in the sunlight he realised he was hungry. Beside the Flood Building was John's Grill.

The restaurant was one of the first to open after the quake in 1906. Its wood-panelled walls gave a sense of intimacy. Inside it was fairly full. The usual assortment of politicians on the make, police on the take, journos eavesdropping and minor celebrities shouting across the tables to one another hoping to attract the attention of someone, anyone.

Hammett nabbed a table by the window that was being vacated by a young couple. He sat down and a waiter put a glass of water on the table. Hammett opened the file and began to read. With each sentence his heart began to sink.

It was the same every time. A new file, a new hope of something interesting. Then reality arrived like a sap on the head. This was a variation on the old story. A man wanting

31

someone to follow a woman. He read on until the waiter came and took his order. He was young and Chinese. Hammett wasn't sure why he was surprised by this. He ordered chops, potatoes and tomato.

He read the file for a few more minutes then he lost interest. He closed it and indulged in a more interesting activity: looking around him. The constantly changing current of humanity. The Grill never failed to interest him. So many different people. Old, young, rich and not-so-rich, white and every other colour under the sun. San Francisco in a room, eating great food. It was always full, yet he usually found a place to sit.

He looked at the different tables. A man sat alone at a table across the restaurant. He was writing in a notebook, drawing with words, probably, the patrons. Not a bad idea, thought Hammett. He fished a notebook from his pocket and began to do the same.

5

Grosvenor Square, London July 1920

Kit breezed through the front door of the Grosvenor Square mansion with a smile and a good morning to the aged Fish, his Aunt Agatha's increasingly befuddled butler. He was racing towards eighty with all of the speed and purpose of a tortoise in mating season.

'The dining room,' said Fish to the unasked question.

Kit strode forward and opened the double doors. Aunt Agatha was sitting alone finishing her breakfast. Kit noted the platters on the sideboard. Aunt Agatha had never been one to pick at her food. Agatha looked up and registered the features of her favourite nephew.

'Do you have to look quite so disappointed, Christopher?'

Kit scolded himself. He suspected that Agatha was not in the least bit hurt, but he had given her an opening which no aunt would pass up.

'Sorry Auntie, may I ask...?'

'Mary is upstairs finishing her packing, although I suspect that once...'

This sentence was interrupted by the arrival of a young woman who swept into the room and fell into the arms of her fiancé rather more dramatically than was acceptable when septuagenarian aunts are in the vicinity.

'...she realises you've arrived.' Aunt Agatha paused for a few moments until she decided that matters between the two young people were getting dangerously out of hand. Raising her voice, a decibel or six, she pointed out, 'I'm trying to finish my

33

breakfast. Would you mind joining the other animals in the field or desist from this exhibition?'

'Lord Aston, you're back,' said the young lady, disengaging herself from the embrace she had initiated.

'I think you proved that point to your own satisfaction a moment ago young lady,' observed Aunt Agatha before finishing the last piece of bacon. 'Now, I know that I may be aging and weak-minded,' she was neither, 'but can you both move your hands, please, back to a more respectable resting place?' Kit and Mary did as they were bid.

'Both hands,' added Agatha without looking up.

Kit removed his right hand from an area that would decently be described as his fiancée's lower back. Agatha was, meanwhile, dabbing her mouth with a napkin. She looked up at the two young people and said, 'I hope this isn't a portent of what I can expect on our trip to America.'

Kit glanced down at Mary. From the look in her eyes it was abundantly clear that this was exactly what she could expect over the next four weeks. The moment was noticed by the good lady and she shook her head.

'You know it's not too late to bring your Aunt Emily, Mary,' said Agatha in her best school-mistressy tone. 'She stands ready for my call.' This was not strictly true, but Agatha had long since abandoned Queensbury rules in the execution of her duty regarding Mary's virtue.

Mary and Kit immediately moved a foot further apart, one adopting a military stand-at-ease posture with his hands behind his back, the other a demurer pose with both hands folded in front of her waist.

'Good,' said Agatha. 'As long as we understand the rules and consequences, we can all be better friends.'

The Frisco Falcon

Mary glanced up at Kit again and broke into a wide grin which nearly caused a breakdown in the iron discipline of her betrothed.

'How was your golfing trip?' asked Mary as they walked towards the dining table. Agatha overlooked, gracefully, that they were holding hands.

'I managed to keep out of mischief, mostly,' replied Kit enigmatically.

Mary shot him a look which was an intoxicating cocktail of frown: curiosity, humour and something else which had Kit counting the days to their wedding seven months hence.

'Meaning?' pressed Mary.

'Romantic shenanigans with Reggie Pilbream. You haven't met him. He's a ...'

'Fathead,' interjected Agatha rising from the table.

'A little unfair, auntie. He's a noted archaeologist.'

'I imagine that you could spend a long time digging for a sign of intelligent life in that young man. I think we'll find Atlantis sooner.'

Kit ignored his aunt and continued, 'Aside from that, we played a bit of golf in conditions that were poisonous. Then back down to make sure Harry and Sam hadn't killed one another.

Harry was Harry Miller, Kit's manservant who had broken his ankle several weeks previously while working on a case. He and Sam, Kit's dog, had a notably volatile relationship.

'How is Harry?' asked Mary.

'He's out of the cast, thankfully. Hopefully by the time we return, he'll be right as rain,' replied Kit. They watched as Aunt Agatha rose from her seat and walked to the doors.

A few seconds after Agatha had left the room, Mary skipped over to Kit and sat on his knee, 'Where were we?'

The door opened and they heard an intake of breath. Looking up they saw Aunt Agatha looking sternly at them. Mary hopped off Kit's knee and patted the front of her skirt.

'I shall finish overseeing the packing.'

Agatha's eyes followed Mary as she made her way slowly, and to Kit's mind, suggestively towards the door. Looking at Kit she held her finger up, 'Last warning, Christopher. I mean it. You must leave this young lady alone.'

Kit felt it would be un-gallant to point out that he was the innocent party. Thankfully, one of Agatha's better qualities was her ability to move on to the next topic of interest as rapidly as it was seamlessly.

'Ah there's someone I want to introduce you to,' said Agatha, gesturing to someone outside the room. 'Natalie, can you come here please?'

Kit glanced at Mary whose eyes lit up like a bonfire. Clearly suppressing a smile, she turned around to greet the newcomer. Seeing Mary's reaction, Kit looked up at the housemaid who had entered. Dressed in a black, she was a brunette in her mid to late twenties, clearly very attractive and slightly taller than Mary. Her waist was as impossibly thin as her bosom was exuberantly exuberant. In short, she would, and probably had, stopped traffic on Oxford Street.

'Natalie, pleased to meet you,' said Kit with what he hoped was not a lascivious smile. He was aware of a pair of blue eyes keenly directed towards him. Discipline was not only important; it was potentially life-saving. Kit kept his eyes above neck-level for his entire interaction with the young woman.

The Frisco Falcon

The young lady curtsied before replying, 'It is an *honneur* to meet you, Lord Aston.' She was French, too. Kit couldn't bring himself to look at Mary but from the corner of his eye he could see that the smile on her face had widened, clearly enjoying every second of his discomfort.

'Come along, Natalie,' ordered Agatha.

The housemaid followed Agatha out of the room leaving Kit and Mary alone. Mary burst into a fit of giggles whilst brushing the front of her chest.

'I never thought I would feel quite so deficient,' said Mary before seeing Kit's reaction and holding her hand up. 'Don't worry. I know you wouldn't change me for the world. I don't think I want to change either.'

'Not even an inch or two?' said Kit. Mary burst out into another fit of giggles. '*Eet eez attracteeve non?*'

'I see I shall have to pay very close attention to you,' said Mary stepping forward, putting her arms around Kit's neck. 'Very close attention, indeed.'

I am your prisoner, would have been Kit's reply but Mary interrupted the thought.

*

Euston Station in London was like a beehive in summer. Passengers, porters, servants and guards buzzed around the concourse knowing exactly what they needed to do. Ordered disorder. Noise levels were high enough to render conversation futile as newspaper boys shouted the headlines and stall holders offered fruit and tobacco to passengers making their way to the train platforms.

Temperatures were rising also, and this was just Aunt Agatha, whose tolerance of crowds was marginally less than her acceptance of migraines. Kit saw the gauge rising to dangerously high levels. Her umbrella would soon be put to use rather as a pirate might deploy his cutlass while paying a surprise visit to a nearby schooner. Natalie, with Mary's help, shepherded Agatha toward the train. Bernard, the chauffeur, accompanied them to ensure a safe passage through the throng.

Kit, meanwhile, paid for a couple of porters to transfer their luggage onto the train. There was a lot of luggage. The trip to America was to last nearly four weeks, although much of that would be spent in transit. For a chap, such an undertaking might require at least one valise to cover the essentials: dinner suit, tweed suit and plus fours in case a chance game of golf should arise. For the gentler sex, travel is altogether a more complicated enterprise. Each week away requires as much time again to pack.

The plan was to travel to Liverpool where the RMS Aquitania would take them to New York. There would be no time spent in New York on the way over and a train would convey the party to San Francisco.

Kit watched the porters transfer the various trunks and suitcases onto the trolley. They departed just as Bernard returned from his mission to ensure the safety of the other passengers by getting Agatha on the train without incident or physical violence.

'You didn't, perchance, manage to remove the umbrella? She'll hardly need it in California,' asked Kit hopefully.

'Sorry sir, she was most insistent on this point.'

Kit rolled his eyes. The conversation with her that morning had proved equally fruitless. Agatha's view of the United States was firmly based on her reading of the western novels of Zane Grey and her taste for the more ferocious and lurid penny bloods. The impression thus gained was of a lawless country, teeming with gun-toting outlaws. Quite what defence her umbrella could muster should they confront anyone pointing a gun at them was open to question. Although to be fair to Agatha, Kit acknowledged she wielded her umbrella like a samurai's sword.

'Bernard, can you just check the luggage makes it onto the train? The last thing we need would be to lose our belongings. I've no desire to see Vesuvius erupt quite so early on the passage.'

'Yes, sir,' replied Bernard and followed the porters with the trolley.

Watching the exchange was a small man dressed impeccably in a dark suit, white shirt with a stiff collar and a silver tie. His jet back hair was greying at the sides. The large moon eyes were blade-black. When Kit turned around, he made as if he was looking for directions.

Kit set off toward the train platform. The small man followed him from about ten feet away. At a certain point, satisfied by what he saw, the man stopped following Kit and headed towards the baggage car where Bernard was overseeing the removal of the luggage. He walked over to Bernard.

'I say, I think your master wants to see you,' said the small man to Bernard. His English was perfect, his accent middle-eastern.

Bernard looked at the small man in surprise. The tone adopted was just short of peremptory. This was only less surprising than Lord Aston entrusting such a commission with a man that Bernard would have adjudged, shady. The two men looked at one another for a moment as the last piece of luggage left the trolley. As it was put on the train, Bernard smiled and said, 'Yes, sir.'

He left the baggage car and went up the platform in search of Kit. The train car was near the engine, at the other end of the platform. Up ahead he saw Kit about to board and he called out.

'Lord Aston.'

Kit turned around and stopped as he saw Bernard coming towards him.

'Yes, Bernard, is there a problem?'

'Did you want me, sir?'

'No, is the luggage on the train?'

'Yes, sir. A man approached me, sir, and told me that you had requested I go to you.'

It was clear from the look on Kit's face that this had been a ruse. Kit climbed down from the train and said, 'Let's go to the baggage car. I don't like this at all.'

The two men started back down the platform with Bernard jogging ahead as Kit's injury prevented him moving too quickly. Bernard arrived at the baggage car nearly a minute ahead of Kit. It was apparent immediately that the small man was no longer present. By the time Kit arrived Bernard had confirmed all the cases were present. Kit looked at one of the guards and motioned for him to come over.

'Did you see a fellow here a few minutes ago? Bernard, can you explain what you saw?'

Bernard described the small middle-eastern man he'd seen. The guard shook his head and replied that he had not seen anyone interfering with the luggage.

Kit looked at Bernard and shrugged. Then he thanked the guard and left the baggage car.

'All of the bags are present and correct?'

'Yes, sir,' replied Bernard.

'Well, not a lot we can do now. Can you stick around for the time being, at least until the train leaves, just in case he returns?'

'Yes, sir.'

*

'What was all the kerfuffle about?' asked Agatha, straight to the point. In fact, the absence of shilly-shallying was a guiding principle of her life.

'Bernard thinks there was a small, foreign-looking man hanging around our bags, but none of the cases seem to have been tampered with,' explained Kit. He looked at Mary. Her eyes had widened in excitement. Kit rolled his eyes and said, 'I'm sure it was nothing.'

'Let's hope not,' responded Mary with a grin.

'You're impossible,' suggested her fiancé.

'You're going to marry me,' responded his intended, which was irrefutable and could not happen soon enough.

A man knows not just when he is beaten. There is another level of defeat, often solely associated with the fairer sex, where one must accept not just a setback but also a trouncing. The only response is to acknowledge meekly that a reverse is impossible and move on to higher ground, if it exists, and hope for a better outcome on the next engagement.

Kit wisely nodded but could not resist adding, 'You know, I shouldn't wonder that both of you are hoping for some unfortunate event on the train or the cruise.'

'It happens all the time,' pointed out Agatha, defensively.

'In the penny bloods you read, perhaps,' responded Kit.

'You should broaden your mind, Christopher,' replied Agatha, thereby ensuring that the last word on the subject was hers.

41

Jack Murray

The Frisco Falcon

6

San Francisco, July 1920

Hammett looked down at the address in the file and then gazed up at the apartment building. The name on the building matched. He took out a photograph and looked at the young woman in the picture. She was pretty swell in his estimation. Dark hair, hard-to-pin-down eyes and a million-dollar smile.

He sat in the car and waited. How he hated this. The heat. The waiting. The interminable waiting. His chest began to tighten again. It was back. The coughing started. He grasped for breath like a child for a new toy. Trying to keep one eye on the front of the building, he put his handkerchief to his mouth. No blood. At least, that was something.

After ten minutes the fit passed, he got out of the car to stretch his legs. The muscles in his leg had turned to stone and his back felt like it was being repeatedly stabbed by a butter knife as coughs wracked his chest. He grabbed a newspaper. He needed something to read. A long day lay ahead. Standing by the car he watched the world pass him by. One or two people entered the apartment block under surveillance, but no sign of the woman. It was early afternoon. He hated the waiting. His mind began to wander.

The sounds and sights began to pass through him, travelling up through his ears to his mind. A New York accent, a Hispanic voice. An argument in a nearby shop. Or perhaps a conversation between two Italian friends. It was difficult to tell the difference sometimes.

Jack Murray

The sun felt like it was blasting his forehead. Summer in San Francisco wasn't so cold after all. Hammett regretted the drinks he'd taken in the morning. And lunch. He felt like a drink now. It wasn't so much a physical need as something to hold, to do. The newspaper had nothing of interest. He threw it in a trash can and walked up to a shop to buy a soda, keeping his gaze fixed firmly on the front entrance of the apartment block.

The white stucco on the front was beginning to blind him. Sweat trickled down his forehead, spewing from every pore in his body. He wanted to take a cold shower. The soda lasted seconds. He threw the bottle towards the trash can basketball style. It missed. He stood for a moment and debated whether to walk over and put it in. Then he realised some other poor bastard would have to do it. Wearily he pushed himself off his car, bent down and put the bottle where he had originally aimed. As he did so, he saw her. She was walking up the steps of the apartment building. She nodded to the young doorman and walked inside.

Hammett watched her go through, then into an elevator. As soon as she was out of sight, he crossed over the road. He waved at the young doorman.

'Hey, kid,' said Hammett taking out a couple of dollars. The doorman was a boy of eighteen, or so. He looked at the two dollars in Hammett's hand and then back up into his eyes. 'Do you want to earn more of these?' asked Hammett handing the money to the boy.

'Yes, sir,' replied the boy.

'Good,' replied Hammett. 'What's your name, kid?

'Cyrus, sir. Cyrus Dundy'.

'This is your lucky day, Cyrus. Answer a few questions, keep your eyes open and you can earn more of these, son.'

'Yes, sir,' replied Cyrus nervously.

'Tell me, who's that young lady just went in?' asked Hammett.

The boy called Cyrus looked at the two dollars again. This was a day's pay if he was lucky. He stuffed the money into his pocket. What the hell, he thought. Looking at Hammett he said, 'That was Miss Collins.'

'Has anyone been visiting that young lady, Miss Collins?'

'Yes, sir. She has a boyfriend,' said the boy, looking up and down at Hammett. Not a chance thought Cyrus, she's a different league. Hammett smiled when he saw how the boy was looking at him.

'Don't worry, I'm not after her, if that's what you're thinking.'

'No, sir,' said Cyrus in a voice that suggested he would agree to differ on that topic.

'What's the boyfriend like?'

'Seems like a nice guy. Always friendly. Tips me usually.'

Hammett showed a photograph to Cyrus, 'Is this him?'

'Yes, sir, that's him.

"Good work, kid. Anyone else come to visit her?"

'No sir, I haven't seen anyone else come. She's only been here a couple of weeks though, so I don't know from before then.'

'How long is she staying?'

'I don't know, sir. I can find out.'

Hammett handed him another dollar, 'You do that, Cyrus.'

Cyrus thanked Hammett profusely while Hammett turned and started to walk back towards his car. Out of the corner of his eye he saw a man reading a newspaper in the fashion of someone who was new to tailing people.

The newspaper was upside down.

Hammett went to his car. Once inside, he sat and thought for a moment. It was clear he was not the only one tailing the girl. Out of the corner of his eye he saw that the man was looking at him. He had seen him when he crossed over the road initially. He was young, the suit was ill-fitting, and he had a small head.

It was obvious that when he left, the man would either try to follow him or, more likely, try to find out more from Cyrus. For the time being it was a waiting game. Neither could move until Miss Collins made a move herself.

*

Ella-Mae walked into the library carrying a telegram. In the corner sat Alastair reading the evening newspaper. She watched him flick over the page, his eyes partially covered by half-moon glasses.

'This just came.'

'What is it?'

'I believe it's called a telegram,' said Ella-Mae very slowly, emphasising every syllable of the last word.

Alastair shook his head and snatched the telegram from his housekeeper. He glanced at it and then looked up, 'They're on their way.' He was delighted and gripped the piece of paper to his chest.

'Can't wait,' said Ella-Mae. It was difficult to say if this made her happy or sad. Alastair made a face at her. Then he turned and looked out the window. The evening sky was a glorious riot of turquoise and salmon pink. Alastair rose from his seat and opened the French doors of the library. He stepped out onto the patio and walked towards the end of the garden which provided a spectacular view over the bay.

His mood was mixed, as it often was these days. Missing Christina was one thing, but as delighted as he was by the impending arrival of his sister and nephew, he couldn't shake off the weight that lay heavy on his chest. Or was it fear? Then he realised it was guilt. He doubted. It was a feeling. Fleeting, perhaps. It was unmistakable and he had to know the truth. Actions have consequences. He, of all people, knew this. For a moment he thought of his brother, Lancelot. Thirty years since they'd spoken. The ultimate betrayal. But who betrayed whom?

He sat on a bench at the end of the garden and looked up at the sky. The pinks were slowly dissolving, and the turquoise had a purplish tinge suggesting evening would soon transform into night. It was still warm. He removed his tweed jacket and set it down on the free space where once she had sat with him on so many magical evenings like this.

A gin and tonic appeared magically beside him. Alastair spun around and shivered, 'I'm convinced you are of the undead.'

'You'll be joining me soon, then,' replied Ella-Mae as she walked away.

'Maniac,' said Alastair, sampling the gin. He raised his eyebrows and smiled with pleasure. 'Very good.' He lifted the glass to his lips again.

'Hey, pops,' shouted Algy from the library causing Alastair to spill a few drops of the gin. He turned around irritably. Setting the drink down he dabbed his shirt with a handkerchief extracted from his trouser pocket.

Algy was soon beside his father. He looked like a friendly dog, only the wagging tail was missing. Alastair glanced ruefully at him, 'I do wish, oh never mind.'

'I'm going out now, pops.'

'Yes, you go, my boy. This young lady of yours is transparently better company than I.'

Algy looked sympathetic, 'Don't say that, pops. You know how it is. I'm sure you were young once.'

'Perish the thought,' responded Alastair, picking up his gin again, a smile of anticipation returning to his face.

'See you later, pops,' laughed Algy. A few seconds later he headed back to the house leaving Alastair alone on the bench with his drink. The sky was painted a greyish purple now. A bird flew across the cloudless sky. He followed it for as long as he could. Perhaps he was worrying too much about nothing. Hadn't it always been so? He was the worrier. Lancelot never. Consequences meant nothing to him. He acted without restraint. Stole without guilt. Loved without caring.

Alastair often wondered if he envied his brother's freedom from shame. He was a scoundrel. Nothing less but nothing more, either. He couldn't bring himself to hate Lancelot. Next year, he would go to Kit's wedding. How could he not? They would meet again. They would speak once more. It would begin again as it had ended.

With Kit.

RMS Aquitaine, July 1920

The RMS Aquitaine cut through the waves of the Atlantic Ocean on the first morning at sea. The liner had set sail from Liverpool the night before, its first voyage carrying commercial passengers in five years. It had operated as an armed merchant cruiser during the War. The carnage in Flanders had somewhat undermined demand for luxury cruises.

Mary and Kit stood by the rails on deck looking at the horizon. The morning sky overhead was an intense ultramarine blue. Every so often a mischievous cloud would drift lazily into view and then disappear again without explanation.

The sea below hissed and groaned and slapped against the full one thousand foot length of the liner. Waves dived beneath the hull, sloughing under the ship, ensuring a gentle rise and fall. The colour of the sea was a dirty greenish hue, bubbling white foam that dissolved into navy, further away.

Mary's eyes shone with excitement as she stood by the rails of the ship. She breathed in deeply and looked up at Kit.

'I'd propose to you now,' said Kit.

'If I wasn't already spoken for?' smiled Mary. She looked around at a bird flying alongside the ship. It seemed to be following just them. Kit and Mary looked at the bird and laughed.

'Do you think Aunt Agatha sent it to check on us?' grinned Mary.

'I wouldn't put it past her, my love. Are you excited?'

'Very. We're on an ocean liner going to America. There's bound to be a murder or a jewel robbery.'

'I think you've been spending too much time in Aunt Agatha's library. When we're married a course of improved reading may be in order.'

Mary executed a perfect salute before grinning. 'You have to admit, though, it's probably not without precedent.'

Kit rolled his eyes but could not suppress a smile. The couple turned and looked out again at the vast ocean. After ten minutes they walked to the end of the ship to view better the enormous four tilted stacks, each billowing smoke into the cloudless blue sky.

Around the upper deck they could see many of the first-class passengers promenading. Mary could have stayed all day watching them pass, inventing stories for each. Around eleven, they made their way to the lounge, where they had arranged to meet Agatha.

The lounge was inspired by classical architecture: ceiling murals overhead supported by Ionic columns that descended to the floor. Agatha was sitting in the middle of the lounge, giving orders to Natalie. Mary glanced up archly at Kit before grinning at his innocent shrug.

'Ah, you've arrived,' said Agatha. 'I've ordered tea and biscuits; I hope you don't mind.'

Kit sat down after Mary, facing outwards. Agatha soon began what, Kit suspected, would become a recurring topic of conversation for the voyage, at least until the liner had docked in New York with the same number of passengers disembarking, who had come on board.

'I don't like the look of him,' said Agatha indicating what, to Kit, looked like a perfectly innocent man of forty or so. Yes, his hair was a poorly judged length, and the tie was more colourful than good taste permitted, but a murderer?

'Yes,' agreed Mary, 'I noticed him on deck, earlier. Decidedly fishy. White slaver I should say'

'Indeed, looks the sort,' said Agatha nodding sagely although her knowledge of this mercantile class, even after many years spent in the Middle East, was decidedly sketchy.

Kit picked up a newspaper and made a great show of ignoring the two ladies and their invariably criminal-themed comments, mostly directed at the male passengers. He read more about the case he had picked up on when holidaying in Scotland, about a murder associated with a medium.

A few minutes of character assassination were followed by Agatha's impression of the liner. She motioned her eyes upwards and said, 'Not sure about the attempt at Tiepolo on the ceiling but altogether an improvement on some of the ships I've been on. Kit, I noticed there is a fencing room. If your leg is up to it, you might want to have a go.'

'It's been years. I suppose I'm pretty rusty,' said Kit from somewhere behind a newspaper. Mary frowned at Kit for a moment. Kit realised he was heading towards an iceberg. He lowered the paper and apologised. 'Sorry, I was looking at a story on a murder in York last week.'

Mary immediately brightened up and then in a heartbeat looked crestfallen. 'Not much use if we're on a boat heading to the other side of the world. With any luck there will be a few more.'

Kit lowered the newspaper and looked askance at Mary. The smile on her face and on Agatha's told him he was being jested with.

'Very funny.'

Mary, took up Agatha's suggestion, 'I'd like to see the fencing.'

The newspaper lowered again. 'I could teach you if you like,' said Kit.

A grin erupted over Mary's face, 'Would you?'

Kit looked delighted and said, 'I'd love to.'

Mary turned to Agatha who was staring at her future niece. Mary smiled innocently, tilting her head submissively and raised her eyebrows in the manner of an *ingenue*.

'This should be interesting,' said Agatha, more to herself.

*

After tea, Agatha retired to the garden lounge to read a book while Kit and Mary walked along the port side of the liner. Along the way they passed a small man with tawny skin, wearing a dark suit and a white panama hat. Mary looked at the man. He was looking at her unashamedly.

Mary turned around as they passed him. He also half-turned his head.

'How odd,' she said.

'Really?' asked Kit.

'Yes, did you see how he looked at me?' pointed out Mary.

'I can hardly blame him for that. Most of the men and a goodly portion of the women are looking at you,' pointed out Kit.

Mary smiled up at Kit and said, 'Thank you for the compliment, but you know perfectly well that is not what I meant.'

'You're wondering why he didn't raise his hat to you,' said Kit glancing archly at his fiancée.

Mary stopped and turned to face Kit. Standing on her tip toes she kissed him gently on the lips. She narrowed her eyes and said, 'I do love you, Lord Aston.' Overhead a seagull squawked, causing Mary to widen her eyes in fear. She giggled embarrassedly as Kit put his arms around her. Looking up she said, 'My knight.'

'Strictly speaking, that would be a demotion.'

*

Luncheon was served in the dining room from midday. Kit and Mary arranged to meet Agatha around one o'clock. Arriving a few minutes early, they spied Agatha sitting beside Natalie, deep in conversation. Mary looked up at Kit and said, 'I didn't think Natalie's English was so good. They both seem quite animated.'

'So, I see,' said Kit. He looked unusually troubled by what seemed a highly familiar interaction. 'Of course, Agatha is fluent in French.'

Mary looked up at Kit and replied, 'I'd forgotten that. In fact, I think it would be a good idea for me to speak more French. I'm depressingly out of practice.'

Kit glanced down at Mary. He seemed pensive. Mary frowned in response. By way of explanation, Kit said, 'Perhaps it would be better to keep all interaction in English for the moment.'

Mary was surprised momentarily then grinned. She looked back at her future aunt and the housemaid who were still oblivious to their arrival. She said, 'Curiouser and curiouser. I do love a mystery.'

Natalie saw them first and immediately rose to her feet. Agatha turned in the direction of Natalie's gaze. If she was in any way surprised or dismayed by the early arrival of her nephew and his fiancée, she quickly dispelled it by slipping seamlessly into her normal bearing of heroically-controlled exasperation.

'That will be all, Natalie,' said Agatha, addressing the housemaid.

Natalie curtsied unnecessarily and went on her way. Kit glanced at Mary to confirm they should not say anything on the subject. Instead, Mary took the opportunity to probe more into the politics of the family Aston.

'Is Algy like his father?'

Well, unknown to Mary, this was a fairly incendiary opening gambit. Agatha shifted uncomfortably. This was picked up by Mary. She glanced at Kit who smiled beatifically.

'Forgive me,' said Mary, genuinely concerned. 'I didn't mean to pry.'

'Nonsense, young lady, of course you did,' replied Agatha. 'And I don't blame you.'

Mary looked non-plussed by this answer then grinned, 'Well, yes. I did mean to pry. So, who's first?'

Kit looked at his aunt and shrugged. Agatha picked up the gauntlet and said, 'This family is,' she stopped and looked at Kit for inspiration.

'Byzantine in its politics?' suggested Kit.

'Thank you, Christopher, I shall think twice about asking you anything in future.'

'Happy to help,' replied Kit, grinning happily.

'As I was saying,' continued Agatha, 'My nephew has chanced upon a young lady that I must confess, to your credit, I am keen that he keep hold of. For this reason, I've been mindful of sharing too much about the family's ...'

'Dirty linen?' offered Kit as Agatha searched for the right expression.

Agatha glared at Kit and continued, 'The more disappointing aspects of recent choices made by our senior family members.'

'Father and Uncle Alastair fell out over a young woman: my mother. They haven't spoken in over thirty years,' said Kit, getting to a point that, despite Agatha's protestations and by her standards, shilly-shallying, she seemed to be avoiding.

Agatha looked at Kit, but her eyes had softened. She took a deep breath to compose herself then spoke again.

'Penny was in love with Alastair before she met Lancelot. However, Alastair did not count on the duplicity, the charm and, clearly, the advantage of his brother's title. He stole her from Alastair using, I'm sure, all manner of tricks to turn her head. It caused a schism between the two that has never been repaired. I think Penny realised her error and spent many years regretting her decision. But it was too late. I don't think I'm being unfair in this assessment, Christopher?'

'I think you're being too kind to my father. He acted like a scoundrel to win her and acted like a scoundrel ever afterwards. He treated her abominably. My mother was the sweetest and most generous person I have ever known, and he rewarded her by betraying her.'

It was there for a moment. A shadow. A look in the eye. Or maybe Mary imagined it. Agatha could be unreadable when she chose but for a moment, and it was just a moment, Mary saw something. She sensed Agatha knew Mary had seen the guard slip.

'He treated her abominably,' agreed Agatha. But the voice, like the eyes, is not always faithful to the message you want to convey. Mary wondered if Agatha, recognised what had passed between them unintentionally was, this time, a communication. The two women looked at one another for a few seconds.

Families have secrets, thought Mary.

Then, Kit spoke again breaking the link between Mary and Agatha. 'Uncle Alastair left for America immediately before the wedding. He did not return. He went over to California to be as far away from England as possible and met a young woman who had been ill-used by another man. He fell in love with Christina and raised Algy as his own child.'

This clearly surprised Mary, 'I hadn't realised. Good for him.' She saw Agatha nodding her head at this. Her eyes seemed moist, or perhaps she imagined this. A thought struck Mary and she asked, 'But there were no other children?' She looked to Agatha again. This time Agatha looked directly at Kit and let him continue the story.

'No, alas not. I understand the birth was difficult and Uncle Alastair swore he would never put Christina through such an ordeal again.'

'How sad for them,' said Mary.

'Uncle Alastair adores Algy, although you wouldn't always know it. They adore one another, in fact, but they also drive one another crazy.'

Mary laughed, 'Really? How so?'

Agatha rolled her eyes at this and said, 'He's a sweet boy but not the quickest horse in the race, if you take my meaning.'

'Always falling in love,' added Kit. 'And I mean always. He's been engaged several times. This isn't the first time we'd made plans to go over for a wedding. We're only over this time because Uncle Alastair said he thought it really would happen.'

Mary turned to Agatha again, but her face was once again, inscrutable. Her feminine sense told her this discussion was now closed. She moved on to other subjects as lunch was served. The story was far from complete. However, enough ground had been covered for the time being, perhaps more than Agatha had intended, or perhaps not.

A black automobile drew up outside the apartment building with the white stucco front. The car was an open-topped Ford. A young man wearing a white shirt and blue bow tie emerged from the car. He grabbed his hat and seersucker jacket from the passenger seat and headed toward the apartment building, allowing a very fat man to pass through first. Each doffed their hats.

From across the street, Dashiell Hammett looked on. He opened the file Geauque had given him. Inside, there was a photograph of a young man. It was very like the man who had just gone up into the apartment building. An open friendly face, even good-looking, light hair combed back off the forehead. Dark eyes, straight nose and a firm jaw. A man without enemies. A straight man concluded Hammett.

Within a few minutes both the young man and the young woman emerged from the building entrance, holding hands. They headed for the young man's automobile and soon sped off.

Hammett followed them. It looked like they were driving downtown, probably for dinner. It was after seven now and Hammett also felt hungry. Or was it something else? He needed a drink more than anything. As soon as he thought of alcohol he began to cough. He spluttered all the way through the centre of San Francisco.

The couple seemed to be heading towards Fisherman's Wharf. Their automobile pulled up to a large fish restaurant near the boats. They went inside, greeted by a maître d' who obviously knew them or, more likely, had received big tips.

The Frisco Falcon

The kid was not short, judging by the car, his manner and his girl.

Hammett extracted the photograph of the young man from the file. Attached to it was a sheet containing a biography. He began to read:

Algernon Aston (1892 -)

Born San Francisco. Father: Alastair Aston (1860 -), Mother: Christina Aston, nee Alvarez (1870 – 1917). Engaged to Dain Collins (1900? -). See separate sheet.

Algernon Aston, also known as 'Algy', is Vice President of Aston Associates, the large advertising firm on Van Ness. The firm is owned by Aston's father (see above) who is semi-retired but still works occasionally.

Aston is around six feet tall and around one hundred seventy-five pounds. His hair is a sandy brown. He has no beard or distinguishing marks.

Aston majored in law at UCLA leaving in 1913. He joined Daniels & Bloom, a law firm in San Francisco, until he resigned in 1917 to join the US Army. He fought in the war, returning in early 1919. Rather than go back to law, he chose to enter his father's advertising firm where he has remained ever since, taking over from his father at the beginning of the year.

Aston Associates is one of the largest advertising firms in San Francisco. Founded in 1897 as Aston & Gutman, the original co-owner Sidney Gutman was jailed for embezzlement in 1906. He was released in 1910. Gutman's present location is unknown.

Hammett stopped reading at this point. The file on Dain Collins had much less detail. He sat outside the restaurant, drowning in the smell of fish. He wasn't sure if he was hungry or feeling ill. Or both. Couples streamed into the restaurant. It was obviously a popular hangout. He began to cough again. It lasted for a minute and then subsided. He really needed a drink now. He took out a cigarette instead.

Across the car park, a cab drew up. Out stepped the man he'd seen earlier near the apartment. His suit really was ill-fitting. Someone should tell him. Or perhaps he was attempting to hide the tools of his trade. There was a tell-tale bulge in the coat pocket Hammett noted. Hammett walked over to a wall in a heavily shaded area and sat down. He wasn't sure if the kid had made him, but he would soon enough. Hammett certainly wasn't attempting to hide his presence.

It was dark now, but the night air was still warm. Hammett felt like his body was beginning to corrode. Even more than a whisky, he was desperate for food, a shower and sleep. Across the car park, the kid was smoking a cigarette, looking straight at him. Hammett wondered who had sent him. Geauque had said nothing to him about back up, so it was likely to be someone also interested in the girl. But who? A jilted boyfriend? A parent? It was tempting to stroll over and find out. There were ways. Then he remembered the gun. Perhaps not.

Another thought struck Hammett, as he sat in the car. How did the kid know to come here?

Two hours later the couple emerged from the restaurant, much to Hammett's relief. He saw the kid hail a cab. The convoy would start soon. Hammett's intention was to follow them wherever they went but he would not stay. There were only two possibilities at this point: the guy would stay, or he would drop her off.

A third possibility existed, as he was soon to discover.

The Frisco Falcon

*

Algy Aston watched his fiancée step up into her apartment block. She turned around and gave him a light wave. She even smiled. Then she was inside, a silhouette now in the dim light of the lobby. Once she was in the elevator, Algy drove off.

He felt as happy and as troubled as any soon to-be-married man would feel, happy to be marrying Dain Collins, the most beautiful girl he'd ever met. Also troubled by the prospect of marrying her. Someone he realised with each passing day; he barely knew. What else did he need to know? He loved her. She loved him. At least, he was sure she loved him. Sometimes there was a distance in her that was unbridgeable. Most of the time, though, she was smart, sweet and fun. If she didn't want to talk about her past, then fine. If she didn't want to invite family to the wedding, then it made him love her more. It made him want to take care of her. Protect her.

He was back at the house fifteen minutes later. His father was up, as usual, reading in bed. Their housekeeper had long since gone to bed. He looked in through the door on his father.

'Hey, pops,' he said with a grin. His father looked up at him with exasperation. 'Solved the case?' continued Algy nodding towards the book in his father's hand. It was called 'A Murderer Lurks'. The cover showed a young woman being tracked by a giant shadow.

Alastair glanced down at the book in his hand and said, 'A mere trifle for a mind such as mine. I shall be reading Wittgenstein in the original tomorrow.'

'Sure you will, pops,' laughed Algy leaving him to his sleuthing.

Alastair watched his son leave the room. He went back to the book but found he could no longer read. Closing the book, he leaned over towards his bedside lamp and switched it off. He lay in bed for a few minutes but felt distinctly restless. The light went on again. He threw the bedclothes off and got out of bed. He was wearing a nightshirt that went to his feet, which were clad in warm socks.

The corridor was dark as he padded down the stairs. At the bottom of the stairs, he made for the kitchen. It was dark and he took a moment to adjust his sight. He went to the cupboard and took out a cup. As he turned around and he found himself face to face with Ella-Mae.

'Good Lord, woman,' he exclaimed, 'Why do you keep doing that?'

Ella-Mae looked at the cup and then back to the master of the house.

'I can't sleep. I want some warm milk,' explained Alastair. Ella-Mae rolled her eyes. She took the cup from him. Five minutes later Alastair returned to his bedroom carrying the warm milk she had made him. He set it down on his bedside table and got into bed. He picked up the cup of warm milk, which had been supplemented by a dash of brandy and put it to his mouth. The liquid raced down his throat, warming his heart, his stomach and his mood. He was asleep within seconds of putting the empty cup back onto the bedside table.

*

Around eleven, after Hammett had watched Algy Aston leave the apartment building, the gunsel arrived again. He climbed out of a cab smoking a cigarette, pretending not to look in Hammett's direction. So, they both stayed at different points outside the apartment block ignoring one another out of the corner of their eyes.

At eleven thirty, there was a wrap on the window of Hammett's car. Hammett glanced up.

''Lo, Dan,' said Hammett. His heart sank. He looked at the big former-detective but could not muster any desire to be friendly. The feeling was unquestionably mutual. He and Dan Cowan, as far as Hammett was concerned, occupied different ends of the moral spectrum.

''Lo, Dash,' said Cowan.

'Your turn now?'

'Looks like it.'

'Read the file?' asked Hammett.

'No, do you have it?' Hammett handed him the file. 'Anything I should know?' asked Cowan. Hammett told him about the kid and their convoy down to Fisherman's Wharf. Cowan's eyes scanned the place where Hammett had said the kid was standing. He nodded to Hammett and said, 'Got him.' There was little else to report from Hammett. He watched as Cowan's eyes stared at the file.

'Seen something?' asked Hammett.

Cowan shook his head. He put a paw up to his mouth and picked at one of his teeth. He did this as much to irritate Hammett as to stop being irritated by the piece of chicken stuck between his molars. When he had finally extracted the offending piece of food, he flicked it into the road. Had he belched Hammett would not have been in the least bit surprised. Thankfully he was spared any further dental self-surgery. Cowan looked at Hammett. 'Want me to do anything about the kid?'

'No, let it ride a bit longer,' replied Hammett. 'I'm curious to see what he does.' They both looked at the kid. He had his arm raised. A cab stopped in front of him and he jumped in. The cab stayed where it was, however. Waiting.

'Well, I guess we know now,' said Cowan.

*

Hammett returned to his apartment just after midnight. He'd hoped to return earlier but as expected, he'd been followed by the cab containing the kid. After taking a detour downtown, then through Chinatown, he'd finally been able to shake him.

Inside the apartment, he went straight to the kitchen and grabbed a small glass from the sideboard. Beside it was a bottle of bourbon, half-finished. He'd bought it yesterday. He took both into his living room and sat down. It was a small room but nicely furnished. A vase with flowers in the window. Beside it a photograph of a couple: a wedding photograph. They looked happy. Not so long ago either. Hammett gazed at it for a moment. Then turned back to the bottle in his hand. He felt a cough rise from somewhere round his feet. It lasted for a minute then the wave abated.

The apartment was small. A living room with a sofa led through to a small kitchen. To one side was a door. The bedroom. Hammett looked around. He could do better than this, he was certain. For now, though, he was a detective. Or, more precisely, a private detective. One of Pinkerton's best.

He put his feet up on the table and thought about the current case. What seemed a straightforward case was now more complicated than he'd bargained for. He'd phone Geauque in the morning after speaking to Cowan. Maybe he'd have some thoughts on how to proceed. Better still, perhaps the drink would help. The first shot of bourbon provided no answers nor did the second. By the third he'd stopped caring. He looked at the bottle and debated whether to finish it or not. It was an easy decision. He fell asleep, fully clothed, on his armchair. A moment later, the glass fell to the carpet. It didn't break but the noise woke him.

Bending down he picked up the glass and brought it back into the kitchen. He put the empty bourbon bottle into the trash can like she had told him. He walked unsteadily towards the bedroom then crept inside. In the double bed lay his wife, Josephine, snoring quietly. She woke as he tried to undress.

'You're back,' she said. Her eyes tried to adjust in the darkness.

'Go back to sleep, darling,' he said gently.

Josephine put her head back on the pillow. Hammett joined her a few moments later. She was already sleeping. He thought about stroking her hair for a moment, then he started coughing again. He rushed out of the room for fear of waking her up.

Why had he signed up for someone else's war, he thought as his body jerked with every wracking convulsion.

Mary looked at Agatha who was having a post lunch nap in the cabin they shared. "Cabin" somewhat understated the size and the relative opulence of the accommodation. Their rooms were very large and, for most, utterly unaffordable. One large twin-bedded room adjoined a generous living area. Mary walked into this room where Natalie was rummaging through a large trunk.

Natalie lifted out a dark skirt and looked at Mary who nodded. She set the skirt to one side and then bent over the trunk again. Mary peeked over.

'There it is, the white one,' whispered Mary.

Natalie lifted a white blouse out of the trunk. As she did so, Mary noticed an object in the trunk. She lifted out a small, rectangular box wrapped in bright blue paper. Rather luridly coloured, thought Mary and she gently shook it. There was clearly an object inside, not very heavy. The package was barely a foot high and not very wide. She looked at Natalie who shrugged Gallic-style. Mary, for wont of any response, shrugged also and replaced the object.

'Must be a last-minute wedding present,' said Mary.

'Shall I put it with the others, mademoiselle?' asked Natalie.

'Yes, perhaps you should,' agreed Mary with a smile.

Mary took the clothes into the bedroom to change. A minute or two later, she emerged wearing the new outfit. The skirt was long and roomy, the white blouse fitted and emphasised her slender build.

'Beautiful, mademoiselle,' said Natalie and she meant it. Lord Aston is a very lucky man, she thought. For a moment

Natalie thought about the conversation she'd had with Agatha earlier. She smiled at Mary and said, '*Bon chance*,' as Mary headed out of the room.

'*Merci*,' replied Mary with a smile.

Out in the corridor, she met Kit, clad in a light fitting shirt and white cotton trousers.

'Aunt Agatha?' said Kit, making no attempt to disguise his happy assessment of Mary's apparel.

'Sleeping,' replied Mary grinning.

Kit took Mary's hand and they headed into his cabin. A few minutes later they emerged, hair and clothing slightly less pristine-looking. They ran into Natalie who had, herself, just emerged from Mary and Agatha's cabin.

'Natalie,' exclaimed Kit and Mary in unison.

Mary said, 'Lord Aston forgot his epee.'

Natalie glanced down at Kit's hand which was, by anyone's assessment, empty of any kind of cutlass. She looked back up at Mary, with a half-smile and said, 'I won't tell, but be more careful.'

She curtsied and in a moment was on her way. Mary looked ruefully up at Kit and said, 'Sorry, best I could think of. I should really have checked what was in your hand.' At that moment, one of Kit's hands was resting companionably on his fiancée's seat.

Kit laughed and said, 'Don't worry, she's French. They understand these things. Still good to know she's on our team.'

Mary looked up at her fiancé and said, 'Indeed. Now, let's go to the fencing room. You can show me the ropes, so to speak.'

Moments later Aunt Agatha appeared in the hallway outside the cabin, 'Ahh, glad I caught you,' she said, plainly oblivious to the fact that she hadn't. Mary glanced at Kit; eyebrows raised.

'I wanted to come along and watch. I haven't fenced in, my word, fifty years probably. I was the fencing champion at St Crispin's three years running. It would have been four but for some foul play from the villainous Joyce Holman.'

'It's good that you've forgiven her,' said Kit.

'Don't be silly, Christopher, I never forgive,' said Agatha marching forward, eyes straight ahead. Then she stopped, spun around and acknowledged, 'Now, I don't know where I'm going, lead on.'

Kit walked ahead, with Mary and Agatha following.

'How long have you fenced?' asked Mary by way of conversation.

'Since I was a boy. Mind you, as I mentioned, I'm a bit rusty. Apart from an incident in Moscow, I haven't fenced since, well, I can't remember. Maybe a bit at Cambridge.'

'I can't wait to learn, it sounds frightfully D'Artagnan-like. Any fencing tips for me Aunt Agatha?' asked Mary sweetly.

Agatha looked at Mary archly and replied, 'I doubt I can teach you much, young lady.'

The gymnasium was located at the opposite end of the liner. It wasn't a short walk through the crowded deck, but the sun was shining brightly, and the ultramarine calm of the sea made their circuit of the boat quite pleasant.

They reached the gymnasium ten minutes after setting off from the cabin. It was the size of a generously proportioned tennis court. The beautiful day outside meant it was relatively empty. Kit went over to the gym attendant and requested two foils and masks.

While the attendant went to retrieve these, Kit turned to Mary and began to explain the rules, the etiquette and the technique of fencing. Every so often he would dance forward and backward to demonstrate the correct movement. Agatha occasionally chipped in also, invariably to disagree with her nephew. Mary's smile grew wider and wider.

*

'Well, I hope you learned your lesson,' said Kit, twenty minutes later. His face was flushed, bathed in perspiration.

'I certainly did, Lord Aston,' nodded Mary. There was only the merest hint of a glow on her face. One might have concluded she'd had to work much less.

'Good,' replied Kit, 'because you definitely have a lot of promise. If you can get more practice in, you have the makings of a pretty decent fencer.'

'Bit off more than you could chew, Christopher?' suggested Agatha, who was sitting very contentedly by the wall. She had a glass of gin in her hand, which may have contributed to her general mood of good fellowship.

'Well, I felt a bit rusty out there. A bit slow at times, the old leg and what not,' suggested Kit.

Agatha made a sound that was as close to a harrumph as one was likely to hear. 'A bit slow? I've seen calendars move more quickly.'

'Tad harsh,' said Kit sorrowfully.

'You lost eight on the trot,' pointed out Agatha.

'I stopped counting after the fifth. Was it really that many?'

Mary shrugged and put a hand on his shoulder, kissing him gently albeit briefly on the lips. 'I wasn't counting either.'

This cheered Kit up. A thought occurred to him and he said with a grin, 'What if I'd won?'

69

'Christopher,' scolded Agatha, stopping just short of wagging her finger but thereby ending this avenue of inquiry. The look on Mary's face suggested a follow up on the subject would be of mutual interest to both parties. She might even let him win.

*

A few hours later, a slow waltz caressed the ears, the bodies and the senses of the passengers in the Aquitania ballroom. The orchestra was small in number, but each note filled every corner of the room. The floor was brimming with couples, exquisitely dressed floating like they were on water, which, of course, they were. Men wore white tie and tails, the ladies were clad in beautiful dresses of all colours, except yellow, which appeared to be out of fashion this season.

Kit looked down at the woman in his arms and smiled.

'What are you grinning at, boy?' said Agatha, looking back up at her nephew. 'You have a lifetime ahead of you of dancing with that young lady. A few minutes with me won't kill you.'

Kit laughed and replied, 'I haven't said anything, and I certainly wasn't thinking anything so foul. You jump to conclusions too quickly to be a good detective.'

Agatha harrumphed, 'I was in the detection business while you were being toilet-trained.'

Kit looked at his aunt in surprise. A story for another time, perhaps. He smiled and wondered how well he really knew the lady he had known all his life.

'I'm delighted you're dancing, Aunt Agatha. It's my pleasure.'

'I'm sure it is. I've always loved dancing. But you're too good to be true, sometimes, and I'm not referring to your dancing either,' said Agatha but not harshly. There was a hint of wistfulness. She continued, 'If I were engaged to that young lady, I'd regret every minute spent away from her.'

Kit looked at his aunt affectionately, 'As you say, I have a whole life ahead with her. They both looked over at Mary. She was wearing a pastel-coloured Grecian-style dress by Madeline Vionnet. She was, to Kit's wholly unbiased view, the most beautiful woman in the room. It was clear he was not alone in this opinion.

A few men, whom they'd met on the voyage, were attempting to play court to her. She smiled serenely but kept her eyes on Kit. One particular Frenchman had inveigled his way into their company on the pretext of having once met Kit during the War. Comte Jean-Valois du Bourbon claimed a distant connection with the Bourbon family. Kit doubted the veracity of this but there was no question he was a glamorous figure in the manner of a knight-errant. He was tall, dark-haired, with a pencil-thin moustache and dark eyes that Mary claimed genuinely flashed.

'That Frenchman has returned, I see,' noted Agatha, who was proving a surprisingly light-footed waltz partner.

'Shall I name you as my second?' suggested Kit.

'By all means,' replied Agatha sardonically, 'Just don't choose swords.' This made Kit laugh, his humiliation at the hands of Mary, all too fresh. It was not a particularly sore point. The waltz finished, and Agatha and Kit returned to their table.

Bourbon clapped enthusiastically and rose from his seat. He bowed to Agatha and took her hand, kissed it and followed it up with more compliments than Agatha had received in over thirty years of marriage to Eustace 'Useless' Frost. Agatha was too long in the game to be affected by such inconsequential flattery and too much a woman not to appreciate the effort by the Frenchman.

'My boy, if I were fifty years younger you wouldn't be looking anywhere else,' said Agatha, pointedly.

'But madame, I am not,' pointed out Bourbon chivalrously, 'I have only eyes for you.'

'Humbug,' replied Agatha, 'However, you may ask me to dance if you wish.'

Bourbon rose immediately, bowed flamboyantly and asked humbly for the next dance with Agatha. She accepted gracefully and accompanied Bourbon onto the dance floor, turning around long enough to give Kit and Mary a wink.

'Shall we, my love?' replied Kit. 'I must remind you, though...' He left the sentence unfinished.

Mary looked at Kit, her eyes glistened with tears. Nothing needed to be said. She rose from her seat and took Kit's hand and led him to the floor. The music played a slow waltz. Dancing with Mary, it seemed to Kit, transported him above the waves and into the air. He was no longer a soldier with a stump, but a bird darting and diving and gliding above the earth. Her eyes never left his. The music seemed to melt into them, both its sadness and its beauty as well as its joy.

They returned to their seats. Bourbon was with Agatha but glanced down at Kit limping, He looked up and caught Kit's eye. They nodded to one another. The War. Kit wondered how it had affected Bourbon. No one emerged from the conflict unscathed. Bodies and minds would bear testimony to the horror of what Europe had undergone.

The dance floor cleared for the moment as the orchestra took a short break.

The Frisco Falcon

'Well, we arrive in New York tomorrow,' said Kit as he and Mary sat down. 'Excited?'

'Yes,' replied Mary, sitting down between Agatha and Bourbon, 'But a little disappointed we haven't had a murder to solve.'

'I agree,' said Agatha.

Bourbon looked up at Kit with alarm. Kit shook his head and put his palms in the air in the manner of a chap who will not take responsibility for the foolishness of his companions.

'Your aunt and fiancée never stop delighting, Lord Aston,' said Bourbon laughing.

'I assure you they are entirely serious. Too much time reading the very worst literature,' said Kit with a smile.

'I must disagree, I think the ladies have excellent taste,' said Bourbon, gallantly. 'The ingenuity of these writers never fails to entertain me. Crime is the very highest peak of the pyramid in literature.'

He finished this speech with a toast to detective fiction. The others joined in good-humouredly albeit with varying degrees of enthusiasm.

*

Kit bade goodnight to the ladies outside the cabin door. Once inside he collapsed on the bed. His leg hurt damnably. As much as he wanted to dance with Mary, there was a price to pay. He was happy to pay it, however. Aunt Agatha was right; he begrudged every minute spent away from Mary.

There was an urgent knock at the door. Kit looked up. The knocking did not stop. He rose slowly and opened the door. Mary was standing in the corridor. Kit's hopes rose immediately. They went crashing to the floor immediately when he saw her face.

73

'Come quickly,' she ordered.

Kit followed Mary into the cabin. He could see Agatha in the other room, sitting on her bed. But then his eyes were drawn to the trunk. Its contents had been emptied onto the floor.

'Someone's been through it. I can't believe it was Natalie,' said Mary.

'I agree. I'll go and fetch her. In the meantime, do not open the door to anyone but me,' said Kit having a quick look around the room and then the bathroom. 'I'll be back soon.'

True to his word, there was a knock at the door five minutes later.

'Kit?' asked Mary from inside.

'Yes, I have Natalie with me.'

Mary opened the door to allow them inside. Natalie gasped when she saw the room. She looked at Mary and then Kit. She was obviously upset. In a frightened voice she said, 'I did not do this, mademoiselle.'

'We know,' reassured Mary, 'Please sit down. Can you tell us everything you did tonight?'

Natalie sat on the chair and drank a little brandy handed to her by Kit. She began to explain, 'I stayed here, after you and madam left. I tidied up for a while. Everything was folded and returned to the trunk. When I had finished, I left the room. I checked to make sure the door was locked. I always do this.'

'What did you do then, Natalie?' asked Kit.

'I went back to my cabin downstairs,' replied Natalie.

'You didn't stop anywhere?'

'No, Lord Aston, I went straight to the cabin.'

'Did you see anyone on your way back near the cabin, or, in fact, can you describe anyone you can remember seeing?'

The Frisco Falcon

Natalie took a sip of the brandy as she tried to recall the faces of the other passengers.

'There were a number of people I saw on this level. An older man, his wife. He doffed his hat to me. Another man, definitely a foreign gentleman, also passed me. He looked at me in a way I did not like but you know men.'

Mary glanced archly at Kit. 'Can you describe him, Natalie?' asked Mary.

Natalie described the man: short, well-dressed, definitely not English. Mary looked at Kit when Natalie had finished. Kit nodded slowly.

'Yes, it sounds like the same man.'

''Lo, Dan.'

''Lo, Dash.'

Cowan was stood by his automobile outside the apartment. There was no sign of the kid, nor had there been for over a day and a half. The girl had not left the apartment the previous evening nor, apparently, received any visitors.

'Dan, would you mind staying an hour longer? I want to follow up on something.'

The big Pinkerton man grinned malevolently, 'Sure. Hey, I'll stay all day if you want. Who needs sleep?'

Hammett attempted a smile. He wasn't sure how the smile looked; but it sure hadn't felt very pretty to him.

'I need the file,' said Hammett and he reached inside and lifted it from the passenger seat of Cowan's car. 'I won't be long.'

A quick nod and he returned to his automobile and headed to the east of the city to a gym where he knew some people who knew things. It was another hot day. By the time he reached the gym, he was probably sweating more than the boxers inside. He parked across the street and dodged a few cars as he jogged across the road to get out of the heat.

It was an unnecessary effort. The gym was also at cauldron levels. He walked inside and scanned the interior. In the middle of the room was a boxing ring. A bell sounded and a youth in his teens and an older boy, who looked Italian, advanced to the centre of the ring.

'Dash,' shouted a middle-aged man from the other side of the gym.

The Frisco Falcon

Hammett made his way over to the far side, his eyes now glued to what was happening in the ring. Whoever described pugilism as the noble art had clearly not had an opportunity to watch these two kids, thought Hammett. They were tearing strips off one another. Defence was based around the simple principle of trying to kill the other person first.

Hammett reached his friend, 'Hey, Joe.'

'Dash, what brings you here?' said Joe shaking Hammett's hand.

'Work.'

Joe rolled his eyes and then, indicating the two kids in the ring, 'What do you think?'

'Not much science.'

Joe laughed, 'I know. If either ever learn to defend themselves, they could go far. They're aggressive as hell.' Joe wasn't lying.

Hammett glanced back to the ring. The white kid made a swing at the other with a punch that started somewhere in the mid-Pacific. It missed, leaving him open to a wild swing coming from the other direction.

'He's Irish,' said Joe, by way of explanation.

'You Micks,' said Hammett with a grin. The round ended with the bell. Joe called into the ring, 'Hey, Huston, Pelosi, that'll do. Get on the heavy bag for ten minutes.' Joe watched them climb out of the ring, both laughing. 'I don't get that kid Huston. He has talent, brains but as soon as the bell goes, it becomes a tear up.'

'Huston? I'll keep an eye on how he goes.'

'Yeah, John Huston. Listen out for him. Anyone with that much aggression could go places. Anyway, what can I do for you?'

Hammett showed him a photostat of Dain Collins. Joe whistled his appreciation.

'A looker.'

'She is,' agreed Hammett. 'Can you find out anything about her? She's come from nowhere. People are interested.'

Joe took the picture and said he would and added Hammett owed him another beer. Hammett laughed and said, 'You drink too much as it is.'

'You too, Dash. Be careful eh? I mean it, don't be a sap'

Hammett said he would which his friend took to mean he would not stop drinking. Giving a casual salute to his friend, he turned and walked towards the exit. He glanced back at the kid again. The heavy bag was having the hell beaten out of it. Probably deserved it.

The next stop was the Hall on Dr Carlton B Goodlett Place. A sergeant passing Hammett as he walked through the double doors of the detective bureau nodded to him.

'Cells are that way, Hammett, make yourself at home,' cackled the policeman.

'You kill me,' replied Hammett. He walked through to the offices behind and up the stairs. Paint was peeling off the walls in the old building. Hammett ran his finger along the wall. Arriving at the first floor he hurried down the corridor and went into an office without knocking.

Lieutenant Sean Mulroney looked up at him and said sardonically, 'Come in.' They shook hands. Hammett sat down and faced the policeman. He was in his forties, lean-faced, hard blue eyes. A man that could easily have been on the other side of the law. Probably was once, thought Hammett. He knew Mulroney well enough now to bet there was no man less likely to be on the take than the Irishman.

'Anything?' Hammett got straight to the point.

'Nothing. It's like she never existed and then she did.'

Hammett shook his head and thought for a moment. He stubbed out a Fatima in the policeman's ash tray and asked, 'What do you make of it?'

'She's changed her name. Not against the law. It'll take more than what you've given me to dig more, Dash. I can't just start asking for this stuff without a reason. Have you a photograph of her?'

Hammett nodded and let out a sigh, 'I'll get you a photostat of her face.' He rose from the seat and saluted the policeman. He was outside the door moments later. There was no farewell from either man.

*

Dan Cowan looked at his watch. He said mirthlessly, 'Fifty-seven minutes.'

Hammett shrugged. 'Told you I'd be back in an hour,' he said before glancing over at the apartment. 'Anything?'

Cowan shook his head. No visitors either apparently. 'Later,' said Cowan. He walked off without looking back. Hammett didn't bother looking at him. Instead, he scanned around the area. He assumed the kid was somewhere nearby looking at them. It was strange, perhaps even concerning, he wasn't showing himself. It confirmed he was taking orders from a more nuanced mind.

An automobile tooted him on the way past. Cowan. He heard a cackle and then both it and the driver were receding into the distance like a bad memory. Hammett lit up a Fatima. A drink would have suited him now. Not water either. A little after twelve, Dain Collins made an appearance. She seemed cool as an ice cream.

79

Jack Murray

She was dressed in a grey sleeveless, cotton dress. It hung nicely in all the places it was meant to hang nicely. Hammett stayed in the car and waited to see what she would do. Cab or foot? Foot, it seemed. Her curly brown hair bobbed daintily as she glided along the sidewalk.

Maybe he needed a walk. He needed it like a punch in the gut. It was too hot for anything except sipping a cold beer. Hammett reluctantly climbed out of the car and followed her down the street. The reaction of men as she passed was by turns amusing and shaming. It made him wonder if he ever did what they did. Not the wolf whistles, certainly, but the undisguised staring, or even the disguised staring.

She stopped at one point to look in a shop window. Hammett stopped also. He felt a slight prickle in his skin that was not related to the heat. Just for a second, only a second, he wondered if he'd been made by her. Was there just a second's glance using the reflection?

She moved on after a few moments. A tram came to a halt nearby. She boarded the tram. Hammett followed her on. He guessed she was going to Van Ness. This would probably mean she was meeting her fiancé, Aston.

Hammett's hunch proved accurate. The tram came to a halt near Van Ness and she exited along with Hammett. He followed at a distance. Up ahead he saw her boyfriend. They embraced and then he took her hand and led her towards a nearby restaurant. They went in but Hammett stayed outside. There was nothing in there for him. He had at least an hour to kill.

A cab stopped nearby to let out an elderly woman. Hammett climbed in. It pulled up outside the James Flood building on Market Street, where Hammett hopped out. His lungs felt tight as he entered the building and he had to stop as another coughing fit overcame him. People walked past shaking their heads. He was holding a cigarette.

Hammett took the elevator and made his way to the Pinkerton office. Geauque saw him first. He looked at him questioningly.

'Should you be here?'

'She's having lunch with Aston,' explained Hammett.

Geauque motioned for him to follow. They walked into Geauque's office. It was small and files sat on every piece of free real estate. How the boss ever found anything in this office escaped Hammett.

'Looks tidier,' commented Hammett sourly.

'Yeah, I like to be organised. So, what's new?'

'Nothing. I asked Mulroney. He says she didn't exist four months ago.'

Geauque nodded. Dain Collins was a mystery, not just a new name. 'What else are you doing?'

'I need a photostat for Mulroney, I gave the one from the file to a contact. We'll show her face around, but it won't be much use if she's from out of town. There's been nothing from the other offices?'

'No,' replied Geauque. 'Quite a mystery this lady.'

Hammett rose from his seat as Geauque looked for another image of the girl. It took a few minutes of hunting among the files before he was able to fish out a picture.

'Great system,' said Hammett escaping the office before Geauque could make a suitably off-colour reply.

On his return journey, he stopped by the Hall and left the photostat for Mulroney. He was back at the restaurant in time for dessert. It looked like cheesecake. He hadn't eaten all morning, but the sight of the cheesecake made him feel a bit nauseous. Or maybe it was the TB. To stave off the hunger and the nausea he lit up a cigarette and waited. The sun overhead caused sweat to drip down and sting his eyes. He felt uncomfortable. He felt ill. He felt he wanted to do something else with his life than this.

11

The deck thronged with people eager to get a view of New York and the Statue of Liberty. It was early morning, but this had not stopped every available place on each deck being full. Even Aunt Agatha seemed carried away by the excitement of arriving in the New World. Of course, she referred to the United States as one of the colonies and even made a particular point of this when near anyone who might conceivably hail from the land.

'I hadn't realised it was quite so big,' said Mary looking at the enormous statue.

Agatha, whose tolerance of all things French was matched only by her love of spiders, replied, 'A little vulgar if you ask me.'

Kit glanced down at his aunt and said, 'I think it marvellous. It is a wonder of the modern world, especially in what it stands for. "Give me your tired, your poor, your huddled masses yearning to breathe free". I think this is one of the most profound statements of what a nation can stand for. Long may it continue.'

Agatha looked at Kit archly, 'I wonder what Americans with darker skin would say to that?'

'I hardly think we're in a position to preach to them, Aunt, do you?' said Kit, although not unkindly.

'No, we are not,' acknowledged Agatha, 'But if a nation puts such a potent symbol of its values so prominently on display for the world to see, is it not then incumbent upon that nation to live those values for all its citizens?'

'It is, Aunt Agatha, but if you don't mind me saying, I have an idea what this country stands for, even if it does fall short sometimes. After Amritsar, I wonder what we stand for now.'

The port was as crowded as the deck of the Aquitania. People had come out in their thousands to see the arrival of the liner, its first commercial voyage since the start of the Great War. The liner glided serenely into the dock. The cheers of the crowds drowned out the brass band playing below.

They stood and looked down at the crowds lining the dock. Mary felt a surge of excitement and even fear. She was caught between staying on the deck and the desire to rush down and take the first steps by a Cavendish in the New World. Kit saw the gleam in her eyes and smiled.

'Shall we?'

'Yes please,' nodded Mary. Kit took her arm and Aunt Agatha's also. They walked towards the ramp leading down onto American soil, well, slate grey and rather wet concrete. Mary stopped a couple of times on the ramp to wave at dozens of children looking on excitedly from the quay. It seemed New York had turned out en masse to greet the enormous arrival from England.

A surge of electricity seemed to surge through Mary as she set foot on the dock. The band was playing 'Yankee Doodle' which resulted in a "Well, really" comment from Agatha.

'I'm sure they mean nothing, Aunt Agatha,' reassured Kit.

'I'm sure they know exactly what they're doing, young man.'

Kit rolled his eyes at Mary, but he was also smiling, excited to be back in the United States. Up ahead newspapermen and photographers were roaming around speaking to the passengers as they disembarked. One of them addressed Agatha.

'Who are you, lady?'

'If I was interested, I might ask you the same question, you impertinent young man,' replied Agatha haughtily. Then a thought struck her, and she stopped. 'How did you know that I'm a lady?'

The newspaperman looked at Agatha unsure of how to answer this. To his eyes, the elderly woman in front of him was definitely female, albeit long of tooth and, clearly, sharp of claw.

'Whaddya mean, lady? You're a lady, ain't ya?'

'Well, yes, I'm Lady Agatha Frost as it happens,' said Agatha drawing herself up to her full five-foot height. This mattered little to the newsman who seemed closer to seven feet than six but was now becoming increasingly cowed as well as confused by the old woman's belligerent tone. He tried flattery.

'You're royal?'

'Hardly,' said Agatha realising that the man was probably an idiot and moving on regally. This left the newsman shrugging to his colleague in bewilderment.

Mary had also attracted a number of reporters, for altogether different reasons. Their excitement became almost feverish when she mentioned her name.

'Yes, that's Mary Cavendish, she will marry Lord Kit Aston.'

This revelation prompted several men with cameras to abandon some of the less attractive passengers and attempt to capture the potentially royal and unquestionably beautiful female passenger.

Kit looked on in amusement until he felt his arm grabbed by his aunt.

'Mary looks to be enjoying the attention a little too much. I think it's time we moved on.'

In fact, Mary's revelations were causing a near riot to develop as the press and photographers tried to gain her attention. Aware that matters were beginning to spin out of control, Mary turned to Kit with an expression which suggested it was time for him to mount his steed and, if not rescue, then extricate this particular damsel.

'Pardon me, Aunt Agatha,' said Kit. Reading Mary's look, he removed her hand from his elbow, 'Duty calls. Back in a moment. Stay here.'

Agatha's initial disgruntlement gave way to a smile of satisfaction as she became aware of the scrum encircling Mary. She nodded her head and called after Kit, 'Serves her right.'

Kit smiled when he heard the comment but continued striding towards Mary. A few yards from Mary, his attention was drawn to a scene twenty yards further ahead. Mary looked up at Kit as he arrived on the scene, 'Perhaps you can...'

But Kit kept on walking past Mary, his eyes looking at a distant point behind her.

'Oh,' said Mary bemused. She ignored the shouts of the journalists and looked in the direction Kit was heading. Just at that moment she saw what Kit had seen. Kit suddenly made an about turn and came back towards her.

'Excuse me, gentlemen,' said Kit to the press and took Mary's elbow, 'Come and see this.'

'I've just seen it,' replied Mary jogging alongside Kit. Up ahead they saw a number of uniformed policemen. They were forcing one of the passengers into a police wagon. It was the small man they suspected of having broken into their room.

'Should we tell the police our suspicions?'

'No, I don't think we can,' said Kit watching the car drive away. 'We have no proof and besides which, nothing was taken.'

The car receded into the distance. They turned back to locate Agatha. Mary looked up at Kit, 'I wonder why they've taken him away?'

'Indeed, I wonder also. But that's not the main thing that attracted my attention. Did you see who one of the arresting officers was?'

'No, I just saw that horrible little man,' replied Mary.

'It was your admirer, Le Comte.'

'Jean-Valois?'

'Yes.'

Kit brought Mary over to Agatha and Natalie and guided them towards the terminal. Then he disappeared for a few moments. Mary noticed him handing a note to a porter. When he returned, she asked him, 'What was that you gave to the man?'

'A couple of telegrams,' replied Kit. 'Letting Uncle Alastair know we've reached New York.'

'What do you think Jean-Valois was doing?' asked Mary, after she'd explained to Agatha what they'd just witnessed.

'Unless I miss my guess, I think he's with the police.'

Penn Street Station, New York

'They're very...,' said Mary, looking at the train, searching for the right word.

'Yes, very,' said Kit.

The silver train seemed to stretch into the distant horizon. The platform was crowded but they were now all old hands at the travelling game. Kit saw the three women onto the train. They agreed to meet in the restaurant car.

'Home stretch,' said Agatha cheerfully as she was helped up onto the train.

'Still time for a murder,' suggested Kit hopefully, but which his companions quite correctly interpreted as sarcasm. He was ignored, pointedly, by the two ladies who immediately turned their backs leaving him standing on the platform alone.

Kit turned to Natalie and said, 'I'll check on our trunks. Can you manage the hand luggage from here, Natalie?'

Natalie nodded yes and Kit left the train to move down the lengthy platform. Ahead he saw an enormous trolley containing the bags being pulled by a black porter. The man looked like he wouldn't see seventy again. Kit walked alongside him.

'Do you mind if I join you?'

'No, sir,' said the porter with a smile which Kit interpreted as a yes.

'Looks rather heavy,' commented Kit glancing at the bags.

'Oh, you get used to it, sir. Can I help you, sir?'

'No, uhm,' said Kit raising his eyebrows.

'Hank, sir.'

The Frisco Falcon

'No, Hank, I just wanted to make sure the bags are safely on the train. We had an incident in London,' said Kit by way of explanation.

The walk down the platform took a few minutes and the two men chatted about Hank's job. He'd started working on trains just after the end of the Civil War.

'Do you remember much of that period?'

'Trying to forget, sir. A terrible war. A terrible, terrible time.'

Kit nodded sympathetically. Hank glanced down at Kit's limp. Kit smiled ruefully and said, 'A lesson we never seem to learn, sadly.'

*

Mary and Agatha were sitting in the restaurant car drinking coffee when Kit re-joined them twenty minutes later. They watched the train slowly depart from Penn Street and emerge into the city. Both ladies looked on in fascination as New York went swiftly past their eyes. The redbrick and silver buildings soon became a blur. The further out from the centre they went, the more forsaken the houses became. The tall buildings slowly changed into wooden shacks in varying levels of disrepair. It was a far cry from the marvel of Manhattan.

'My word, it has changed since I was here last,' said Agatha. She answered the unasked question, 'I think it was 1907, with Useless. We made this trip to see Alastair and Christina.' She was quiet for a moment as she remembered her husband with sadness and affection. Mary took her hand and Agatha smiled gratefully. 'A lifetime ago, it seems. Still, here we are. No point in dwelling on the past. Do you think it's too early for a...?'

'Yes, Aunt Agatha. It's barely gone ten o'clock in the morning,' pointed out Kit.

Agatha rolled her eyes and looked at Mary.

'Stiff neck.' She wasn't complaining about the discomfort she was feeling, either. With just the merest hint of a sulk, she took a book out of her handbag along with a pair of spectacles, 'Well, if you won't let me have a little snifter, I shall have to entertain myself in other ways.'

Kit and Mary both stared down at the book: 'The Clue of the Blood-Red Dagger' by Guinevere Grufnutz.

'Let me know when you've finished it,' said Kit innocently. Mary covered her mouth to stifle a giggle.

Agatha fixed him a beady glare, 'When you get to my age, Christopher, you'll welcome anything that keeps your mind active. I'm afraid your brand of prep school repartee isn't quite up to the mark.'

Mary nodded in a that's-told-you manner. She looked at the lurid cover and said, 'Interesting name, I wonder if it's a *nom de plume?*'

This drew an arch look from Kit, who decided to take the comment at face value. 'If it isn't, I suspect she'll be wanting to be married sharpish,' said Kit.

*

Two days later:

'It's possible to tire of flat landscapes,' said Kit looking out the window of the train. Hour after hour of the Mid-West was beginning to tell on the good humour of the travelling party, although deadly violence had been kept to a minimum.

'No murders,' said Mary glumly.

'No murders,' agreed Agatha.

Mary glanced down at the finished book on the table: 'The Widow Murders' by Max Bloode.

'*Nom de plume?*' asked Mary.

'I hope so, I can't imagine anyone would admit to writing such rubbish,' said Kit. 'It's a nice touch adding an "e" to the end of his name.'

'Adds a little bit of class, I agree,' said Mary.

'Did you deduce who the killer was?' asked Kit.

Agatha glared at Kit in a manner that confirmed the redundancy of such a query. Silence returned for another few minutes and then Mary observed, 'I can still hardly credit Jean-Valois was a policeman. He seemed so...'

'Fat-headed?' offered Agatha.

'No, but he was so French and charming. It's difficult to imagine him chasing after criminals through the back streets of Paris or the docks of Marseilles,' responded Mary.

'It's difficult to imagine a teenage daughter of a lord nursing on the front line of the worst war in history, but this is also possible,' retorted Kit wryly.

Mary looked at Kit evenly in the eye, then grinned, '*Touché.*'

'Congratulations, Christopher,' observed Agatha drily, 'You finally landed one. Took you long enough. You're losing it. Of course, I knew there was something about him from the off.'

'Who?' inquired Kit, credulously.

'Le Comte, or whatever he is,' said Agatha.

'How did you find him out,' asked Kit eyeing his aunt closely.

Agatha took on a certain it-was-obvious-really *mien*. She looked at her nephew and said, 'Well, it was in the eyes, actually. He always seemed to be looking around.'

'At Mary,' pointed out Kit. Mary grinned as innocently as a final year schoolgirl.

Agatha's eyes narrowed. 'One can hardly blame him on that score. I had my eye on him very early.'

'I wonder if we'll see him again?' asked Mary.

Aunt Agatha looked up suddenly and put her finger up to attract the attention of one of the waiters. She finished the discussion with what in England, constitutes the end of any debate, or session in cricket for that matter.

'Could we have a pot of tea, please? And bring some milk, not lemon.'

Hammett stood over the dead body of Dan Cowan whose white shirt was stained red by the head wound. The back of his head had been mashed by a heavy object. Hammett knelt down and looked at his sometime colleague. He rose almost immediately.

'I figured you'd want to see him before we took him away,' said Mulroney, smoking a small cigar, which stayed in his mouth as he spoke.

'Thanks, Sean,' said Hammett lighting a Fatima.

They were outside Dan Cowan's house in the east of the city. It was night but still very warm. Hammett looked at Mulroney. The policeman was sweating profusely. He dabbed his forehead with a handkerchief.

'Is his hat anywhere?' asked Hammett, looking around the area next to the body. 'I don't see it around. Did someone lift it?'

Mulroney shrugged and turned to another uniformed policeman. He asked him if he'd seen a hat. The answer was no.

'Do you think he was brought here?' asked Mulroney.

It was Hammett's turn to shrug now. He walked over to a nearby automobile and looked underneath. Nothing. As he stood up, the medics moved the dead body onto a stretcher.

'Any idea who might have done this?' asked Mulroney.

Hammett laughed mirthlessly, 'Where do you want me to start?'

'I thought as much. What was he working on? Is it anything to do with that girl?'

Hammett nodded.

Mulroney said, 'I guess we'll start there.'

Hammett held his hand up, 'Wait, Sean. We're tailing her.'

'She didn't know?'

'Not as far as I know. There was someone else though. A kid.' Hammett described the kid who had also been hanging around the apartment. Mulroney made some notes.

'Where were you an hour ago?' asked Mulroney, semi-joking.

'Very funny. Look, I didn't like him but he's one of ours. Let me follow up on the girl. You guys speak to Geauque and see what else he'd been working on. In fact, if I don't miss my guess....'

Phil Geauque hove into view. His big frame moved with the grace of an inebriated rhino. His face and body were bathed in sweat. He looked at the body of Cowan being loaded into the ambulance and then walked over to Hammett and Mulroney.

'What happened?'

Mulroney's summary of the known facts was brief for the very good reason they knew very little. Geauque nodded but said nothing. His face resumed in its usual aspect: a sphinx. His eyes showed compassion, but his manner remained business-like. When Mulroney had finished, he said, 'D'you mind if we tag along on this?'

'Yeah, it'll be great to have you hot shot sleuths to point us in the right direction.'

'Funny,' said Geauque. 'We'll tell you what we know, and you share with us too, right?'

'Sure,' said Mulroney. 'What can you tell me now?'

'The guy was a rat. We know this. It's why you guys kicked him out. But he knew his job. I know, I hired him. He put away a lot of guys over the last twenty years. There's many would like to have used whatever clubbed him.'

'What about Dain Collins?' asked Mulroney. 'Hammett tells me he was working with him on that.'

Hammett and Geauque exchanged a look.

'That was good of Dash,' said Geauque in a tone of voice that did not suggest it was in the least bit good. Hammett felt uncomfortable.

'*Quid pro quo*,' said Hammett, defensively. 'Sean will let me handle the Collins end for the moment.'

'For twenty-four hours,' said Mulroney, from the side of his mouth not dealing with a cigar.

'Twenty-four hours, then,' said Hammett. 'I better get on it.'

*

'Hello, Mr Aston,' said a young secretary as Alastair Aston walked into the offices of Aston Advertising. Alastair took off his hat and smiled down at her. Margaret had been one of his last hires. She was one of his best. In her mid-twenties, she was blonde, smart and industrious. His clients loved her. She played them like a pro.

'Hello, Margaret. Is my son in?'

'No sir, he went out to lunch an hour ago.'

'With a client?' asked Alastair innocently, knowing the answer. His heart sank before Margaret responded.

'I believe with Miss Collins, sir.'

'Since?'

'Before eleven, sir.'

'Ahh young love' said Alastair with a wide smile which turned to a grimace the moment he went into his old office, now occupied by his son. 'Young love,' he repeated more bitterly. The phone rang. He picked it up.

'Put him through, Margaret. Hello James, how are you?' Gone was the not-so-kindly old uncle. In his place was a man who had built up one of the most successful advertising agencies in the city.

For the next ten minutes, Alastair dealt with a client who, if not quite annoyed, was far from 'noyed either. At the conclusion of the call, Alastair replaced the phone wearily. He took out a handkerchief and mopped his brow. At that moment Algy arrived.

'Hey, pops,' said Algy. It was an Algy-thing to say but the usual brio was missing. Alastair at once sensed something was awry. But he'd been out for nearly two hours.

'You're back, I see,' said Alastair with undisguised irritation. 'I've been dealing with a rather unhappy client while you've been out romancing the mysterious Miss Collins.'

'Don't say that, pops.' For once Algy was quite serious and he was clearly unhappy for reasons that had little to do with his father.

Alastair immediately felt contrite. 'Is something wrong, my boy?'

'Nothing, pops. Who were you speaking to? James Bosworth?'

'Yes Bosworth. He's refusing to pay us for the work we did.' Alastair looked at his son but Algy did not return his gaze. The only sound in the room was the clock on the wall.

'Where are Jefferson and McKay? The only person I could see in the office was Margaret.'

Finally, Algy looked up at his father. There was sadness in his face. A deep sadness. Alastair looked with concern at his son, 'Son, what's wrong? Tell me.'

'I had to lay them off, pops. We've had a run of bad luck.'

The Frisco Falcon

'What do you mean?'

Algy collapsed in a chair and put his head in his hands. His father rose from his seat immediately and went to comfort him. Finally, when Algy had regained control, he began to explain.

'We lost a couple of clients, new ones I had brought in last year. They wanted a New York agency to handle the national account. They liked us but they were given no choice. Then Laidlaw's said they wanted to end our contract.'

'Laidlaw's,' exclaimed Alastair, 'But Fraser Laidlaw has been a client of ours for twenty years. Why would he leave?'

Algy sighed.

'He wasn't a client of ours, pops; he was a client of yours. When you retired, I think he felt it was an opportunity to leave. Same with Nathaniel & Webster. Same with Fred Johnson. We lost 'em all.'

'Why didn't you say something, Algernon? I could have done something about it.'

'No, pops. They were obviously apologetic. They said our work was still good, but they felt it was time to have fresh thinking. I didn't say anything because we won the Bosworth contract and a few others. But it looks like they're all going. I had to let go Cy Jefferson last month, so I've been writing all the copy.'

'Who's doing the accounts, if not McKay?'

'Well that was not much of a loss, pops, as you well know. The man was incompetent.'

Alastair nodded dolefully, 'Yes, that was a bit of a hospital pass, wasn't it? I'm sorry son.' He patted Algy on his back.

'It's been going wrong for a while now, pops. The only good thing in the last few months was meeting Dain.'

'Ahh yes, the enigmatic Miss Collins,' said Alastair rising from the side of Algy's seat.

'You should give her more of a chance.

'I would love to, son. But I wish she was more forthcoming about her life. Her family.'

'We're not in England now. Family isn't as important here.'

Alastair eyes widened in anger, 'Don't say that. Family is important.'

Algy now returned his father's glare. He said, 'Then why don't you talk to your brother? Why haven't you spoken with him in thirty years? Why have I never met him? Why isn't he coming to this wedding?'

Families also have secrets, thought Alastair. Deep secrets that sometimes see the light of day in our thoughts, in moments of weakness when we hold onto them like a drowning man to an outstretched hand. But sometimes those secrets are the weeds dragging us deeper into the water, covering our eyes, our mouths, stopping us from breathing, enveloping us and slowly, ever so slowly, suffocating us.

Alastair rose up and put on his hat. He looked again at his son, 'I accept what you say. We're having a bad run. It happens from time to time. But when it happened to me in the past, Algernon, my way of dealing with it was to fight. To get back up off the ground and fight. Fight,' said Alastair, clenching his fist, 'fight and fight until you're winning again. Your mother would have killed me had I swanned off for two-hour lunches while the business was in trouble.'

The mention of his mother, realised Alastair, was too much, no matter how true. Algy's face crumpled. He began to weep uncontrollably. Alastair went over to him, tears stinging his own eyes, 'I'm sorry, son. I'm sorry.'

The Frisco Falcon

Kit stepped off the train first at San Francisco Station. The platform was swarming with people running around like they'd spilt hot tea on themselves. Porters fought for air with the human wave of passengers. Mary followed Kit off the train then both turned to help Aunt Agatha. Natalie joined them a few moments later. The noise on the platform was deafening. Conversations in the United States seemed to occur across platforms such was the din.

'Why do Americans insist on speaking so loudly?' asked Agatha, rhetorically. Kit glanced down with some alarm as he saw the umbrella. The last thing they needed was for his aunt to assault some innocent passenger who had the misfortune or poor judgement to be standing in her way.

The party headed towards the exit with Kit and Agatha looking out for a familiar face. When they reached the concourse, Agatha saw Alastair and waved at him to attract his attention. It took a few moments, helped by Agatha nudging a few passengers out of the way, and then he saw them. Moments later they were embracing one another like long lost family, which they were.

'You haven't changed, Agatha,' lied Alastair with a wide smile.

'You have,' said Agatha glancing upwards at his head.

'Ah yes, I think the last hair went in 1918,' admitted Alastair ruefully. He shook the hand of Kit and then, overcome with emotion, embraced him also, 'Kit, my boy, so good of you to come.'

The Frisco Falcon

Finally, he took a step back and looked at Mary with the relish of an art historian gazing upon an undiscovered Madonna by Raphael, 'Miss Cavendish, what a great honour.' He turned to Kit and with a stage whisper that was meant to be heard by all, 'My word, Kit, congratulations.'

'My word, indeed, Uncle Alastair,' agreed Kit smiling broadly.

Mary looked at the tall, slim man in the ridiculous tweed suit and dark bow tie. Ridiculous because of the stifling heat. The expressive eyes were bordered by bushy eyebrows and his grin was saved from being maniacal by the obvious sweet-nature of the man. Mary decided immediately she was going to like Kit's uncle very much. Instinctively she took his hand and he rewarded her with an embarrassed giggle.

'I don't want to make an enemy of my...' Alastair hesitated a moment before saying nephew. 'Come this way, we have a car waiting. I'll send for your luggage. And do you have...?'

'This is Natalie, my maid,' said Agatha, emphasising the last two words to Alastair. The older man turned to the younger woman, sized her up, literally, in a moment and smiled almost with delight, 'Pleased to meet you, too, Natalie.'

Was it Kit's imagination that his aunt and uncle exchanged a look? Almost inaudibly he heard Alastair say to Agatha, 'Very good, Agatha. Very good.'

Kit turned to Mary. She looked at him and raised her eyebrows. Apparently, it wasn't just him then. The group followed Alastair towards the exit of the station. Suddenly he stopped. It was just for a second. Kit noticed the momentary pause and looked at a sea of faces. Had he seen someone? Alastair was moving again. It had happened so quickly that the two ladies hadn't broken their stride.

'Where's Algy?' asked Kit.

Suddenly, Alastair stopped and turned around, 'I have something to tell you. Perhaps when we are back at *Bellavista*.'

*

One day earlier:

Hammett stood outside the apartment block and watched Lieutenant Mulroney arrive with another cop he didn't know. Mulroney introduced him as O'Hara. He scowled at Hammett when he saw a smile crease the Pinkerton man's face. Yes, another Irishman. He could read Hammett's mind sometimes.

The three men walked up into the apartment block. Hammett nodded to Cyrus. They took an elevator to the third floor. The doors opened and they walked down a corridor with pale brown wallpaper to the door at the end.

They knocked on the door. No answer. Impatient, Mulroney knocked again, harder this time. Then he used his fists and banged the door like he meant it. Just as he said, 'Police, open up,' the door opened. A man answered the door. He was tall, well-made and about as far from being a criminal, thought Hammett looking at the bow tie, as it was possible to get.

*

Algy looked at the three men standing in the corridor. His first thought was they were as likely to be robbers as policemen. The grim faces on the three men prompted his second thought, a realisation that this was not going to be good. He was right. Then the man at the front showed him a badge. Algy had never been arrested before but he recognised a police badge when he saw one.

'How can I help you, gentlemen?'

The Frisco Falcon

Algy's first rule of dealing with policemen was politeness. In fact, he used this rule with most every person, but with policemen it was especially important. He finished off the question with what he hoped, was a winning smile.

'Is Dain Collins at home?' said the man holding the badge. It read Lieutenant Sean Mulroney.

'Yes, come in,' said Algy, still smiling, but hope was fading fast. This was definitely not going to be good. The three men walked in without another word. 'This way,' added Algy somewhat superfluously.

They entered a generously sized living room. The ceiling was high, the furnishing second hand but tasteful. Some paintings on the wall, in the modern style. Two brown leather Chesterfields sat opposite one another. On the table between the two Chesterfield's was a cup of coffee and an ashtray with a half-smoked cigarette. Hammett's first view up close of Dain Collins was the back of her head. She remained seated as Mulroney asked, 'Dain Collins?'

She rose from the seat. Up close she looked younger than her twenty years, thought Hammett. And beautiful. A porcelain beauty. Flawless white skin, and then there were the eyes.

'Yes,' said the young woman. Her voice was just barely audible. She was nervous. The arrival of the men was clearly not a surprise, Hammett noted. Confused yet not so confused. Yes, she was beautiful, that much was clear but in a way that was difficult to define. There was an innocence, an unworldliness in the green-brown eyes. She seemed remote but he sensed fear also. Of course, he had met many like her before; the manner was unmistakable and easily explained. He examined her more closely as she looked at the two policemen.

The longer Hammett gazed at her, the stranger her beauty seemed. The ears were without lobes; the hair was a mass of reddish-brown curls, the vacant-but-amused eyes, the sculpted cheekbones. She was compelling while she, at the same time, kept you at a distance. She was not tall, but she was very slim, perhaps too much so.

'Do you mind if we sit down and ask you a few questions?' asked Mulroney.

Dain Collins looked at Algy, who nodded. She nodded dumbly also and sat down, reaching for the cigarette. Lieutenant Mulroney sat in front of Dain Collins. Mulroney got to the point very quickly. 'Miss Collins, a man has been murdered. Daniel Cowan. Does the name mean anything to you?'

She shook her head. Algy moved around the back of her chair and sat down. He took her right hand in his. On her left hand, Hammett saw an engagement ring. It didn't look new. This surprised him. The Aston family were rich, weren't they?

'Miss Collins, look, we know your name isn't Dain Collins.'

'It is, though.' The voice was soft, refined, expensive.

'It wasn't always. What was it before?'

'You don't have to answer that, Dain,' said Algy. 'Lieutenant, unless you are charging my fiancée with something, anything, then I don't see why she should explain a name change that is legal.'

Mulroney glanced at Algy and removed his cigar, 'Are you her lawyer, bud?'

'No,' replied Algy amiably before adding, 'I'm her fiancé. I used to practice, Lieutenant. I think we both know Dain is under no obligation to answer your questions.

Mulroney scratched his head and pointed out what seemed obvious to him.

'A man has been murdered. Your refusal to answer even the simplest of questions makes us kinda suspicious.'

'Dain's told you she didn't know the man, has never met the man. Why do you believe she is connected to this man?'

Mulroney looked at Hammett and shrugged.

Hammett said, 'He was working with me.'

'And you are?' asked Algy.

Hammett told him.

All this time Dain Collins said nothing. In fact, she did not look at either the policemen or her boyfriend. She seemed to be either uninterested in the conversation or she was trying to use a cool façade to hide her fear. Hammett suspected the latter, but another thought was gnawing away at him.

'Why is some two-bit shamus following my girlfriend?' Algy was clearly rattled or angry or both.

Hammett smiled at him, 'Two-bit? You rate my abilities more highly than my boss. Speaking of which, he would be disappointed if it was me answering the questions rather than you and your girlfriend. One of our men has been murdered and I mean to find out who did it. I think you'd be doing yourself and your fiancée a favour if you told us what you know because I know my friend here has a low tolerance for obfuscation.'

Mulroney turned to Hammett in surprise and said sardonically, 'Whatever that means, I agree. Look, I can go downtown and get a warrant, or you can come with us and answer questions real friendly like.'

Dain Collins seemed to wake up from her reverie at this point. There was fear in her eyes. This was clear. Algy also seemed less sure of himself. There seemed to be no way out.

'Have it your own way,' said Algy, 'but Miss Collins is not answering any questions without a lawyer present.' He stood up and went over to the phone.

A few minutes later they left the building, Dain Collins and Algy first then the three detectives. After being indoors, the heat punched them all in the face. Across the road, Hammett could see the kid again. Out of the corner of his mouth he whispered to Mulroney, 'Ten o'clock. Who's the kid?'

Mulroney made a show of looking to his right and pointing at something then he glanced left and caught the kid directly in the eye. The kid bolted.

'Did you see him?' asked Hammett.

'Yes,' said Mulroney. 'I could be wrong, but I think his name is Cookson. William Cookson. He's pretty new. Did some juvenile time. Seems to be a hired heavy these days. Why do you ask? Is he connected to this?'

'Maybe,' said Hammett. 'He's been hanging around the apartment, but I hadn't seen him in a few days. Makes me wonder if he knew Cowan and was laying low.'

Mulroney shot Hammett a look.

'Seems to me, Dash, I should be putting you in a room too.'

'Wise guy,' said Hammett. He wasn't smiling. 'Say, can you do me a favour?'

Mulroney laughed mirthlessly, 'Protect and serve, it's what we do, right?'

'Sure you do,' replied Hammett. 'Can you find out more about Cookson?' asked Hammett. 'Who's paying him?'

'What do I get in return?' shouted Mulroney as Hammett walked away.

A salute, apparently.

The Aston residence in San Francisco was named *'Bellavista'*. Mary gasped when she saw it. At last, after years of searching, she had found a home as spectacularly ill-designed as her own at Cavendish Hall. Built on almost a similar scale, it was made of wood, like most of the American houses she passed on her journey from the station. The front door made a half-hearted attempt at a Palladian entrance, perhaps the only part with any material not made from wood. At each end of the house were wooden turrets which, no doubt, offered impressive views across the bay although probably little else by way of function.

Alastair saw the look on Mary's face and decided, once again, that Kit was the luckiest man in the world. He grinned at Mary and said, with a tone of voice that one might have said was gleeful, 'Hideous, isn't it?'

Mary looked at Alastair in shock. This was replaced by a wide smile as she realised he was serious. Incredibly, he actually seemed to share her enjoyment of the extraordinary spectacle that was *Bellavista*. She took his arm, looked up at him and said, 'It's gruesome. You really must see Cavendish Hall sometime. I think you'd love it there. We combine Palladian, with Gothic and Tudor.'

'No,' exclaimed Alastair delightedly. 'Are such things really possible?'

'The evidence at Cavendish Hall,' replied Mary, 'suggests possible, yes. Advisable, no.'

'Well I'm now doubly excited at the prospect of your wedding, my dear. My wife and I fell in love with this place at first sight. Lord knows what the architect was drinking when he designed it. American houses are so protestant and serious, it was a genuine delight to come across a folly such as this.'

Agatha looked on at the conversation with head-shaking exasperation while Kit merely laughed. He had been looking forward to Mary's first sight of *Bellavista*. Mary's reaction had not disappointed him. Oddly, though, both Alastair and he were extremely fond of the building which seemed a wonderful example of the New World's take on Gothic, albeit in....

'Mint green, in case you're wondering my dear,' said Alastair pointing at the paint on the wooden walls of the house.

'The colour is just too perfect, Uncle Alastair. You don't mind if I call you...?'

'I should be insulted if you didn't,' replied Alastair in mock alarm to Mary, before grinning with delight. They climbed up onto the front porch together. The door opened just as Alastair was about to open it.

'I do wish you'd let me do that sometimes. I'm not a child,' snarled Alastair at Ella-Mae.

'You could've fooled me,' responded Ella-Mae, scepticism sculpted into every syllable.

Mary looked at this exchange initially with alarm and then had to cover her mouth to stifle a giggle. She glanced at Kit who was smiling affectionately at his uncle and housekeeper.

Agatha made a sound that resembled a tut to Kit. She repeated it thereby confirming Kit's initial hypothesis. She stepped forward, past Alastair towards the elderly housekeeper.

'Lady Frost', said Ella-Mae warmly, taking Agatha's coat from her, 'It's a pleasure to see you again.'

'Ella-Mae,' said Agatha regarding the housekeeper, 'I'm glad there's at least one person in this house with some sense.

You've hardly changed.' Which was hardly true, but she grinned her thanks anyway.

Alastair introduced Mary and then turned to Kit, 'You'll remember my nephew.'

'I do, and my, haven't you grown to become such a handsome young man,' said Ella-Mae regarding Kit happily.

Kit bent down and kissed Ella-Mae on the cheek, 'It's good to see you again, Ella-Mae and thank you for looking after my uncle so well. He's mellowed thanks to you.'

Ella-Mae rolled her eyes at this. Then she saw Natalie. The French woman was last to leave the automobile, arriving at the door a minute after the others. Her appearance prompted a remarkable transformation in Ella-Mae. The smile immediately left her face and she glared at Alastair, who avoided her eyes. Mary observed all before Kit took her elbow and led her into the main entrance hall. Meanwhile, Ella-Mae nodded a greeting to Natalie and took the remaining coats before silently leaving the group.

Mary twirled around the enormous entrance hall. It was not as large as Cavendish Hall, but it was impressive. It was certainly more tastefully decorated inside. Even more exciting was the collection of paintings dotted around the hallway and on the staircase leading up to the first floor. On first glance, Mary counted three Sargent watercolours, a Whistler pastel of Venice and a number of landscapes of the Hudson River school.

'My wife,' said Alastair, unable to hide the sadness in his voice. 'She loved art and collected many of these pieces. I'll take you around later. Let me show you the rooms. Kit, Agatha, you'll have your usual rooms. Mary, come with me.'

'Be careful, Mary,' warned Kit, 'He may be old....'

Mary laughed and followed Kit's uncle up the staircase, occasionally stopping as Alastair pointed out a notable painting or photograph. They stopped at a painting of a beautiful Hispanic woman. Mary heard the catch in Alastair's voice.

'She was beautiful,' said Mary simply.

'Yes, in every way.' Desolation was etched on Alastair's face. Then he collected himself and said, 'But we push on. We must.'

*

Mary looked out across the bay from her window. The view was undeniably beautiful. Sunlight glistened on the water like tiny jewels cast over a cobalt-coloured silk.

'My word, Uncle Alastair, I can see the reason why the house is called *Bellavista.*'

'Not my choice,' confessed Alastair, 'Christina's idea. I went along with it. Happily, I might add. But the view is remarkable, certainly. Now, I won't get in your way. I'll see you downstairs for tea.'

A few minutes after Alastair had departed, there was a knock on the door. Mary heard Kit say, 'Special delivery.'

She smiled and replied, 'I'm hardly dressed.' Which was not true.

The door practically burst off its hinges.

'Well, Lord Aston, I thought you were a gentleman.'

Kit joined her at the window, and they gazed across the bay. In such circumstances there is only one thing for a gentleman to do when in the presence of a young lady of his liking. This duty lasted several minutes before the noise in the corridor suggested the imminent arrival of a septuagenarian bodyguard. They returned to their previous pose just in time as the door opened.

'Ahh, there you are,' said Agatha obliviously. 'Tea is being served downstairs. When you've stopped all this romantic nonsense, you should join us.' The door closed when she finished.

Kit glanced down at Mary, 'Come on then.' They turned from the window and walked towards the door. 'Is the room to your liking?'

'Everything is to my liking. Your uncle is adorable, and I think we'll get on famously.'

'I thought you might. Don't take any notice of him and Ella-Mae. I should've mentioned that, on first sight, they can seem to have a fairly abrasive relationship. He'd be lost without her. I rather think she'd be lost without him.'

Mary laughed, 'I think it's rather sweet. By the way did you...?'

Kit looked at Mary and replied, 'Yes, I did notice her reaction to Natalie. What did you think?'

Mary frowned as they stepped into the corridor. In a more serious tone she said, 'Well, I have a feeling that your aunt and uncle are up to something.'

'My thought also,' agreed Kit. 'Algy is rather prone to marriage proposals and then being ditched or ditching the poor girl. This one has reached a more advanced stage in a shorter space of time than normal for my dear cousin.'

'Do you think Aunt Agatha and Uncle Alastair are testing him?'

'They're certainly testing him,' said Kit seriously before seeing Mary's reaction which had much of Aunt Agatha's disapproval albeit in younger and prettier form. He added quickly, and sheepishly, 'If you like that sort of young woman.'

The Frisco Falcon

'I can see you do,' said Mary with a straight face but the raised eyebrow suggested amusement rather than jealousy. 'She's certainly striking.'

Kit moved the subject on from Natalie's obvious attractiveness to the more pertinent issue raised by her arrival on the scene. He had a good idea of what his elderly relatives were planning.

'If this has been cooked up by the pair of them, it suggests there's no question that Algy wants to marry this girl.'

'Did you really doubt it?'

'You don't know Algy, darling,' replied Kit. 'I mean, it's possible Uncle Alastair disapproves. Hence the recruitment of our new maid by Aunt Agatha. Incidentally, Uncle Alastair mentioned he wanted to speak to me about why Algy hadn't come to meet us. I wonder if there's a problem.'

Mary tilted her head, 'Aside from Uncle Alastair trying to split them up?'

Kit smiled and then his face became more serious. He paused for a moment before saying, 'Something else. I'm sure of it. Anyway, we'll find out soon enough.'

*

The library in *Bellavista* reminded Mary, once again, of Cavendish Hall. It was large, well-stocked with beautiful, leather-bound volumes of the classics. Two leather chesterfield sofas and armchairs surrounded a low coffee table made from oak. A couple of Winslow Homer watercolours adorned the walls. Two differences were notable: the view from the large windows provided another opportunity to enjoy the bay, and then there was the bookcase near the entrance of the room. Agatha lifted one book and showed it to Alastair.

'Worth reading?' she asked hopefully.

113

'Let me see, which book is that?' replied Alastair putting on a pair of round tortoiseshell spectacles. 'Ahh, "The Case of The Wrong Corpse". Enjoyable but a mere trifle for you, my dear. You'll have the killer by page forty-five. No, let me find you one more devilishly clever.' He walked over to the bookcase and scanned the contents.

Mary glanced at Kit archly. He smiled back and whispered, 'We're in the presence of highly skilled sleuths.'

'So I see. It's certainly an impressive collection of...'

'Training manuals?' suggested Kit.

They listened to Alastair pronounce "Flash Fraser and the Love Nest Murder" a light read but promises several twists of interest. Agatha looked sceptically at the rather lurid cover which showed a somewhat underclad young lady standing before a man in a suit and a fedora that cast a shadow over his eyes.

'Very much of the American school, I see,' said Agatha, clearly an expert in the genre.

'Oh very,' chuckled Alastair, 'but unusually intelligent nonetheless, given its provenance.' This high recommendation of both the literary tome and the country that gave it birth, seemed to set the seal on the matter. Agatha took the book from Alastair before joining Kit and Mary at the table. Ella-Mae had entered stealthily as ever to serve some sandwiches and tea from a silver pot. Agatha noted with satisfaction there was not a lemon to be seen and Ella-Mae stirred the tea pot well before pouring and adding milk.

Once the tea was poured, all eyes turned to Alastair. For a few moments he looked non-plussed and then he remembered something important he'd meant to share with his family. He giggled nervously at his forgetfulness.

'Ahh, yes, we've had something of a hitch develop in the smooth-running course of true love, and all that.'

'The hitch being?' asked Agatha.

'Dain, Algy's fiancée, was arrested yesterday for murder. She spent the night in a cell.'

The sound of a cucumber sandwich being eaten would have felt like a scream in the middle of the night, such was the silence that greeted this announcement. All eyes turned to Kit. Realising, the ball was in his court, he pressed for more details on what had happened.

'Perhaps you could expand' said Kit for wont of anything better to say about such an extraordinary statement.

Alastair, somewhat oblivious to the shock he'd caused, happily explained all that he knew of the case: the murder of the Pinkerton man and the subsequent arrest of Dain Collins due to her refusal to answer questions on her past. All throughout his relaying of the story, both Kit and Mary had the distinct impression that the news was neither as surprising nor as alarming to Alastair as a prospective father-in-law might, otherwise, be feeling. More surprisingly was Agatha's less-than-worried reaction.

'I'm sure the matter will soon be sorted out satisfactorily,' she offered before biting into a sandwich which, as she held it up and nodded, clearly met with her approval. 'Ella-Mae has lost none of her facility, I see.'

'No,' agreed Alastair, 'She does at least one thing right.'

Kit noted they were veering alarmingly off topic and tried to steer matters back to what one might reasonably have concluded was the important issue of the moment.

'But this is madness. Surely, she can't be guilty? Shouldn't we be trying to get her out of jail?'

'We are,' said Alastair, finishing off another sandwich. 'I have Saul dealing with it.'

'Saul Finkelstein? Is he still alive and kicking?' exclaimed Agatha.

'Alive and certainly kicking, particularly when his opposite number is rolling around the ground,' replied Alastair with a titter. He dabbed his chin with a napkin.

'Who is Saul Finkelstein?' asked Mary.

Saul Finkelstein rose to his full five-foot and half an inch height. He leaned forward onto the desk thereby looming over Lieutenant Mulroney, insofar as it was possible for someone with a deficit in altitudinally-directed inches. The impact on the good lieutenant would have been amusing had they not been in the second hour of the interrogation in a room that might easily have doubled as one of the increasingly popular saunas in the city.

Finkelstein was seventy if he was a day, and that day was a wet, windy Tuesday in February. His heavily-lined, jowly face wore the permanent scowl of someone who disliked people he disagreed with. That he disagreed with most everyone, practically as a matter of principle, meant that a smile was a rare commodity on the face of the little lawyer unless he had succeeded in winning a case.

He thrust his hands in his waistcoat and took a deep, deliberate breath which had Mulroney's heart sinking as quickly as the air entered the lungs of the lawyer. Without removing the cigar which, like Mulroney's, was permanently wedged in the side of his mouth, pointing like a revolver towards the unfortunate object of his ire, he addressed the detective in an accent that hailed somewhere between New York and the Bronx.

'Look, Mulroney, enough is enough. Either charge my client or release her. You've nothing, admit it.'

Mulroney didn't even have that much but was reluctant to be browbeaten by an old nemesis. The interrogation of Dain Collins was failing on all fronts. She was a distant spectator to the verbal tennis between the detective and the lawyer. Her occasional answers were inaudible mostly, and monosyllabic when she was allowed to speak by Finkelstein, which was rarely.

Sweat rolled down Mulroney's head and he envied, for a moment, the ability of the little lawyer to wear a three-piece suit and not suffer heat stroke. Even Dain Collins looked unnaturally cool. Ice seemed to inhabit her veins. Meanwhile, Mulroney drummed his fingers on the table before the weakness of his position forced him to acknowledge defeat for the moment.

'Blow,' he said finally. 'Don't leave town though. We're not through with you Miss Collins, or whatever you're called.'

A smile, of sorts, creased the features of Finkelstein. He'd won. He usually did. Anger, perseverance and smarts. He'd made a career based on these three qualities of which he had an abundance. A fourth quality he never considered but which was appreciated by his clients, and hated by his opponents, was his gargantuan insensitivity to what people thought of him. He genuinely, profoundly even, did not care. Making enemies was a badge of honour. The more enemies he made, the more successful he became.

And, wealthier.

*

There was silence for a minute while Phil Geauque digested the information from Hammett. They looked at one another. It was difficult to read his boss's mood. The blue eyes were friendly but distant. Hammett doubted he would ever understand the man before him. There always seemed to be wheels within wheels. The arrest of Dain Collins had been reported to their client earlier that day. The brief had not changed, however.

Find out who she is.

'Does he want us to find out before the cops?'

'I don't think he's too worried,' answered Geauque. 'So, as long as he pays us, we stay on the job. Any leads?'

'Possibly. I had a call from Joe Cusack. He's arranged for me to meet someone down at the gym later. He says this guy may know Dain Collins. Just a question, but is our client in any way interested whether or not she's guilty?'

'I didn't ask. Why are you asking?'

Hammett leaned forward, 'I didn't like Cowan much. Nor did you, but he was one of ours. It doesn't look so good if we can't look after our own.'

'I agree. We keep on this until we find out who's responsible. At the moment, the Collins girl is our only lead. Some of the other guys are working other angles. You stay with this one.'

This was Geauque's way of ending a meeting. Nothing else needed to be said. Hammett stood up and offered his boss a half-hearted salute. He made it out of the office before the coughing started again.

A car ride to Joe's Gym took ten minutes longer than Hammett's good fellowship was ever likely to last in the summer heat. By the time he emerged from his car, he was sweating like Custer facing the Sioux with a broken sword and an empty gun. He strode into the gym. It was full of young men battering bags with a violent intensity. Hammett heard Joe before he saw him.

'Dash,' yelled a voice. It came from the doorway of an office.

119

Hammett wandered over. Inside, Joe was standing beside a nervous-looking Italian dressed as a waiter. At least Hammett deduced he was a waiter. The two men nodded to one another. Joe took the photostat of Dain Collins out of his pocket and put it on his desk.

'Do you know her?' asked Hammett.

The Italian looked up at Joe, greed in his eyes. Fear, also.

'I promised him ten bucks if the information was good. Five now, five later and a broken arm if he was messing with us.'

Hammett nodded and took out his wallet. The Italian grabbed the five dollars.

'I don't know her name, but she called herself Danielle in the club. Pretty sure it's her. Different hair. She was blonde but it's her, I'm sure of it.'

'Where?' pressed Hammett.

The Italian looked nervously at Hammett and then at Joe. He said, 'Look, they can't know I told you alright? I work at a small place just outside the City. Rich men go there. They show films. There are girls, dancing. You know the sort.'

Hammett did.

'Name?'

'Lehane's, d'you know it? Redwood City.' said the Italian.

Hammett nodded, 'Yes, I've heard of it. Nice place,' he said sardonically. The Italian looked either hurt or guilty, the look of a man who had to make a buck. For a moment Hammett felt remorse. Who was he to be so pious? 'Tell me more. Was she on the game?' he asked.

'No, I don't think so,' replied the Italian. 'Some are just escorts. Hostesses. The ones who speak nice. She was one of them. They don't wear much, mind you.' The Italian half-smiled at this. Clearly the guilt he felt at working in such a place was mitigated by some non-financial benefits.

'Anything else you can tell me? Did she have any friends?' pressed Hammett.

'No, she kept herself to herself. Didn't get involved with any of the guys working there. I think she's a bit strange.'

Hammett didn't disagree with the Italian on that one. Dain Collins was strange. He waited for a moment then said, 'There was no one special then?'

The Italian thought for a moment. Then a light appeared in his eyes as he remembered something that might be important.

'Yes, one other thing. There was an old guy, in his sixties or older. Came regularly. Always asked for her.'

'Do you have his name?'

The Italian confirmed what Hammett suspected anyway. He laughed dismissively, 'No, but these men give a different name anyway.'

'Sure,' said Hammett nodding.

But the Italian wasn't finished. 'One other thing about him you should know.'

'What's that?'

'He's English.'

It was later in the evening when Algy returned to *Bellavista*. He wasn't, it must be said, looking his usual dapper self. The tie was loosened; the evidence of the heat of the day, or more specifically, the Hall, was all too evident in the tell-tale stains underneath his arms. His face badly needed a shave. He ran a hand through hair that had not seen a comb for a few days also.

All things being said, there was a distinct lack of pippedness about Kit's cousin that only a day spent on the wrong side of the law can set off. The sight of Kit and his fiancée, as well as Aunt Agatha, a favourite target for his repartee, did serve to pick the young man up and the smile returned to his features when he saw his cousin in the library.

'Kit, my word, old man you're a sight for sore eyes.'

Kit smiled and looked Algy up and down as they shook hands, 'Same might be said for you.'

It was not in Algy's nature to take offence at much of anything and this was greeted with loud laughter. He held his arms out wide and regarded his unkempt appearance with something approaching embarrassment and good humour.

'You're not wrong there,' replied Algy before spying the disapproval on Aunt Agatha's face. 'My favourite aunt,' he exclaimed.

'Your only aunt,' sniffed Agatha.

Algy strode over to Agatha and planted a kiss on her cheek, 'It's good to see you again.' Moments later he noticed Mary. She was everything Kit had described her as being and a bit more besides. The blue eyes were clear and sparkled with an electricity that would have been intense had they not also radiated such obvious delight at the world around her. Algy glanced at Kit and noted the amused look on his cousin's face as if he had anticipated the impact Mary would have. Every time.

'Miss Cavendish,' said Algy, bowing theatrically, 'I am your servant for life.'

Her laugh felt like a splash of fresh water on a hot summer's day. She held out her hand and Algy kissed it like a knight errant, with a flourish saved from caricature only by its evident sincerity.

'Dear God,' said Alastair shaking his head in horror, 'The boy's a fool.'

Algy glanced at his father affectionately, 'So what have I missed?' There was a moment's embarrassed silence. Despite appearances, Algy was not a fool and he immediately gauged the situation. He nodded slowly, 'I guess pops has told you?'

'Yes,' confirmed Kit. 'Can you tell us what's happening? You've been to the police station.'

'Hall of Justice,' corrected Alastair.

'The Hall,' added Agatha in an American accent. This caused amazement on the face of Alastair and amusement on the faces of Mary and Kit.

'Have you taken leave of your senses?' exclaimed Alastair. Agatha merely shrugged and held up the book she had been reading before Algy's arrival by way of explanation.

Algy sat on the other side of Mary and ran his hand through his already unruly hair. 'I won't tell you the whole story; it's a mess. Dain was arrested two days ago but not charged. She was held last night in a police cell. Initially we didn't take it seriously and we were somewhat, shall we say, scathing in our approach to answering questions. Of course, I don't know what it's like in England, but over here that's like waving a red rag at a bull. Next thing we knew they're telling us that Dain has to stay in the cell for the night and that they're getting a warrant for her arrest.'

'But why?' pressed Kit.

Algy exhaled and pressed both his palms against his face for a moment. 'Look, the thing about Dain is that she's changed her name. I didn't know this until she was arrested. She's never talked about her past and I haven't asked her. I love her; she loves me. That was enough. But her refusal to talk about her past, or at least her real name, means that the cops won't discount her from the investigation. I said to her just tell them, but she refuses.'

Kit looked at Algy. His face betrayed the question that was now on everyone's mind. Algy looked at Kit and said, 'Look, I know this could mean a number of things like, she's been married before, or may even be still married. I don't care. I'll do whatever it takes.'

This seemed to satisfy Kit, but he noticed Alastair, sitting facing him, rolling his eyes. He also saw an exchange of looks between him and Agatha. This confirmed his suspicion that the two of them had cooked up the plan involving Natalie.

Kit asked Algy, 'But is she still in jail?'

'No, Saul saw to that. It took a long time to track him down; otherwise, she'd have been out of the Hall with our cop friends getting a flea in their ear. He was staying up at Pebble Beach. We managed to track him down on the fifteenth hole. Anyway, he was at the police station within a couple of hours and he sprung her an hour or two later. I've been down at the Hall since they took her in.'

'We'd noticed,' said Alastair staring pointedly at his son. 'And is Miss Collins joining us for dinner tonight?'

Algy shook his head. 'No, she's too shook up.'

'I'm sure she is,' said Mary. 'A warm bath and an early night would be my prescription.'

Algy laughed, 'That's exactly what she's doing. You'd make a swell nurse, Mary.'

'She did once' said Kit, looking at his fiancée.

'I remember,' smiled his cousin. 'I'm glad you found her in the end.'

Outside in the corridor the telephone was ringing. They heard Ella-Mae answer the phone. Moments later she entered the room like a breeze in summer. She looked directly at Alastair. Kit's uncle looked irritably back at his housekeeper but rose anyway, as ordered, apparently.

'Excuse me, important business I'm sure, otherwise my housekeeper would never have dreamed of interrupting such an important family get together.' He glared at Ella-Mae on his way past. She ignored him.

'So, am I to take it that you still plan to proceed with the wedding, Algernon?' This was Aunt Agatha at her sternest.

'Of course, two days from now Dain Collins will be my wife. There's no force on earth will stop this happening,' replied Algy staunchly. 'Now if you will excuse me, I think we can all agree on one thing, I need a bath.'

Kit and Mary laughed. Agatha raised her eyebrows and frowned. Algy passed his father on the way out of the room. Alastair sat down and said, 'I'm terribly sorry, but I must leave you for an hour. Something's cropped up. Don't worry,' he reassured them when he saw the concerned looks on Kit's and Mary's faces, 'It's a small matter. I'll be back soon. In the meantime, I recommend a walk in the garden, Mary. You might even find a handsome young man to accompany you. The views, you may have noticed, are rather wonderful.'

'I shall do so, Uncle Alastair,' said Mary with a smile. She rose from her seat as did Kit and Alastair. She pecked her soon-to-be uncle on the cheek causing a blissful flush to the cheeks of the older man. She held out her arm to Kit, who gallantly took it and led her out through the French doors into the garden.

When they'd left, Agatha looked at Alastair, 'Do you want me to come?'

'No, best if you stay and keep your ears and eyes to the grindstone, so to speak. We don't want to tip our hand.'

That was quite enough mixed metaphors for anyone, so Agatha merely nodded and watched Alastair exit the room from one door and her nephew and Mary from the garden doors. She rose immediately from her seat and went to the door Alastair had left by. She opened it enough to peek outside. She just managed to see Alastair place a hat on his head and leave through the front door. Another check to see that the entrance hall was clear, and she was out of the library and climbing the stairs more rapidly than any septuagenarian had a right to. Reaching her bedroom, she found Natalie.

'Ah, good. I was hoping I'd find you here.'

Natalie had unpacked the luggage and placed Agatha's clothes on the bed for hanging in the wardrobes. She was holding a wedding gift in her hand. Agatha looked at the bright blue paper wrapping with some distaste.

'What on earth?'

Natalie shrugged, 'Mademoiselle Mary did not know either.'

'Must be Christopher's. No matter,' responded Agatha. 'Right, onto business. The young man has returned home. Now, I'm about to ask you do something which, God forgive me, you may not like. You do not have to do this.'

'I'm happy to help, Madame.'

'That's the spirit. My nephew has gone to his room to take a bath. I think this is a wonderful opportunity for you to get lost, so to speak. His bedroom is the last on the right.'

Natalie smiled, curtsied for reasons that surpassed either her or Agatha's understanding, and headed out of the room. As she left, Agatha gave her a brisk nod and said, 'Thank you. You shall be well-rewarded.'

'*Merci,* Madame.'

The corridor was empty. Natalie darted along to the last room as instructed by Agatha. A light knock at the door, just enough to ensure no court in the land could accuse her of breaking in, then...

She opened the door.

The room was empty. Then the realisation hit her: Algy was in the bathroom. In fact, she could hear noise from another room. Thinking quickly, she opened the door again and looked out into the corridor.

It was empty.

Across the corridor she could hear the sound of a bath filling up. Natalie Doutreligne was a young woman made of stern stuff. The prospect of seeing a man in a state of undress was neither new nor frightening. And she was being very well paid for what was, on the face of it, a task that had very much been her hobby since the age of eighteen. Ten years, and the random endowments of mother nature, had turned her from an amateur hobbyist into a highly skilled practitioner of *affaires de coeur.*

Taking a deep breath, she plunged into the bathroom.

Standing in front of her, in all his glory, albeit with the serendipitous good luck of a modesty-covering towel he had just lifted to dry his hands, was all six feet and one hundred and eighty pounds of Algernon Aston.

There was a shocked moment of silence. Well three moments, actually, as both sized each another up and decided that what they saw was very much to their liking. Algy looked at the beautiful young woman in the maid's costume that was in no way ever meant to fit her. The black-brown hair, the olive skin and the dark quick-sand eyes were all perused, assimilated and committed to memory with an efficiency and a certitude that only the stronger sex can manage.

For Natalie, Algy's white skin, which was not necessarily his most appealing feature nor a particular preference of the young Frenchwoman, was stretched tautly over a well-muscled body, which most certainly was.

And he was rich, apparently.

In those split seconds Natalie realised that this task could actually be considerably more enjoyable than the first few weeks had given her to suppose. Her early attempts at attracting the attention of the old lady's other nephew had fallen sadly, short.

Natalie reacted first, courtesy of greater training in these delicate situations. She immediately averted her eyes and uttered, '*Je m'excuse, monsieur.*'

Hearing the French accent was, perhaps, the last piece of excitement that Algy needed at that moment. Out of the corner of her eye Natalie could see that Algy was, quite literally in the horns of a dilemma. Thinking quickly, she put her hand to her forehead, palm facing outward, and pretended to faint. She fell backward, hoping for the best.

Algernon Carlos Aston was the son of a gentleman. As such, he needed no second invitation to come to the rescue of a young damsel whose purity and modesty had been so traumatised by the sight of a partially clothed man. In fact, reaching to save the young lady meant his exposure was now complete, a consequence of the towel, he had previously gripped for dear life, falling to his feet as he prevented said damsel from hitting the floor, with a thud.

At such moments, in the very lowest forms of theatrical entertainment, the actors in the scene will be greeted by the inconvenient arrival of someone new. Real life was about to prove every bit as farcical for young Algy. Ella-Mae arrived, as noiselessly as ever, just in time to see a sight she had not seen in around twenty-seven years: the unclothed appearance of her master's son.

'This isn't how it seems, Ella-Mae,' said Algy cradling the groaning young French woman.

Sadly, the evidence that everything was exactly as it seemed was, to Ella-Mae's startled eyes, considerable although not, paradoxically, incompatible with the impression that young Algy had certainly grown up a fine figure of a man.

*

Kit and Mary walked hand in hand towards the end of the garden. It was late afternoon, and the sky was a livid blue, cloudless, empty of anything except a single bird swooping and climbing with abandon. Across the bay, yachts skimmed and twisted and fluttered like butterflies unable to decide which leaf to land on.

'Uncle Alastair and Aunt Christina used to sit here,' said Kit pointing at the wooden bench which overlooked the bay from the end of the garden.

'I can see why. It's so peaceful.'

'Yes,' said Kit sitting down. He looked at Mary, 'Not wishing to break into your sense of wonderment of the view, but what do you think of Algy?'

Mary grinned, 'I like him. He seems to me every bit as honest, guileless and big-hearted as you suggested.'

Kit nodded in agreement. This was as good a summary as any.

'Did you see Uncle Alastair and Aunt Agatha? The looks?' asked Mary.

'I was going to ask you the same thing,' agreed Kit. 'Yes, they're cooking up something alright.' Kit was silent for a moment before adding, 'I think I understand their concerns better now.'

Mary frowned a little, which both attracted Kit and worried him in equal measure.

'I don't think we should be rushing to judge her, Kit. She may have good reasons for not discussing her past. I can think of a few. It certainly doesn't mean she's some sort of fallen woman. Not that I can believe we are even considering such ideas in 1920.'

Kit looked at Mary. Her tone had not been harsh. Instead she was clearly torn between a natural feeling of sisterhood and the adverse evidence. Kit felt emboldened to continue.

'True, I want to believe she's the one for Algy, notwithstanding his past record in these matters. But it's still an issue. It can't be ignored. It wouldn't be fair on Algy. I think you accept this also but, as ever, I love that you want to support her too.'

Mary's eyes narrowed as she looked at Kit and then she looked out towards the bay. He saw a smile gradually appear on her lips and she turned to him again.

'I seem to remember a young man who had not one but three names, none of them his. I still fell in love with him before I found out who he was. I believe he also entertained similar feelings towards a young lady who, it transpired, was being less than honest about her name.'

'The folly of youth,' laughed Kit. 'Now, can we return to your strikingly open-minded views on the topic of fallen women.'

'You'll find my views very open-minded, Lord Aston,' smiled Mary, putting her arms around his neck.

Outside the apartment of Dain Collins were two men Hammett recognised. One was a Pinkerton operative, a new guy whose name he couldn't remember. The other was the kid, Will Cookson. The new guy was clearly a little bit smarter than either he or Cowan as he was sitting well out of sight of the kid. For the moment, one watcher was unaware he was being watched.

Hammett parked one block up from the apartment and walked towards the new operative. He was sitting on a park bench, wearing sunglasses and holding a walking stick in front of him. Hammett knelt down behind the bench and said, 'It's me, don't turn around. You see the kid over by the tree?'

The Pinkerton man nodded curtly.

'That's William Cookson. He's a thug connected to those watching the Collins woman. Keep an eye on him. He's dangerous; might have been the one that popped Cowan.'

Another curt nod. Garrulous, thought Hammett.

A few moments later a taxicab drew up outside the apartment building. Hammett tensed, unsure if he should get to his car or wait and risk attracting the attention of their friend in the ill-fitting suit or stay and see what happened. Inside the cab was a man. It was difficult to see his face and he was wearing a hat. He did not look young. Then Dain Collins appeared in the lobby of the building. She rushed out the door and climbed into the cab. It sped around the corner, stopping just long enough to pick up William Cookson. Then they were gone.

Both Pinkerton men gave vent to an impressive array of swearing that caused one old woman walking her dog to look venomously at both of them. They apologised. Hammett ordered the other operative to stay in position. Meanwhile he returned to his car and set off for the Hall of Justice. Inside the car he punched the steering wheel in frustration. Amateur. Geauque would blow a gasket. And he would be right to, also. Amateur night.

After a short journey, Hammett arrived at the Hall and made his way up to the detective bureau where Mulroney's office was located. He entered without knocking.

'Come in,' said Mulroney sardonically.

'I've just seen Dain Collins leave in a taxi with an old man. What happened?'

'Saul Finkelstein happened,' explained Mulroney. He stubbed out his cigar which had long since gone cold and looked at the private eye. 'What do you know?'

Hammett told him about the car picking up Dain Collins as well as William Cookson. He also told Mulroney about the connection with Lehane's near Redwood City. Mulroney whistled when he heard the name.

'What' so funny?' asked Hammett.

'You'll run into half of San Francisco's politicians there, from what I hear.'

Hammett laughed, 'A few policemen also, I suspect. Senior policemen too.'

Mulroney didn't try to deny it. This created a problem.

'It'll ruffle a few feathers if we go there,' said Mulroney. 'It's not a career-enhancing idea if you take my meaning.'

'Nothing to stop me,' pointed out Hammett. He was still unsure if he should mention the Englishman. He decided against it for the moment. The Dain Collins case was still his and it was not necessarily relevant to the Cowan murder. Not yet anyway.

'They'll love you, a hot shot shamus.' Mulroney began laughing at his own joke.

Hammett let that one pass. He lit a cigarette and asked, 'What about Cookson? Have you anything on him?'

'Nothing on him here, but that's only a matter of time. The kid's violent. He'll do something soon if he isn't already implicated in the Cowan killing.'

'Do you know who he's working for?'

'Have you heard of Sidney Goodman?'

'I think so. He's a fence?' said Hammett.

Mulroney nodded, 'That's right.'

'I don't know much about him. Our paths have never crossed. I can't see what the connection could be with the Collins girl, though.' The name was familiar, though. Hammett had heard it recently. He wasn't so sure it wasn't in connection with this case.

'Me neither. Goodman's been operating for a few years now under the front of an antique shop on Pine. We've never been able to pin anything on him. The word is Cookson's been hanging around this Goodman.'

Hammett left the Hall and jumped into his car. He felt the tell-tale liquid tremor in his stomach that usually preceded a coughing fit. Right on schedule he began coughing. For the next few minutes he gouged his stomach and throat of catarrh. When a ceasefire was finally granted by his body, he drove to the Pinkerton Offices.

He gave Geauque's office door a brief rap then walked in just as he heard him say 'enter'. The benign blue eyes looked at

Hammett. He might have made a good hypnotist, thought Hammett.

For the next few minutes Hammett updated Geauque about the developments in the Dain Collins case. The head of the agency merely nodded, remaining sphinx-like throughout. A good poker player too, thought Hammett.

'Lehane's won't be cheap,' said Hammett.

Just at that moment the phone on Geauque's desk buzzed. He answered it. As soon as he heard the voice on the line, he covered the phone and said to Hammett, 'Can you wait outside?'. Hammett rose from his seat and left the room. It was a thing of Geauque's. He preferred to keep operatives and the commissioning client apart in these cases. A strange quirk but Hammett let it pass. He'd barely sat down when Geauque peered through the door.

'That was the client. He's fine with the expenses. Do what you have to. By the way, do you have you a gun?'

'No and no,' replied Hammett anticipating the inevitable follow up.

He left the office and took the stairs down to the ground floor rather than wait for the elevator. The cost of information at Lehane's would be high assuming they didn't throw him out on his ear. This was a real possibility although they would have no reason to if, as Hammett assumed, she was no longer working for them.

It was still a little early to go to Lehane's. Nightclubs like Lehane's usually didn't get going until after eight. On a whim he headed in the direction of Pine, stopping briefly in a public library before returning to his car. He arrived at an antique shop called Goodman's Antiques, ten minutes later. He parked the car and walked up to the window. It contained an old oak writing bureau, and chair on one side and several stone sculptures and wooden carvings in the other. Hammett took from his pocket a pair of spectacles and put them on. He quickly checked on how they looked via his reflection in the window. It made him look smarter, he thought. Then he walked inside.

The shop was smaller inside than it had seemed from the outside. The front windows had only provided a small clue as to the contents in the shop. Hammett was no expert in antiques, but he could see items from various countries: an Egyptian sarcophagus, Roman statues, woodblock prints and swords from Japan, and a wall full of leather-bound books, with a sign above claiming they were first editions.

He headed straight towards them. A few moments later a woman appeared and stood beside him. Hammett turned to her. She was in her forties and it looked like she hadn't worn a smile since her twenties. Hammett almost recoiled at the severity of her expression. Collecting himself quickly he smiled openly at the woman.

'How do you do?' he said primly.

The woman's mouth moved slightly in what she may have mistakenly believed was a smile.

'Are you looking for anything in particular?'

'Yes, do you have Julian Aubrey's '*Birds of America*'? First or second edition?'

The woman looked completely confused by this, which she should have but perhaps not for the reasons she should have. Hammett smiled hopefully at her.

'We have a small section over here on nature,' said the woman gesturing towards a group of books on the bottom shelf. Describing this section as small was an understatement. Hammett counted three books.

'It could also appear in your art section,' said Hammett with another killer grin.

The smile, insofar as it could have been described thus, slowly left the woman. She was beginning to feel out of her depth. She moved slowly towards the art section which, to be fair to Goodman's, provided a wider selection of books. However, none matched the title of the book Hammett was after, principally because just over one hundred existed. And the author was called John, not Julian and his surname was Audubon.

'Perhaps,' offered Hammett, 'I could speak to the owner. I'm very interested in acquiring this book. I would be willing to make it worth his while. May I speak with him?'

The woman saw an escape route open up and Sandra Robins was not a woman to allow such a golden opportunity to pass.

'Mr Goodman is not in today. I'm sure if you were to come tomorrow morning, you would find him here. After eleven,' said Sandra Robins before adding needlessly, 'He's a late riser.'

'A man after my own heart.'

'Can I leave him a message?' She handed Hammett a pen and some paper. Hammett thanked her and wrote the following message.

I'm interested in a certain rare Bird. Would like to discuss with you tomorrow. Yours, J. Audubon.

Sandra Robins looked at the message and said, 'I'm sure Mr Goodman will be delighted by your interest.'

Hammett smiled back, 'Yes, I'm sure he'll be just delighted.'

Jack Murray

There was unquestionably a certain atmosphere at the dinner table that evening. The air crackled with a current that managed to be both under, positive and live all at the same time. The key clues picked up by the betrothed sleuths were the unusually flippant mood of Agatha, more than matched, it must be said, by Alastair, and the despondency of Algy.

Kit discounted the idea of pre-wedding nerves or second-thoughts. Algy seemed far too smitten even by his own high standards for this to be the case. Clearly the fact that Dain had been implicated in a murder was uncommon even by the standards of modern matrimony. This left two possibilities. He discussed them with Mary afterwards *sotto voce.*

'He must have met Natalie,' suggested Kit.

Mary looked wryly at Kit, 'Are you suggesting, Lord Aston, that it is Natalie who has turned his head?' The implication was clear.

This was dangerous territory under normal circumstances for any chap talking innocently with his intended to negotiate. Kit dealt with the potential pitfalls adeptly, aided by the certainty that Mary was less interested in testing his love for her than turning any situation into an opportunity to tease him.

There was only one response.

'Certainly. Natalie would turn any man's head,' declared Kit, straight-faced. 'One look at her...'

Mary held her hand up and managed both to grin and frown at the same time. This was an extraordinary natural gift of hers and left Kit, once more, regretting that he could not take his fiancée for a romantic walk, ideally somewhere secluded. For a week or three.

'I think I understand your point, Lord Aston,' interrupted Mary. She ran her hand down the front of her dress slowly before adding, 'Even I can see how some men might have their head turned.'

Kit's eyes narrowed and they both began to giggle. After a few moments his face grew more serious.

'Either something happened with Natalie or the mystery surrounding Miss Collins is beginning to wear his resolve down. I think the former,' said Kit glancing in the direction of Alastair and Agatha who were all but clinking glasses in celebration.

'I agree. Can you ask Algy, you know, man to man?' The last part of that sentence was said in a deeper voice. Then Mary's face erupted into a smile at her own foolishness.

'Remind me, when are we getting married?' asked Kit plaintively.

'Why wait?' pointed out Mary, eyebrows arching upward.

Indeed, thought Kit. Why wait. It was 1920. Times had changed. He felt torn between a rational respect for his fiancée and more emotional feelings, needs even.

They were joined by Algy at that moment. He tried to smile and be the good host. Kit decided to put him out of his misery.

'Let's go outside, old man. I can't stand to see you so miserable. Tell me what's on your mind.'

'Is it so obvious?' said Algy, his face fell vertically, like a teardrop.

Mary took his right arm and Kit the left and they walked outside into the garden. They followed the path down to the seat overlooking the bay. It was night. Lights flickered like fireflies across the other side of the water. A ship went past and blew its horn. Another one responded. The sound of a boat's engine spluttering on the water echoed across the bay. Overhead the cloudless sky provided a spectacular display of stars, blinking lights from the very beginning of time. Algy began to speak of Dain, including their first meeting.

'I was out with a potential client. He said he knew a place that was fun. Good food, dancing, lots of girls. I thought, well why not. Business hasn't been so good lately and we needed a win. We went to this place out of town. Anyway, I didn't like the look of it from the moment I arrived,' said Algy looking at Kit directly in the eye.

'I think I take your meaning,' said Kit.

Mary frowned at both men. Kit shrugged but remained tight-lipped.

'We went to where the music was playing. Actually, the band was pretty good and lots of people were dancing. We ordered some food. It was all wrong, though. This guy didn't want to talk about his business. In fact, he seemed a bit young to me to be even in business.'

'What was his business?'

'Antiques, he said. He was going to be opening a big store in town and wanted to get the word out to as many potential clients as possible. The thing was, when I asked him about his business, he seemed uncomfortable.'

'How do you mean?' asked Mary.

'Like he was reading from a script. Some of his answers had nothing to do with my questions. It was really strange. Then he saw Dain. I didn't know her at that point. She was working in this place as a hostess. Hated it, by the way. Old men pawing at her. Anyway, that's just what happened. This guy snaps his fingers and orders her to come over. I have to tell you; I really didn't like that. Then he grabs Dain by the arm and virtually pulls her down to sit with us.'

'My word, a ruffian,' said Mary.

Kit looked at her archly and said, 'Ruffian? He sounds like one of these American hoodlums Aunt Agatha, and apparently Uncle Alastair, love to read about. What happened then.'

'As soon as I saw the fear on Dain's face, I was on my feet and giving him a piece of my mind. I told him we didn't take thugs like him as clients. And do you know what he did?'

Both Kit and Mary shook their heads.

'He started laughing at me. I couldn't believe it. I mean he was laughing in a strange, mad way. He grabbed at Dain again and tried to get her to kiss him, but, naturally, I wouldn't have it. I was round the table immediately and about to sock him when he let her ago. He was still laughing. I told him to get on his feet and act like a man. I was ready to teach him a lesson. Then he showed me.'

'Showed you what?' asked Mary.

'The gun?' suggested Kit.

Algy nodded to Kit. He shook his head at the memory of the night. 'He was grinning like a maniac. Dain was saying to me, "Please get me out of here. I hate it." I took her hand and we got out of there.'

'Didn't anyone try to stop you?' asked Kit, surprised.

This time Algy shook his head. He said, 'Nobody tried to stop us. It was like they expected their clients to act that way.'

'How horrible,' said Mary taking Algy's hand.

'On the way home, we talked. She told me she'd left home in New York a year ago. Her stepfather was a beast. He was trying to make unwelcome advances on her. She'd changed her name and come out west to make sure he'd never find her again. Her nerves were shot but she managed to find a job as a hostess in that terrible place. It's like she's a Maître d' but she also stays and chats to the clients. Mostly male clients. Some strange women too but I won't dwell on that.'

Mary tilted her head slightly. Enough to mock the ridiculously misplaced sense of gallantry in men that stopped them from speaking about subjects that might, quite literally, melt the ears of well brought up women. Kit suppressed a smile. Algy would learn what Mary was like soon enough.

'I could tell, even on that car journey back, that she was not what my father probably thinks she is. You may have gathered pops is not keen on the marriage. He's been perfectly gentlemanly towards her, naturally, but I know he doesn't approve. He's stopped short of telling me outright, of course. He knows what my answer would be.' Algy stopped and looked at Kit. 'Look, Kit, God knows I've made mistakes before. I can be a bit rash. This time really is different. I'm sure about Dain.'

Kit put his hand on Algy's arm to reassure him. 'You said that business isn't going well?'

'Since pops left, we've lost clients. Quite a few. We're not replacing them, and competition has increased. It's tough but we'll survive. Pops says he'll maybe help out a bit. He's great with clients, like a magnet. The business has missed that.'

Kit smiled and glanced back at the house.

'Your father seemed in a very good mood tonight for a man whose son is rushing into an unfortunate marriage, a prospective daughter-in-law who is under suspicion for murder and with a business in trouble.'

143

Algy put his hands over his face and groaned. Then he smiled with embarrassment, 'Oh my God, this so embarrassing.'

'What happened?' asked Mary.

'I don't quite know myself. This new maid, Natalie. She's quite...' Algy saw Kit looking at him directly, eyebrows raised. 'Anyway, I was getting ready for my bath and in she walks. Anyway, she faints when she sees me. I was holding her when Ella-Mae arrived.'

'When you say getting ready, Algy?'

'Let's say I was all but climbing into the bath, Kit.'

'I think I see,' said Kit.

'Me too,' chipped in Mary which earned her a wry look from Kit and a shocked one from Algy.

'Best to ignore her, Algy, I find,' advised Kit.

Algy laughed, 'I'm falling in love.'

'Choose your weapons, sir,' replied Kit with a grin.

'Advertising copy?' suggested Algy hopefully.

'I'm not a box of chocolates,' pointed out Mary in mock irritation.

Kit rolled his eyes and motioned Algy to finish the thought.

'No, Mary, you're so much sweeter,' said Algy.

Mary exhaled theatrically, clasped her hands together dramatically and pronounced Algy her hero.

'I can see why your business is in trouble,' said Kit sardonically.

It was close to midnight when Hammett pulled up to the large parking lot outside Lehane's. A big neon sign blinked over a single-story building that looked like a gaudily painted garage. A pretty big garage. There were no windows. Hammett sat in his car and listened to the first drops of rain hitting the roof. Little by little the sound grew louder. Soon the windscreen was a mass of rivulets running downwards, distorting the view of the club.

The parking lot was half full. The cars were a mixture of waiting taxicabs and larger, more expensive automobiles. Hammett had no doubt his local taxes paid for the taxicabs. He felt the anger rising.

The thought of visiting a joint like this sickened Hammett. He hated it already. He hated the owners running the place. He hated the customers more. A politician he half-recognised left the club. He was accompanied by a younger Hispanic woman. Much younger.

Finally, Hammett emerged from the car and strode towards the club like a man who had every right to be there. He was dressed in his best dark suit and a recently acquired blue silk tie with light blue polka dots. If he didn't have a million dollars then he sure as hell had set out to make people think it. As he got closer to the entrance, he heard music playing. A poster at the entrance showed a scantily clad woman behind a microphone. It read Elsa Nichols. Hammett had never heard of her, but he doubted it was her voice that audiences were interested in. He also saw the doormen. They were big. More than big, they looked mean. Thankfully he didn't recognise any of them. This meant the chances of him being recognised were slim.

He nodded to the smaller of the two men at the door. The smaller man was better dressed. This seemed to satisfy the man and Hammett had passed his first test. He realised as he walked in that his heart was beating very quickly. In a moment he would begin to cough. He covered his mouth. A young woman came over to him.

'Are you alright, mister?'

She was in her early twenties. Heavily made up. He looked at her and wondered why she'd bothered. Mother nature had been kind enough to her.

'Water,' croaked Hammett. Then he tried to smile, 'Add it to the whisky.'

The woman said, 'Come this way.' Hammett followed her towards a door where the music was coming from. He saw some other men walk through a different door. She saw him look at the other men.

'They show films. Do you want to go?' she asked. Sadness filled her like tears. She seemed to want him to say no.

Hammett frowned and shook his head. The coughing wasn't as strong now, but he could still feel the tickling sensation in his chest. She led him into a large ballroom. A small orchestra, dressed in white dinner jackets which looked pronounced against their dark skin, was playing jazz music. The dance floor was empty. The room was not very bright. A dim light emerged stealthily from behind cornices on the beige-coloured walls. They walked over a dark red carpet towards the dance floor where most of the remaining free tables were situated.

The Frisco Falcon

The dance floor was a light brown parquet, probably made from an odd assortment of hardwood. A bronze railing surrounded half the dance floor and led to the orchestra who, thought Hammett, were actually rather good. They occupied around a third of the stage. Elsa Nichols was singing. She was not bad either. Maybe he'd done her a disservice. What little there was of the dress was very pretty too. Reluctantly, Hammett drew his eyes away from the dress to his new companion. They sat down and the young woman went to collect a drink for him. A minute later she returned with a half-bottle of whisky and a glass.

'You not joining me?'

She shrugged, 'Do you want me to?'

Hammett pushed the glass in her direction. Underneath it was five dollars. The young woman sat down. She was clearly nervous. Hammett handed her a cigarette and lit it. The music suddenly switched from jazz, which had failed dismally to attract any dancers, to a slow tango. Several older men and several clearly reluctant young women trooped onto the dance floor.

'I'm looking for a girl,' said Hammett.

The young woman looked bored now, 'You've come to the right place.'

'A particular girl. Name's Danielle. D'you know her?'

'Look, mister, I just work here.'

Up ahead Hammett could see some of the men belonging to the club looking over at his table. Eventually one strolled over.

'Is everything alright?' he asked. There was no trace in his voice that he cared either way what the response might be.

Hammett smiled up at him, 'Just dandy.'

The young woman got up to leave, 'Thank you for the drink, mister.'

The man watched the young woman go and then looked down at Hammett. He said, 'Perhaps it's time you left, too.'

Hammett nodded, perhaps it was. The young woman had been pulled aside by a man in an expensive dinner suit. They were both talking and looking over at him. He turned away from Hammett and walked off. Moments later the man he had been speaking to came over.

'Come with me.' It wasn't a request. Hammett stood up and followed him away from the dance floor. They walked towards the foyer of the nightclub but turned suddenly into a shallow corridor that led to a door. The man knocked then opened without waiting for a reply.

Hammett entered the office. There was a leather sofa by the wall. Above it was a painting that Hammett suspected was a Picasso. There were other paintings that looked like they would cost Hammett's annual salary. The room was dominated by a large oak desk. Behind the desk was the man who had been looking at him earlier. He was smoking a cigarette. From the cigarette holder, Hammett guessed this was the great man himself: Eddie Lehane.

The door shut behind Hammett. He stood alone in front of the desk like a schoolboy about to be punished. The man regarded Hammett in silence. No doubt he was trying to intimidate him. Hammett could have laughed. Finally, he spoke.

'I don't like people coming to my club asking questions.'

'I missed the sign saying that' replied Hammett. 'Sorry.'

Lehane's eyes hardened.

'Wise guy. Listen up, I already have an arrangement with the local johns. Understand? Now, beat it.'

How do you do, too, thought Hammett. He kept his eyes on Lehane.

'I'll go, but just so as you know, I'm Pinkerton, not one of your boys on the force. You don't own me.'

'Yet, shamus, yet,' sneered Lehane. Neither his veneer of wealth nor polished dress could hide the obvious: he was a crook. And probably a mean one, too. His hair was turning to grey but with the suit and the general well-heeledness that provided its own level of self-assurance, he was not bad looking. The eyes were hard though, even if the smile wasn't.

Hammett took a chance. He showed a picture of Dain Collins. He said, 'I'm looking for information on her. I know she worked here.'

Lehane took hold of the picture and looked at it closely then handed it back to Hammett.

'Danielle. We haven't seen her in months.'

The door opened behind Hammett. The other man entered again. Lehane nodded to the man. The conversation was over, and Hammett felt a hand grasp his elbow, far from gently.

'Wait up, Mr Lehane,' said Hammett rolling the dice. 'I know where she is now. That's not what I want.' Lehane stopped and turned around again to Hammett.

'Go on.'

'I want to know where she came from.'

'Why?'

'My client. She's about to marry some guy. She's under suspicion for murder and no one, police included, knows who she is.'

149

'That about figures. You're climbing the wrong tree here, shamus. You may have gathered we don't do background checks,' said Lehane with a mirthless smile, and gesturing around his club, 'If you take my meaning.'

'Who's the English guy?'

Lehane, removed the cigarette holder from his mouth and walked up close to Hammett. He stared deep into Hammett's eyes. Hammett stared back. A slow grin crossed Lehane's lips, 'I don't know why, but I like you. You seem straight.'

'My partner's dead. I didn't like him. But that means something to me, anyway. If this girl is connected, I want to know why.'

'You think she killed your partner?' Lehane seemed surprised.

'I don't even know her name and I've been tailing her for days now. I don't know. Who's the English guy?'

'Sorry, shamus, I'm not in the business of informing,' said Lehane and turned away. He was gone in a moment.

Hammett turned to the man and grinned, 'Looks like it's you and me, sister. Do you dance?'

The man growled at him, 'Blow.' Hammett felt his arm being handled roughly. Another man came over towards the table. This was becoming distinctly unpromising.

'Alright, Clyde, I'm going.' Hammett shook his arm free and brushed past the other man on his way to the exit. He could feel a hard object in the man's pocket as he passed him.

The automobile slowed down as it passed each house. Finally, it reached its destination. Overhead the night sky was a black blanket, the rain cloud had arrived and dispensed its gifts generously. It was after two in the morning. A single streetlight shone. Gutters were flooding. Even the criminals were indoors with their feet up.

'That's it. Look up there,' said the young man in the ill-fitting suit. 'Some house, huh?'

The other man in the car looked at him, trying to disguise his contempt. He was dressed neatly: dark trousers, dark shirt, dark overcoat. He regarded the house for a moment. It was a monstrosity. He looked back at his companion driving the car.

'Some house.'

It was difficult to say if he agreed with the driver. The foreign accent hid all manner of nuance. Not that the young man would have understood sarcasm rooted in tone rather than words.

The car drew to a halt, and the two men sat and viewed the house. The young man was surprised that his companion had made no move.

'What are you waiting on?' he asked, nervously.

The other man looked at him again, without expression. The silence in the car lasted a few moments but felt like minutes to the young man.

'I'm waiting,' said the foreign gentleman, pausing almost for dramatic effect, 'for the rain to stop.' As he said this, he was mentally shaking his head. Where did the fat man find these people?

The fat man.

He hated the fat man; worse, he didn't trust him. But he had no choice. They were bound together by the one thing that is thicker than blood: money. When this was finished maybe he would retire. Not in America, though.

Barbarians.

Barbarians like the man beside him. Without culture, without a spiritual or intellectual impulse unless it involved money. There was no love of beauty, of finer things such as art, music, jewellery, ideas. These people were not like him. Without refinement. However, there was something to be said for the openness of their society that allowed people from the bottom to rise to the top. This was an improvement on Europe, unquestionably. He looked again at his young companion who was chewing gum. Then again...

They sat in silence while the rain fell heavily onto the car beating metronomically. It was hypnotic. The young driver began beating his fingers on the wheel in time to the falling rain. The other man looked at the fingers and then at the young man. He stopped immediately.

The foreign gentleman closed his eyes and waited. His senses were filled as surely as the gutters on the road by the sound of the rain falling. They waited. Half an hour passed with little change in the intensity of the rainfall. Beside him, he heard the crack of thunder, or, at least, snoring. The foreign gentleman opened his eyes and looked with disgust. Once again, he wondered where the fat man located such low-level hoodlums. He nudged the boy awake.

The kid at least had the decency to look embarrassed. He tried to smile but nerves contorted his face into something less friendly, more maniacal. The foreign gentleman remembered similar smiles on idiots from his village. He shuddered at the memory. A long time ago. He'd escaped.

A few minutes later the rain eased to a point where he felt he could risk stepping outside to brave the night. He climbed out of the car and told the driver he would be back soon. He knew what to do if not.

The night was dagger-black, the air damp like a cold wet towel on his face. He made no attempt to hide the fact he was walking to the front door. He walked up the long garden path silently then onto the porch and stood in front of the entrance. He tried the door. Unsurprisingly, it was locked. Opening it would have presented little or no problem. However, negotiating the stairs brought with it a certain amount of risk, even at this ungodly hour.

He walked along the front of the house and round to the back. There was a garden gate built into the wooden fence. The fence was knee high. The foreign gentleman looked at the picket fence in wonderment. What was the point? He continued on his way. A few moments later he stood in the back garden. He peered through the French doors into a well-stocked library. Turning away from it he saw what he was looking for.

The kitchen was situated on the ground floor of the mansion. It jutted out from the main building. Directly above the kitchen were the guest bedrooms, at least according to the intelligence he had been given from the fat man.

With balletic grace, the man hopped up onto a pipe attached to the wall. He used that as a platform from which to climb onto the windowsill. From there it was an easy manoeuvre to reach the roof of the kitchen. Moving forward he counted two windows over from the end of the house. He jumped up and caught hold of the railings of the first bedroom's balcony. He hauled himself up and over onto the balcony itself. The curtains were closed.

Removing some keys from his pocket he tried a few different options for the French doors. Finally, one slotted in. A few moments of manipulating the lock and the door opened. He slipped inside.

On the bed he saw an old woman. She was snoring lightly. The man padded over to a large valise and opened it. Empty. He went over to the wardrobe and searched it, with no success. The drawers were equally unproductive. There was no sign of any wedding present in the room. He crept out of the room and went to the next room. With great care he opened the door.

On the bed was another woman. She was young. He recognised her from the boat. Such beauty, such elegance. He stood over the bed and admired the serenity of her features at rest. Even in sleep she was the very definition of refinement. Exhaling dejectedly, he tore himself away from the vision before him and conducted a similar search of the room with a similar lack of success.

The next option was the one he had been looking forward to least. He had been briefed on Aston. In all likelihood he was a light sleeper. This was now heading towards risky territory. He reached inside his pocket and felt the familiar cold metal. He was prepared for any eventuality.

Except one.

The man opened the door of Mary's room and crept out into the dark corridor. His first step caught a loose floorboard and he heard it creak. It felt like a rumble of thunder in a monastery. He resisted the urge to scream a volley of oaths. He

The Frisco Falcon

continued on his way, creeping along the corridor like a burglar which, strictly speaking, he was.

He arrived at the final guest bedroom and began to twist the doorknob when he felt a sharp pain on the back of his head and his eyes lit up. He screamed in agony and then he felt a wild animal attack him with what looked like a silver drinks tray. He was hit repeatedly with the edge of the tray, which, it must be said, was rather painful.

'You're hurting me,' he complained, truthfully.

'Take that,' shouted the wild animal, who, the man could see was the rather diminutive housemaid he had been warned about.

The row had, by now, woken the house. The first to appear was Alastair Aston who, sensibly, switched on a lamp sitting on a table in the hall. Next to appear was Kit followed by Mary, who exclaimed, 'It's that horrible little man.'

'Pardon me?' he said in a voice that was as offended as it was clearly not American.

The man glanced hurtfully at Mary, his moon eyes, quite literally feeling a pain that was no longer just physical. Mary felt a stab of guilt for a moment seeing the man's evident distress was not solely a consequence of Ella-Mae's rather violent attack.

Seeing the two, no actually it was three now, Aston men, advancing on him - Algy had made a belated appearance at the end of the corridor - the man remembered in the midst of the battering that he had a gun in his pocket. He pulled it out and pointed it wildly at everyone and anyone who was moving.

'Leave me alone,' he shouted, in the manner of a child who has been set on by his friends. Everyone stopped in their tracks immediately. In fact, everyone, including the man, stood rooted to the spot.

'What do you want from us?' asked Kit. His voice was unnervingly calm; the small man did not like the look in the English lord's eyes. He did not seem afraid. Worse, he looked like he was quite some way down the track of a plan to disarm him. At this point the man bitterly regretted his decision not to load the gun. It was then he registered that the tall Englishman was leaning on a walking stick. Heavily.

He glanced down at his adversary's two legs then back up into the eyes of Kit Aston. One man was in control, and it seemed to the little man holding the gun it wasn't him. He waved it about again, hoping to remind the man facing him of the situation.

Guns and Joel Israel did not get on. He considered them, not unreasonably, dangerous. Joel Israel did not consider himself a violent man. From time to time he had, as a final recourse, resorted to behaviour that resulted in bloodshed. This was not him, though. He was too refined, too cultured, fundamentally too caring not to regret its deployment. He felt it important that the people he was holding the gun on understood this.

Joel Israel's journey to San Francisco's *Bellavista* had begun some forty years previously from the most unlikely of locations. He was born in a small village outside Cairo. His mother had met a young man whom she believed loved her. His departure soon after she demonstrated her love for him was inevitably unexpected. The young man was rich, she was not. He was also married, a detail he had neglected to mention as he wooed her with jewels that subsequently turned out to be as fake as his professions of undying love.

The Frisco Falcon

Thus, young Joel Israel grew up with a hatred of rich men. He channelled this hatred positively by robbing them in a single-minded effort to become just like them. His talent was as prodigious as his success inevitable. By the age of twenty he had moved to Cairo with his mother and, with the opportunities only a big city can provide, he achieved a surprising level of affluence for one so young. So surprising in fact that it attracted the attention of what law enforcement there was in Cairo at that time. They, like many of the neighbours, could not understand the source of the young man's wealth given that he, ostensibly, did not seem to do a tap of work.

He kissed his mother goodbye and fled to Constantinople which was to remain his home for the next fifteen years. His career continued, albeit at a less frenetic pace, and he achieved a level of affluence consistent with his pedigree. Avoiding the same mistake as Cairo was paramount.

To this end, he brought his mother over to join him in Constantinople and set her up as proprietor of a small antique store which acted as a front for his true profession: stealing and fencing stolen goods. He kept his hand in, from time to time, on robbery, but tended, of late, to play the gentleman about town rather than cat burglar. The Joel Israel of today was a dapper little man with a fluency in many languages including the one true *lingua franca* of the planet: money.

Yes, Joel Israel had come a long way, literally, as he stood face to face with the tall, good-looking Englishman. It was clear to the little man that this was someone from a noble background. Twenty years of associating with such people had tempered his view of this caste. Was he not one of them now? Had it not always been so? They were alike, at least in Joel Israel's rather skewed view of the world. Standing there with a gun in his hand was unfortunate. No, worse, it was ill-mannered.

'I regret the necessity of this. But you have something of mine, and I want it back,' he coughed apologetically. 'You will please put your hands up.' He moved the gun upwards to emphasize his meaning lest it was not understood by the native English speakers facing him.

'We have something belonging to you?' exclaimed Kit. 'What do you mean?' His hands remained resolutely by his side. He didn't look happy, thought Joel Israel, before realising he probably wouldn't be either if he had been woken up by a gun-wielding intruder, no matter how well-dressed and polite he was.

Joel Israel looked at the tall Englishman apologetically and glanced down at Kit's hands, motioning upwards with his eyes and gun for him to do as the others, however reluctantly, had done. He was just about to launch in an explanation, of sorts when a door opened to Joel's right. The voice of Aunt Agatha could be heard complaining about the racket outside her room.

Joel Israel knew it was a mistake the moment he glanced the old woman's way. In the blink of an eye he registered, first, her surprise, followed by her righteous anger. However, the volley of abuse that followed from her immediate assessment of the situation served to add to his distraction. To be fair to the old woman, her understanding of the status quo was as rapid as it was accurate and also, surprisingly, colourful; stopping just short of outright swearing.

He felt a sharp pain on his arm. He glanced back wildly at Kit. The gun was on the ground thanks to the Englishman knocking it out of his hand with his walking stick. The

Englishman was on the ground in seconds seeking to retrieve the gun. Time to leave, thought Joel Israel.

Quickly.

He turned and sprinted down the stairs. Agatha looked at Kit who was now back on his feet. The moment he picked up the gun he realised it was lighter than it should have been. To his left he heard Aunt Agatha say, 'Well go on, shoot him.'

'It's empty,' pointed out Kit.

Joel Israel was at the bottom of the stairs now with a set of keys in his hand. He put one in the front door lock.

'Well chase him then,' ordered Agatha. Kit glanced down at his leg, which was missing its prothesis, and raised his eyebrow questioningly.

'Oh yes, I forgot that.'

Algy tore past Kit and Agatha and raced down the stairs three steps at a time. He reached the bottom just as Joel Israel opened the front door. He was at the door a second after it closed. The two men wrestled the door open. But then Algy heard a tell-tale click. The little man had closed the door and locked it from the outside. Algy could hear footsteps racing off into the distance. He went to the window and saw him climb into an automobile which then sped off into the night.

'Who was that?' demanded Algy angrily, climbing the stairs.

'More to the point, what was he after?' mused Kit. He turned to Mary whose eyes seemed more amused than terrified by the experience. She walked over to Kit and kissed him on the cheek.

'That was quick thinking, Lord Aston. I was wondering when you would try something.'

'I'm off to bed,' announced Agatha, 'I trust I can leave it to the men to guard this place for the rest of the night?'

'It looks to me like Ella-Mae did a much better job of that,' pointed out Mary.

Alastair glared at Ella-Mae, 'Welcoming as ever to guests, I see.'

'I try,' replied Ella-Mae, turning and walking down the stairs. As she walked down to the bottom Alastair leaned over the balcony.

'Are you getting...?'

'Yes,' replied the older woman.

A minute or two later she returned carrying a Webley revolver.

'Is it...?'

'Yes, it's loaded.'

'Algy,' said Alastair, 'You go first. I'll take over at five.' Algy nodded and took the gun from Ella-Mae. Alastair turned to his guests, 'Perhaps we should turn in. Let's get some sleep. We can try and make sense of this extraordinary affair tomorrow.'

Downstairs, Natalie appeared. She looked up first at the Astons and Mary standing on the first-floor balcony overlooking the entrance hall, then she registered Algy holding the Webley. Her eyes widened. Putting her hand to her mouth she said, '*Mon Dieu.*'

Indeed, thought Kit, *Mon Dieu.*

The waitress at John's Grill offered Hammett some more coffee. It had been a late night. Very late. He raised his cup and she refilled it. He added some sugar and put it to his lips. He was beginning to wake. Slowly. Around him businessmen and some women were breakfasting. The Grill was full; a couple of people even stood in line for a free table. One of them was the Pinkerton man who had shadowed Dain Collins. His name, Hammett now remembered, was Foley. Strange how he could remember the name so easily now when the day before he couldn't place him. Old age thought Hammett. He was twenty-six years old.

Hammett motioned him over. Foley saw Hammett and moved rapidly through the tables. There was an economy of movement about the small man, not just in words. He nodded to Hammett, sat down and removed his hat.

'The old man sent you?'

Foley nodded.

'The Collins girl. Any sign?'

'None. I just told Geauque. The landlord in the building told me she's paid up to the end of the week. Her apartment was already furnished.'

'So, she's flown the coop.' It wasn't a question.

'Looks like it,' replied Foley, raising his hand to attract the attention of a waitress. He ordered coffee.

'You can save me a trip then, tell Geauque that I'm following a lead I mentioned to him yesterday. A fence named Sidney Goodman. Owns an antique store on Pine. Do you know him?'

161

'Only by rep. The store is a front,' said Foley.

'I gathered that. What about Dain Collins? Do we have anything new on her?' asked Hammett.

'The old man is going to find out what the client wants. I have the feeling he thinks it's case closed.'

'Just like that?' Hammett was unhappy at this news.

Foley shrugged. He had no investment in the case either way. Pinkerton's would assign him something new. He looked at Hammett. The man before him was a similar age but looked much older. He sure didn't look well. The coughing began again in between cigarettes.

Foley asked, 'What's it to you what happens to her?'

Indeed, thought Hammett, what's it to me? Something didn't feel right. That's what. A colleague had been murdered, possibly in connection with this case, although it was just as likely, perhaps more, it was a revenge killing. There were few leads; the girl was one of them. The idea of dropping the case, no, it didn't feel right.

He thought about Dain Collins. She was like a fawn, beautiful, nervous and prey to the men around her. She was vulnerable. That much was clear. Perhaps, rather than being a murderer, she was also a victim. But why should he care? It was just another case.

Only it was never just another case. Hammett could never shake this bad habit of his: a desire to know what and why. A desire to do the right thing even if it was for a partner he detested and a woman he barely knew. She knew about death. He was certain. He was equally certain she knew more about Cowan's death than she was letting on. A killer though? It seemed unlikely. How could a young girl get the better of a man like Cowan? There were plenty of other men who she knew who could have, though: Lehane and the kid, Cookson, just to name two.

'Before we get pulled, can you do me a favour?' asked Hammett, as his train of thought ran its course.

'Shoot,' said Foley.

'Wire a description of Dain Collins to the New York office. Ask if they have any missing persons like her. Actually, while you're at it, anyone who is wanted who matches her description. Mention her eyes, they kind of change between grey and green, and she has funny shaped ear lobes.'

'I thought we'd done all this.'

'That was before we saw her up close. We've got a better description of her now. She's supposed to have escaped a bad situation with her family in New York. There's a detective you could ask, he owes me one.'

Foley took the details of the policeman and also the key points to mention in the wire. He drained his coffee and left without saying goodbye.

'Goodbye to you too, Foley,' said Hammett, sardonically, watching him walk out the door of the grill. Hammett lit a cigarette and considered his options. He wasn't carrying a gun. But his note to Goodman could be like casting a grenade into a still pond. A compromise was to pop into the Flood Building nearby and let Geauque know his movements just in case Foley hadn't. Decision made he paid up and walked over to the Pinkerton's office.

*

Just before eleven, Hammett walked into Goodman's Antiques. Sandra Robins looked up from her book as he entered the shop. The book, Hammett noted, was leather-bound and on the topic of medieval coats of arms. He wondered if she had a magazine hidden inside. The lady's demeanour seemed slightly less frosty this morning. A hint of a smile creased her lips rather like a cat lucky enough to have cornered a particularly dumb mouse.

It was as cold inside as it was hot outside. Hammett shivered involuntarily. He put on his best lady killer smile, the one that had them falling at his feet, never. Sandra Robins was now on her feet and walking around the desk to greet him.

'Mr Audubon, so good to see you again.' She almost seemed to mean it. The owner of the shop obviously had as much respect for her intelligence as he did and hadn't let her in on the joke.

'Hello,' said Hammett brightly. 'Is Mr Goodman in?' For a moment Hammett considered speaking with a lisp; but decided against it. She motioned him to follow her. They walked past her desk in the middle of the store to a door concealed behind a marble bust of Venus. Hammett almost stopped to admire the lovingly-created figure. Business called, however.

'This way,' said Sandra Robins, pointing rather pointlessly at the door. Where else was there to go from here, thought Hammett? In fact, he was about to find out.

*

The office of Sidney Goodman was large, about a third the size of the store out front. Commercially, this struck Hammett as being suicidal. However, the business of Sidney Goodman was not out front. By Hammett's estimate, the shop at the front plus Goodman's office accounted for around two thirds of the store's size. This meant a large storeroom was also part of the building, no doubt where the real business was conducted. As the store was located on a hill, there was likely to be a basement also.

The Frisco Falcon

The office itself was decorated, as far as Hammett could tell, tastefully. The style was Art Deco, minimal, just a desk with a large cubist painting behind and a sofa with two armchairs and a coffee table between. The desk was large, with a small Tiffany lamp at one corner.

Sidney Goodman rose slowly from his seat. The first two things that struck Hammett as Goodman rolled towards him was his size: he really was fat. In addition, he was dressed like a relic from a Henry James novel. He was wearing tails, a grey waistcoat and a blue silk cravat. When he finally spoke, it was with an English accent.

'Mr Audubon, at last we meet,' his hand was outstretched, his voice a treacherously seductive purr. The smile seemed warm, but the eyes were as grey as cold steel. Hammett was under no illusions: this was a dangerous man. For a moment he wondered what had made him come here. 'Please take a seat,' said Goodman, softly as if talking to a small child.

Hammett went to the sofa and sat down while Goodman moved to the other side of the coffee table, extravagantly swiping his tails to either side of the seat. Sandra Robins was still in the room. She seemed to be waiting to be dismissed.

'May I offer you a drink, Mr Audubon, or a coffee?'

Hammett was desperate for a whisky, so he said, 'Coffee would be great, thanks.' Goodman nodded and Sandra Robbins left the room. As the door clicked shut Goodman's attention returned to Hammett rather as a shark might contemplate its next meal, deliberately and with no small relish.

'Well, sir, I must confess I enjoyed your little joke. Audubon, yes, very witty. Gad, sir, it's so rare in my line of work to be able to enjoy a moment of humour. I see you are a man who enjoys such moments also. I like that sir.'

'I thought you'd enjoy that,' said Hammett, smiling to hide his nervousness.

'Capital,' said Goodman, drumming his hands on his knee and smiling. 'I think I'm going to like you, Mr...?'

'Hammett.'

'Now, Mr Hammett, you mentioned something about a bird. I'm intrigued,' said Goodman. Hammett's senses were tingling like a spider meeting a scorpion on its way back from lunch. Goodman's eyes, previously slits hidden behind puffy pink cheeks had widened. It did little to improve his looks, heightening instead the threatening aura surrounding the man.

'I'm sure you are. Me, too.'

The smile broadened on the fat man's face. It was benevolently chilling. He said, 'I can see you are a man who plays his cards close to his chest. I admire that. It suggests character, a quality I find to be in decreasing supply these days, sadly. Now, sir, what do you know of this bird?'

Hammett was confused. It almost seemed as if Goodman was talking about a real bird. Some, but not too much, clarification was badly needed.

'The girl,' said Hammett.

Now it was the fat man's turn to look confused. For a moment he seemed unsure of what to say in response. Then he replied, 'I'm at a loss, sir.' Hammett sensed that he genuinely was at a loss.

Perhaps further prompting was needed. Hammett leaned forward, looked Goodman in the eye and said, 'The one you took the taxi with. The one your boy has been guardian angel to.'

Recognition grew in the eyes of the fat man, and menace also, cloaked behind a smile. Just at that moment Sandra

Robins appeared with a tray containing two cups of coffee. She placed the two cups on the table and received a Thank You from both men for her trouble.

'You were saying, Mr Hammett.'

'Dain Collins,' said Hammett getting to the point. 'Who is she and where is she?'

Goodman put two spoonfuls of sugar into his coffee and smiled, somewhat embarrassedly.

'As you can see, sir, I am a man with some vices,' he said patting his large stomach, 'But, Gad, I can't help myself. Well, sir, you have laid your cards on the table and I appreciate you for doing so. I shall respond likewise. Miss Collins is a friend of mine, I admit. She is to marry a young man named Algernon Aston. I understand the young lady has had second thoughts. The wedding was arranged hastily. You know how it is with young love. She simply desires to have more time. So, to this end, she has returned to her family. I believe they are in New York.'

Hammett reached down and sipped his coffee. It was a decent cup. He nodded to Goodman his appreciation.

'Life is too short to compromise, don't you think?'

Hammett didn't respond but asked instead, 'Why did she come to you? Where can I reach her?'

Goodman drained the rest of his cup, with evident relish. He looked at Hammett and said, 'Gad sir, you are direct. I like that in a man. Well, as to the former, she saw me as an impartial, disinterested even, friend. Why this should be so I cannot say. You would have to ask her. As to the latter, I cannot say either. Even if I knew her address, and I do not, I would be, as a friend, loathe to share such intelligence with someone I do not know. You understand, don't you?'

'I understand plenty, Goodman,' snarled Hammett angrily. 'I understand you picked her up at Lehane's. I understand you probably set her up in that apartment. I understand you're probably feeding her dope. For all I know, your boy may even have killed Dan Cowan. Yeah, I understand plenty, Goodman. What I don't understand is why.'

Hammett felt the blood rushing to his head. He was angry; angrier than he thought he would be. It felt strange. He felt strange. The fat man was smiling at him now. Staring at him. Strangely. The room began to turn like it was a carousel.

'Mr Hammett,' he said. Goodman's voice sounded like he had moved to another room. 'Mr Hammett,' repeated Goodman.

And then everything went black.

The blackness lasted for seconds, seemingly, and then he felt his face being slapped. Gently at first. Was that water being dabbed on his cheek? Let me sleep a bit longer, thought Hammett. But the person trying to wake him was persistent. He tried to turn away, but the gentle slapping continued. He heard a voice say Wake up. Seemed like an English accent. Wake up, it said. Are you alright? No, I'm sleeping you damn fool, leave me the hell alone.

The voice with the English accent was stronger, clearer now. 'Wake up.'

The telegram arrived around ten in the morning. Algy and Kit were still upstairs when it arrived. Agatha and Alastair sat at the end of the garden drinking tea when Ella-Mae arrived and handed the note to Alastair. The misadventure of the night before appeared to weigh more heavily on host than guest. Agatha was positively chipper, so much so, in fact, it began to grate on her brother. He looked up irritably at his housekeeper when he read the name on the envelope.

'It's for Lord Christopher Aston. Can't you read?'

Ella-Mae glared at Alastair, 'I didn't want to disturb him.'

This was a good point, not that Alastair was about to admit as much, 'Yes, well, very good.'

'Thank you, Ella-Mae,' said Agatha, 'The tea was lovely by the way.'

'Thank you, ma'am,' said Ella-Mae pointedly. She left the two siblings to their tea. Agatha looked at the telegram and then at her brother, 'Well, aren't you going to read it?'

Alastair looked aghast at the idea. Agatha stared back at him as if there was nothing more natural in the world than opening someone else's mail. Such was the state of play when Algy arrived. He had shaved and seemed better for it.

'Christopher's just received a telegram,' announced Agatha.

'Strange,' replied Algy.

'My thought exactly. Your father is refusing to open it.'

Alastair looked affronted at this and replied, 'I didn't say I wouldn't open it; I was just pointing out that to do so would be improper.'

Agatha's patience, never the deepest of wells in the first place, finally dried up. She reached over and snatched the telegram from her brother and tore it open. She read the contents for a moment. Confusion descended over her face like a dark cloud, then in the blink of an eye or three, it was replaced by the light of perception.

'Interesting,' she said, keeping hold of the note.

Alastair looked at her expectantly. Agatha looked away and cast her gaze towards the bay. The gentler sex has, over many centuries of practice, developed a system designed to puncture the more impractical principles of men whilst adding, at the same time, a further twist of the knife to tease out the inherent hypocrisy at play.

'Well, come on, woman, out with it,' exclaimed Alastair.

Agatha looked at him piously, eyebrows raised, mouth set firmly to distaste, before handing it back to Alastair. Her brother glared at her before extracting a pair of spectacles from his breast pocket. He looked for a moment at the telegram. Silence followed and then, like Agatha moments before, recognition dawned on him.

'Good lord,' he said and looked up at Agatha. 'But this is extraordinary.'

Mary arrived at this point, looked at Algy and asked, 'What have I missed?'

Alastair held up the telegram, 'This has just arrived for Kit. As he is still resting after his guard duty last night, Agatha took it upon herself to read the note.'

Agatha looked up at Mary and shrugged innocently, 'Seemed the thing to do, frankly.'

'Quite right, too,' agreed Mary. She opened the tea pot and looked inside, 'Is this tea fresh?'

'Never mind the tea,' spluttered Agatha, 'listen to what the telegram says.' Mary grinned and sat down. All eyes turned to Alastair.

Alastair began to read from the telegram. 'You have something belonging to me. We have information that your cousin will consider important. Suggest exchange. Please visit Goodman's Antiques on Pine at two.' Alastair looked up and added, 'There's no signature, so to speak.'

Mary looked at her prospective aunt and uncle for clarification. Algy had walked around the back of his father to view the telegram, much to the obvious irritation of his father who shot him a look and said sarcastically, 'Did you think I missed something?'

A swift glance at Alastair then Agatha provided the explanation., 'We believe the Goodman referred to here is, in fact, Sidney Gutman, Alastair's former partner in the advertising business.'

Alastair took up the story. 'I discovered, much too late, that someone I thought was a friend turned out to be, in fact, a man of the most despicable sort. He was involved in all manner of criminal activity of which I knew only of embezzlement and blackmail. Needless to say, I shared my discovery with the authorities. He went to jail for three years. The last I had heard of him he was in New York; I had no idea that he had returned under a new name. And to think, an Englishman,' said Alastair shaking his head at the wonder that such behaviour could be possible from a fellow countryman.

'Half German,' pointed out Agatha.

'Good point, Agatha,' agreed Alastair, nodding. This seemed a reasonable explanation.

'What will you do?' asked Mary.

171

Agatha and Alastair exchanged looks. They were clearly concerned. Too much was at stake now. Alastair voiced this concern, 'Let's see what Kit says. Gutman or Goodman is a dangerous fellow and he's clearly mixed up with people who would think nothing of going to extreme lengths to get what they want.'

'Can't we just inform the police?' said Mary.

'Yeah, pops, tell the police,' agreed Algy.

'I wish we could, son,' replied Alastair, 'but if what I think is true then we have a much bigger problem than some object Gutman wants.' Alastair looked up sadly at his son. As he did so, he spied Kit walking across the lawn towards them, 'Here's Kit.' His voice sounded fragile, unable to hide the desolation he was feeling.

*

'So, you believe this Goodman, who certainly doesn't appear to live up to his name,' said Kit, 'is possibly holding Miss Collins?' Kit saw Alastair nod; he noticed that Agatha was nodding also. 'May I ask why you believe this to be so? Because I can think of only one way you would know.' Kit looked far from happy.

'What do you mean, Kit?' asked Algy, bewildered by the direction Kit had suddenly taken but clearly aware of his cousin's anger.

'Are you going to tell Algy or shall I?' said Kit. His voice was grim.

Dejection was etched over the face of Alastair He looked up at his son and said, 'No, Kit. Let me.'

Agatha interjected, 'Before you do so, Alastair, I want you all to know this was my suggestion. Alastair went along with the idea reluctantly.'

'No matter, I have to tell the truth,' said Alastair. 'I engaged the services of a private consulting firm through Saul. The purpose was to have Dain followed, Algernon, and to understand more about her background.'

'What?' exclaimed Algy. 'But why?'

'Why do you think Algy? You fall in love. Again, and again, I might add. It was all too good to be true. I decided, after speaking with Agatha and Saul, to find out more about Dain. I'm sorry, but you're my son and Miss Collins was just too much of a mystery wrapped up in an enigma.'

Algy's eyes blazed at his father. Kit was none too happy either with Agatha, who studiously avoided her nephew's gaze. The tense atmosphere was broken by Mary.

'Well, I, for one, would like to meet Dain.'

'She hasn't answered her phone,' admitted Algy dolefully.

Kit looked at Algy and said, 'Algy, why don't you take Mary down to Dain's apartment. In the meantime, your father, Aunt Agatha, and I will deal with this chap Goodman.'

Algy looked at Kit and then his father, 'Are you sure? This guy sounds like he's bad news.' However, it was clear he was desperate to find his fiancée. Mary stood up effectively ending the discussion.

'Let's go, Algy. I think Kit and your father can handle some dusty old antique dealer.'

'Less of the old, young lady, he's younger than me,' pointed out Agatha.

*

Kit said nothing as they drove down to Pine. Both his aunt and uncle knew better than to interrupt his thoughts. For Agatha, the drive provoked mixed feelings. The last time she had been on Pine, her husband Eustace had been alive. She

173

remembered Alastair taking them around the city in a horse and carriage. How times had changed. How the city had changed. How she had changed. Well, not really. A little older, perhaps.

Alastair, too, was lost in his thoughts. The hurt he had inflicted on his son was severe. Had he gone too far in hiring the Pinkerton agency? The reaction of Algy, even more significantly, for Kit, suggested he had. His conscience felt more clouded than winter on the moors. What ignoble actions often arise from noble intentions.

The root cause, and the source of pain for Alastair, was the fundamental fact he hadn't trusted his son's judgement. He had treated Algy like a child. The pain Algy felt was also a form of guilt; his father had most probably been right. This was cold comfort for Alastair as they drove in silence to the antique shop.

The question for Alastair now was how to repair the damage. The wedding would be cancelled; the business was heading for the rocks. Was there anything to keep Algy in the city? He could hardly blame Algy if he chose to leave. Such thoughts caused a wave of despondency to sweep through Alastair. The prospect of confronting Gutman made him feel lower still.

Up ahead they saw the antiques store. It was midway up the hill, a bright white against the grey of the buildings around it. Alastair had passed this store many times. He'd never thought it housed his old friend-turned-enemy Sidney Gutman. He pointed to the shop and was about to pull over when Kit told him to drive on. Fifty yards ahead Kit spotted a parking space and pointed to it.

'Just in case there's funny business.'

'I would work on this assumption, my boy,' said Alastair. He looked at his nephew. His mood brightened a little. He trusted Kit. How he wished he'd been able to watch the boy grow because the man he had become was remarkable. Quite remarkable. Penny would be so proud. He felt proud also.

'Aunt Agatha, you stay in the car.'

'I shall not,' replied Agatha. 'I want to confront that beastly man.'

The horn of a passing car drowned out Agatha's precise view of Goodman, but it was unlikely to be complimentary, thought Kit. He looked steadily at his aunt and said, 'We may need to make a swift getaway. Can you drive the car round to the store front after we walk inside?'

This mollified Agatha considerably, but it was Alastair's turn to be horrified. He stared aghast at Kit and said, 'Have you taken leave of your senses? Do you know how much this car cost?'

'I know how to drive,' said Agatha defensively.

'And I know the principles behind walking on a tightrope, but I certainly won't be attempting it any time soon.'

Kit held a hand up to silence the bickering siblings. 'Enough,' he said, 'Uncle Alastair, we need someone outside with the motor running. It's either you or Aunt Agatha.'

Alastair looked at Kit in exasperation and climbed out of the vehicle. Kit looked at his aunt and repeated the order.

'Yes, yes, yes. I heard you the first time.'

Kit resisted the temptation to say anything else. Taking his uncle by the arm, they walked down the street and across the road to the antique store. A bell rang as they walked through the door.

Jack Murray

Algy held the steering wheel tightly as he and Mary drove into the city. They sped past the harbour; Mary was entranced by everything she saw. It was so different from any city she had seen before: the trams skirting past the automobiles, the grid road system, the hills.

Algy was glad to have Mary with him. He felt so desolate. In his heart, he knew Dain was gone. His father was right. She was a mystery. Too much so. It had been part of her attraction. That and her beauty. And she was beautiful. The eyes that changed shade, seemingly with her moods. And the moods that changed from playful and funny to distant, yet sensual. She teased his imagination as much as she stirred his passion. And the passion that he felt, she reciprocated. It had swept him along. A happy madness. There had been no one in his life like her. Of course, he'd fallen in love.

Algy looked at Mary. Kit was unquestionably a lucky man. Mary was electricity given human form. Her intelligence, her humour, those blue eyes, crackled with an intensity that radiated from her body and lit up the minds of those around her.

Her questions about Dain gave him a chance to open his heart in a manner he couldn't have with either his father or Kit. He talked about his fear, his love and his hopes. They all amounted to the same thing: her.

Mary listened mostly, asking occasionally about things that seemed tangential to Algy. But, as he talked, he realised how little he knew of her and how little it seemed to matter.

'Do you have a key to her apartment?' asked Mary as they climbed out of the car. Algy admitted, with some embarrassment, that he did. Mary wondered for a second why he seemed so self-conscious; then it dawned on her: he was embarrassed by the implication of having a key and what this genteel young woman would think of his fiancée.

'Jolly sensible,' said Mary, shrewdly absolving Algy, and by extension, Dain Collins of any wrongdoing.

Algy brightened immediately. He said hello to Cyrus on his way into the block. They took the elevator, and within a few moments they were outside the apartment. Algy looked at Mary. His heart was beating so loudly he wondered if Mary could hear it. His breathing became shallower. A part of him realised he didn't want to know. Living in hope, seemed easier than dealing with the certain knowledge she was gone. Knowledge was darkness.

Finally, he raised his hand to the door and knocked firmly. He called out her name. There was no answer. He tried again. Silence. Algy put his hand in his pocket and rooted around for the keys to the apartment. When he found them, he put the key in the lock.

Just as he did, the door opened.

*

Sandra Robins watched two men enter the antique store. She had been briefed to expect at least two. The younger one was striking. Tall, light-coloured hair and clear blue eyes. He looked like he could be royalty, such was his bearing. Then he spoke, which as good as confirmed in her mind that he was.

'Good day, we have an appointment with Mr Goodman.'

She looked up at the man whose diction was as crisp as the collar on his shirt. The other man, much older, had a nervous look about him, like he would have preferred to be just about anywhere else at that moment. She didn't blame him. She would too, frankly.

'I will tell Mr Goodman that you're here.' She walked towards a door at the back of the store. They followed her.

'Thank you,' said the younger man. The other one nodded impatiently.

A few moments later she stood at the door and gestured for them to enter. Kit and Alastair looked at one another. Alastair marched forward, his temper beginning to fray. In a moment he was in Goodman's office. His former friend and partner sat behind an expansive desk. He was speaking on the phone and promised to call the other person very soon. He replaced the phone.

'Alastair, it's you. It's really you,' said Goodman.

'Of course, it's me, Sidney, who else were you expecting?' replied Alastair irritably.

Sidney Goodman rose from his seat. Alastair was astonished by how much weight he'd put on. This must have registered on his face because Goodman immediately looked down at his stomach and patted it with pride.

'They feed you well in prison, Sidney? Or did you simply eat your cell mate?' said Alastair archly.

But Sidney Goodman was in much too good of a mood to let a mild rebuke undermine his desire for good fellowship. He laughed at the joke and said, 'Gad, sir, I've missed your jests. And this, if I may be so bold to assume, is the famous Lord Aston.'

Kit noted that he made no effort to shake hands and he decided not to offer his. Nor did he respond directly to the indirect compliment. Instead, he replied, 'I believe you wanted to meet us, Mr Goodman.'

'Very good,' beamed Goodman. 'I like a man who gets down to business. There's much too much small talk in this world. Men have lost the ability to get straight to the point.'

'My thought exactly, Sidney,' said Alastair, his eyebrows raised accusingly. 'We haven't all day for your sub-Shakespearean oratory.'

Goodman's smile faded slightly and the glint in his eye hardened. He gestured for them to sit on the sofa and said, 'Please, take a seat and let me explain why I invited you here today.'

'I better make myself comfortable then. I suggest you do so also, Kit, my boy. This could take a while,' responded Alastair. If Kit didn't know better, and he did, he'd suspect his uncle of trying to provoke the antique shop owner into dropping his façade of bonhomie. For the moment it was holding, rather like the banks of a river in the midst of a flood.

Just.

Kit wondered what it would be like when the real Sidney Goodman was revealed. He was fairly certain, at the current rate of going, they wouldn't have too long to wait. The large man before them threw his tails to either side as he sat down. He intertwined his fingers and they cracked like a Webley revolver.

'You met my associate Mr Israel last night.'

'He broke into my house,' pointed out Alastair.

Goodman waved this away as if it was no more an issue than an unwelcome door-to-door Bible salesman.

'Regrettable, I agree. I hope you will accept my sincere apologies,' replied Goodman. It was abundantly clear from the look on Alastair's face that he was as likely to accept an apology from Goodman as he was to go to a distiller for advice on temperance.

'Well, working on the assumption that you will not,' said Goodman, a distinctly harder edge to his voice, 'I would like to recover an object that found its way into your luggage, Lord Aston.'

Kit looked at Goodman and smiled, 'Would this be a box, wrapped in rather tasteless blue wrapping paper?'

'Mr Israel was unable to find anything more suitable in the time available, probably,' admitted Goodman. 'No matter. We would like the object back. Today, in fact.'

Kit leaned forward and asked, 'How did it end up in our luggage?'

Goodman smiled, 'Why, Mr Israel put it there. How else do you think?'

'Why? And why us?'

Goodman paused for a few moments as he weighed up how much of his hand to reveal. The truth, in Goodman's mind, was like a fine wine. Too little denied you enough of an experience to appreciate it but too much caused problems later on.

'I believe he saw that your baggage was destined for the Aquitania and he did not have a lot of time.'

The ball was now in Kit's court, so to speak. Kit responded, 'He planted stolen goods in our bags. This was clearly in the hope he would avoid the object being found on him when he was searched. He broke into our cabin on the Aquitania and failed to find the object in question. He was arrested in New York yet was able to trace us to San Francisco. It strikes me,

Mr Goodman, that Mr Israel was most fortunate in his choice of importer.'

'Indeed,' smiled Goodman. Kit felt his senses tingle. This was a dangerous man. The smile was like a cobra staring at his dinner sleeping peacefully in the sun.

'What is the object?'

Goodman and Kit's eyes locked for a moment. The mask had slipped. The man before Kit made no attempt to replace the benign veneer for those few seconds. It was enough to confirm to Kit that they had walked into a trap.

'As you will know by now,' replied Goodman, 'it is a small carving of a falcon.'

Kit neither confirmed nor denied he knew what the package contained. Goodman paused for a few seconds. Once again, his mind whirled through the permutations of how much to reveal. Decision made he pressed on.

'This small carving has a certain value for the right owner. It is an antique and, as a result, both the government of Turkey and the United States would feel duty bound either to prevent its leaving their shores, or in the latter case, impose significant duties on its import. You, Lord Aston, presented a solution for Mr Israel as he did not believe for one moment that your bags would be searched. Unfortunately, Mr Israel has attracted, if I may say, the wholly unwarranted attention of various police forces in Europe and, it seems, the United States. The fact that you have this artefact in your safe possession at *Bellavista* proves the wisdom of his choice.'

Kit sensed this was the truth. Some of it at least. He also sensed there was much more to this, but Goodman was unlikely to reveal his hand. Yet.

The Frisco Falcon

'What's so special about this blessed falcon anyway?' interjected Alastair.

The smile returned to Goodman's face.

'Have you heard of Michelangelo Merisi?' asked Goodman.

'Caravaggio,' said Kit and Alastair in unison.

Valletta, Malta 1607

What made Michelangelo Merisi, Caravaggio, move to Malta? Who knows? All we can be certain of is that he went there in 1607, a fugitive from justice. A murderer, or so people believed. Certainly, the courts had decided his fate. He was effectively under sentence of death. His defenders, and there were many, claimed the killing of young Ranuccio Tomassoni was accidental. They pointed to the fact that Caravaggio had also been wounded, badly. Others were less sure. And so, the artist fled to Malta.

Perhaps he harboured hopes of allying himself with the Knights of St John in order to gain some redemption for his crime or perhaps he had always held a desire to join this famous, infamous even, military order. Whatever the truth, the Knights welcomed the runaway artist with open arms.

Who was the Military Order of St John of Jerusalem, Rhodes and Malta? They were missionaries of a sort; the sort that preached the gospel of the love of Christ using stallion, shield and sword.

They were led, at this time, by a Grand Master named Alof de Wigancourt. He was a visionary man. Not for him the idea of being the head of a once great military order located on a far flung, provincial rock in the Mediterranean. He saw the Order as a bulkhead of Christianity. It had been so in the past during the Crusades; it could be again. Attracting the greatest artist of the day was a coup for him. Here was a man that could bring glory to the island through the creation of works of art to decorate the homes of the senior members of the Order and, more importantly, the churches. The Order would, once more, be seen as the first line of defence for the faith against Islam.

Once upon a time the Knights had been a formidable fighting force. They established garrisons and castles along the front line between Christianity and Islam. For centuries they fought, won, and lost battles from Asia Minor to Egypt until they were finally forced to leave the Holy Land in 1291.

Soon after leaving, they captured the Island of Rhodes. The island was used as a base to attack Turkish shipping and coastal settlements. In fact, they became such a nuisance to the Islamic world that reprisals were inevitable. The warriors of the Order held out for decades but eventually succumbed to overwhelming force.

The Knights were defeated by Suleiman the Magnificent in 1522, a man who would reach the gates of Vienna. By 1530 they had a new home. Charles V gave them the fortress of Malta. He hoped their presence on the strategically important island, would protect his underbelly in Italy and ultimately Rome.

The Knights were grateful to the Holy Roman Emperor and in return they promised an annual tribute to him and his mother, Joanna of Castille. This annual tribute was to be a single falcon. Not any falcon, though. This was a bejewelled falcon. Imagine that. Something so small. Priceless.

This is where Caravaggio enters our story. By 1607 he was living on the island and producing portrait commissions for the great and the good of the Order, including the Grand Master himself. These, unquestionably, bought the redemption of the artist. He was invested with the habit of Knight of Magistral Obedience and given the title of 'Fra Michelangelo Merisi'.

185

Such an investiture required Papal permission, which was forthcoming. It meant that by becoming a Knight, the death sentence would become void. As payment for this great honour, Caravaggio delivered a magnificent altarpiece, 'The Beheading of St John'. The altarpiece was to hang in the Oratory of St John, a co-cathedral of St John in Valletta. The finished work was enormous, some ten feet high and fifteen feet wide, the biggest he would ever paint and the only painting that he would ever sign. The signature was written in the blood of St John, a public confession, a penance and a forgiveness of his mortal sin.

So, all was well. Caravaggio was a free man, but he could not stay away from trouble. His nature was too volatile, the violence in his blood too overpowering. He strayed again. An ill-considered quarrel with a noble Knight of Justice and this time there would be no forgiveness. He was imprisoned on the island in a cell cut into the rock of Castel Sant' Angelo. Our story takes a new turn.

Caravaggio escaped.

Yes, this genius, this murderer, this troubled soul broke free from the prison. To escape was, of course not only impossible, it was unimaginable. But this is the great, the mad Caravaggio. The extraordinary becomes ordinary for such a man. He scaled the ramparts of the castle, lowering himself down a two-hundred-foot precipice and boarding a waiting boat that transported him to Sicily.

Did he do this alone? Of course not. He had help. And the price for this help?

This is where our story becomes interesting. Legend has it that during his incarceration, he produced his own falcon. Think of it. A tribute to win, once again, his freedom. And what greater symbol of freedom can there than a bird? His early biographer, Baglione, hints at the existence of the bird, which could only have been a falcon. Later writers mentioned it also, but they suggest it was merely a story. It seemed too fantastic. They said it was out of character. It was just a story to be used by dishonest men to profit from the gullible.

It was not a story. It was true. Many men have searched for this legendary bird. Rumours emerged over the years of its existence. Stories almost as amazing as the falcon itself. Legendary owners such as Catherine the Great, Napoleon and other rich men prepared to pay vast sums of money to own this falcon. Perhaps even to kill.

Then it disappeared again. Or so it seemed.

When Goodman had finished telling the story he sat back in his chair, seemingly satisfied by the impact that he'd had on his two guests. This was punctured in seconds by Alastair.

'I told you he likes the sound of his own voice. Dear God. What next? A long-lost detective novel by Michelangelo?'

The smile leaving Goodman's face felt like a whip cracking. Goodman stood up from his seat. Kit tensed, ready for what would happen next. 'Miss Robins,' he barked at the door. Gone was the cat-like purr voice. Now it was cold, hard like a dagger.

The door opened and Miss Robins walked in followed by a young man. Both Kit and Alastair at the same time as realising their situation was perilous also noted the young man badly needed a new tailor.

'This is William,' said Goodman by way of introduction. 'He will take one of you back to your house to collect the bird.'

Kit and Alastair were both looking at the new entrant when Kit returned his attention to Goodman. He saw a gun pointing at him. A moment later he heard Alastair's surprised voice as he also saw the gun.

'I knew I couldn't trust you, Sidney,' said Alastair. 'You're a scoundrel. Always have been.'

Goodman ignored this jibe and continued, 'My suggestion is that you will stay here, Lord Aston, as our guest, while my old friend Alastair retrieves our possession. As soon as we receive what is ours, then you will be free to leave.'

Kit looked at Goodman coolly, 'At least you're making no pretence that I'm to be anything other than your prisoner.'

'I dislike such a pejorative view of the situation. You're my guest and your time here will be short, I promise, if Alastair does as he is told. It's really just a very simple exchange. There is no need to complicate matters with unnecessary heroics.'

Alastair's irritability breached its, already low, threshold and he poured forth a volley of invective that was as surprising to William Cookson as it was unsurprising to Goodman who knew him only too well. However, Goodman's eyes never left Kit. He sensed that the man before him would only need half a chance to turn the situation around.

'Search them,' he ordered Cookson.

The young man stepped forward and rapidly frisked both men. He looked up at Goodman and shook his head. This seemed to amaze Goodman.

'Really?' he said in a kind of wonder. His eyes hardened again, and he looked at Kit. 'Almost too naïve to be true. I see I must impress upon you the seriousness of your situation. A situation, I reiterate, that we can resolve amicably by the return of the falcon.'

Goodman went over to his phone. A minute later he motioned for Kit to come over. He glanced back at Alastair. Cookson had a gun trained on him. There was little either could do about the situation for the moment.

Things were about to get worse, though. A lot worse.

*

As the door lock sounded, Algy's eyes lit up. He glanced round at Mary, relief surged through his body and love descended on him like a fog, obscuring reality, imperilling him, compelling him to move forward.

And then the feeling evaporated.

'What are you doing here? What have you done with Dain?' shouted Algy, wildly.

Joel Israel smiled at Algy and Mary. He could afford to smile. He was the one holding the gun. He glanced down at it and said, 'I took the precaution of loading it this time. Do come in.' He stood back and motioned them both in with the gun.

'What have you done with her, you animal?' snarled Algy at the little man. Joel Israel, once again, seemed positively hurt by the insult.

'I have no idea where she is,' he replied with as much dignity as a man in the undignified position of holding a gun on someone else could muster. Algy looked as if he was straining to avoid tearing him limb from limb. 'Please don't do that, Mr Aston. I really must insist you calm down. If you'll take a seat, please.'

'Algy, let's do as he says,' said Mary. Joel Israel looked into her blue eyes. My word, he thought, what a woman: without fear, utterly composed. He was even prepared to forgive the mild contempt in her eyes. Perhaps her situation merited such a reaction. The two captives did eventually sit down.

Mary looked around the apartment. The décor was in the modern style: long stemmed lamps, wooden tables, wooden chairs, parquet floor with a Japanese rug that did not look like it owed its provenance to a street market. Chinese watercolours adorned the walls. Someone has good taste, thought Mary. Did it feel female to her? Not in the slightest.

She heard Joel Israel speak to someone on the phone. She heard him say, 'You were right. It's Aston, and he's with the English girl. Yes, I'll wait for your call.'

The Frisco Falcon

He finished his call and sat down looking at the two young people. He wore a smile, the smile of man nearing the completion of a particularly complicated puzzle. And it had been complicated. Stealing the item in Constantinople from a rich, well-known collector of art and antiques with shady connections to crime, then smuggling it out of Constantinople, across Europe, into England, across an ocean and, finally, a continent. It had gone to plan. Almost. Staggering in conception, audaciously executed. The plan was Goodman's, but he, Joel Israel, had carried it off with style and, yes, no little dignity. If any man had earned the right to smile, it was he. If any man had earned the respect of another, it was he.

Yet, as he gazed at the two young people, he knew it would never be forthcoming from people such as them. The smile faded from his face. It became an animal like snarl. How he hated these people. Born into privilege. They had done nothing in their lives. Nothing. They commanded respect, not because of their talent, not because of their achievements, not for how they had overcome the greatest of challenges. They commanded respect because of their names.

His finger tightened on the trigger. As it did so, the phone rang. The pressure of the trigger eased.

*

The hardness of Goodman's features eased again, and the serpent-smile returned as he heard a voice at the other end of the telephone line.

'Mr Israel, I have Lord Kit Aston and Alastair with me now. Do you want to put your guests on the phone?' A voice came on the line and Goodman said, 'One moment, please.'

He gestured for Kit to step forward. Kit did so and picked up the phone.

'Hello?' Kit's eyes widened as he heard Mary's voice. Then the line went dead. 'Mary,' he shouted. "Mary, are you there?' No answer. He put the phone down and stepped towards Goodman. The gun stopped him.

'I wouldn't do that, Aston. Sit down,' ordered Goodman impatiently. There was no choice. He turned around; Alastair looked desolate.

'She's with Algy. They have both of them.'

'We do,' confirmed Goodman, 'but no harm shall come to them. Just return the artefact. We shall make an exchange. Your son Alastair and the girl, for the falcon. Do as you're told; all will be well. I promise.'

Alastair snorted dismissively. Goodman ignored his former friend and focused his attention on Kit.

'What's to stop you reneging on this? You must know the police will become involved,' said Kit.

'They shan't,' replied Goodman calmly. 'By the time they do, I will have moved the artefact on to its ultimate home. All the police will find is a law-abiding businessman, wrongly accused of holding stolen property. Anyway, I have insurance.'

Alastair looked at Goodman, unable to disguise his horror at the man he had once called a partner. He asked, 'What do you mean?'

Kit looked at Goodman and his eyes narrowed. 'You're holding Dain Collins?'

Goodman smiled and shrugged complacently. His voice was a purr again. The cat was in complete control.

'I wouldn't put it quite like that, Lord Aston.'

'How would you put it then?'

The smile evaporated again, 'You will do as you're told, and then you will be free to find out at your leisure. We mean to have our property, Lord Aston. We want it back. We do not want trouble. But if you create any problems, it will surely be the worse for you. I hope this is clear. William, would you be so good as to take Alastair back to his house? I trust, Lord Aston, that you can tell my old friend where to locate the artefact without any coded messages to contact help. I should add that young Will here will have no hesitation in taking the most extreme measures to ensure the safe return of our property.'

Kit did as he was told. They nodded to one another and then Cookson led Alastair out of the office.

'What do you intend doing with me?' asked Kit.

'Can I offer you some refreshment?' asked Goodman, genially, gesturing with his gun towards a tray with several glasses and a decanter containing, Kit surmised, whisky.

'A little bit early,' suggested Kit.

'I quite understand. Then if you will please move towards the door, I would like you to go to another office, in the basement.'

'Sounds rather like a prison cell,' commented Kit, like he was talking to an acquaintance about the weather.

'It can be whatever you want it to be, Lord Aston.' The voice was hard, now. The fat man was nearing the coup of a lifetime. Perhaps his nerve was beginning to fray. His patience certainly was wearing thin.

Kit walked ahead towards another door to the side of the office. He opened the door. It was a stairwell, and it was dark. It was also cold, as if all the life of the world had been sucked out and replaced by death.

'You're not afraid of the dark, Lord Aston, surely?'

'No, Goodman. Not too keen on guns, however,' said Kit, picking his way carefully down the steps. The door shut behind him, leaving him completely in darkness save for the light coming from the bottom of the door. Kit reached the bottom of the stairs and held his hand outwards looking for a wall to support himself against. He walked forward slowly.

Then he tripped over an object on the floor. A body.

Kit rolled the body over and checked for a pulse. As Kit's eyes grew accustomed to the light, or lack of it, he was able to see that it was a man. He began to slap the face of the man gently, urging him to wake up. Finally, his efforts gained their reward as signs of life appeared in the prone man.

After a few minutes, the man uttered a few slurred words, like he was still drunk from the night before. He wanted to be left alone, it seemed. Kit persisted in trying to wake him.

'Who are you?' asked the man, a few minutes later. Reasonable question, I suppose, thought Kit.

'Kit Aston,' replied Kit.

Silence for a moment. Just as Kit was about to repeat his name, the man said, 'Aston?'

'Yes, Kit Aston.'

Kit sensed the man was fully awake now. He was right. The man sat up and they looked at one another.

'And you are?'

The man was silent for a moment. He was, clearly, having difficulty remembering his name. In fact, the truth was much simpler. He was still trying to process the combination of English accent and the name Aston. The last Englishman he had spoken to had slipped him a drug to knock him out. He was still somewhat suspicious, but the Aston name threw a lifeline to another part of his brain. He remembered that

Algernon Aston's father was English. With each second, the fog cleared. Connections began to be made.

'Hammett,' he said holding out his hand, 'Dashiell Hammett.'

They shook hands briefly, then Kit asked in a voice that struck Hammett as unusually casual, given their circumstances, 'So what brings you here?'

'I was about to ask you the same question.'

The gears on the American automobile took a little getting used to for the septuagenarian lady behind the wheel. They seemed specifically designed to make no sense. Thankfully her feet were able to reach the floor. Just.

After a few abortive attempts to move the car, the combination of pedals and gear stick finally registered with Agatha, and she managed to manoeuvre the car forward. She drove forward one block then negotiated a highly illegal U-turn before driving past where Alastair had set them down, arriving at a space immediately outside the store.

There was nothing else she could do now but wait. The sun shone down on the street, drying the remains of the previous night's downpour. The brightness of the sun, and the rather light-coloured road began to irritate Agatha's eyes. Very soon she became impatient, desirous to know what was happening. Patience and Agatha Frost were far from bosom buddies. Rather like the skills of an accomplished snipe shooter, she acknowledged its value in other people but rarely practiced it herself.

And then it started.

Alastair was the first to exit the store. A young man who was carrying a raincoat over his arm trailed behind him. Lady Agatha Frost, nee Aston, following a lifetime of reading dime novels and penny bloods was just the woman to recognise what the young man was hiding underneath a wholly unnecessary raincoat. In fact, '*The Case of the Black Widow Spy Girl*' had dealt with just such a scenario. It was also clear that her nephew was being held in the store, under similar circumstances.

The Frisco Falcon

Alastair spotted his sister immediately as he exited the store. He used his eyes to indicate the man behind. Agatha gave a curt nod. Did he think she was a complete idiot?

A more grateful Alastair gave a silent prayer of thanks for a sibling whose literary tastes were as elevated as his own. Then he climbed into the driver's seat of the car pointed out to him by the young man with the gun.

As he climbed in, Agatha started her car. She slipped out ahead of her brother. By her reckoning there was only one place they were heading. She drove in the direction they had come from, keeping an eye on her brother behind. At a certain point she allowed him to overtake her. She wanted him to arrive first.

A plan was already forming in her head.

*

Joel Israel put the phone down and motioned for Mary to move towards Algy. He set the gun down and pulled out a cigarette case. Moments later he was puffing contentedly on a cigarette.

'Turkish,' he explained. 'Much better than your American ones. Now, I think we should make our way to Mr Goodman's store. If you would be so good as to drive, Mr Aston. Of course, I need not remind you that the gun is loaded. But I think I shall, anyway.' Joel Israel held up the revolver and opened the chamber for Algy to see. It was fully loaded. The two men looked at one another before Joel Israel said, 'She will die first, Mr Aston. Think carefully on this matter as we drive to Goodman's.'

'I will,' said Algy through teeth so gritted it conceivably would take a week to unclench them.

'It's on Pine. I'll show you where.'

The group made their way out of the apartment. The little man indicated the stairs. The elevator held too much risk. The gun was in his side pocket, his finger on the trigger. They walked slowly down the stairs, passing no one on the way. Cyrus was clearly on a comfort break.

Soon they were outside in the bright sunlight. Mary looked at a palm tree silhouetted against the blue sky. There were no clouds. Just the cerulean blue overhead. The street was surprisingly quiet. In the distance Mary heard the sound of a tram bell. A slight breeze lifted from the direction of the bay. It cooled Mary's face as she contemplated the man behind her holding the gun trained on her back.

The choreography of climbing into a car was not something Joel Israel had given much thought to in his life, particularly when he was holding a gun on his two fellow passengers.

'I'll get in first,' suggested Algy, clearly aware of the little man's confusion. 'Then you climb into the back, and Mary takes the passenger seat. We won't do anything funny; I promise.'

Joel Israel nodded in gratitude and within a minute they were driving in the direction of the city centre. He made sure to sit behind Mary, lest the young American proved to be less than true to his word.

Algy glanced at Mary, as he drove to see if she was coping with this unexpected situation. She looked back at him. Those extraordinary blue eyes crackled. She smiled. Without knowing why, he felt there was hope. The only certainty, however, at this moment was the knowledge that Kit was a lucky man. His thoughts returned to her briefly.

She was so different from Dain. One was a compelling mixture of mischief and remoteness. Just as he was getting close to her, really close, the drawbridge was pulled up. Yet they had been close. As close as a man and woman can be. Yet still she held back something of herself from him. He was sure she loved him. Sometimes.

When he felt that certainty, there was no better feeling in the world. But there were other times . Many, in fact. They were part of her enigma. Part of her attraction. The need to protect her was, sometimes, overpowering. The need to wrap her in his arms and hold the dragons at bay. And there were many dragons. He knew this. He accepted this.

Mary was not someone who would ever need the kind of protection a man like him could offer. There was no mystery to her. Her nature, her being, was visible. Palpable even. She was energy and intelligence in female form. A beautiful female form if truth be told. Yes, she was right for Kit, and he, for her. He felt happy for Kit. Not a trace of envy, just delight in knowing that Kit had found someone, as he had, to love and cherish.

At least until death.

They arrived at Pine, and drove for a minute or two until Joel Israel, rather unnecessarily, pointed out the store.

'Excellent,' he said, 'We can park just in front.'

'Marvellous really,' said Mary with a smile to the passenger in the back. Joel Israel looked askance at Mary. What was the possible meaning of this comment? As they walked into the store, his mind turned over the possible significance of what she'd said.

*

'What brings you to this part of town?' asked Hammett. His head felt like two military bands, composed principally of percussionists, who were warming up before battle.

'Easy, old chap. I know what it's like to be drugged,' said Kit, who couldn't, in fact ever remember being drugged. 'I'm here for a wedding but appear to have, inadvertently, transported stolen goods across the ocean. What's your story?'

Hammett began to cough. A loud, wracking and uncomfortable cough. Kit patted his back, for wont of anything better to do. When the coughing fit finished, Hammett looked at the man before him. His features were barely discernible in the light. But the accent was clearly English. Even more clearly, it sounded to Hammett that this was, indeed, nobility.

The next few words out of Kit's mouth were very far from noble as he sought to find some comfort for his stump which was giving him hell.

'What's wrong?' asked Hammett. Kit told him about his leg.

'So much for a quick getaway,' said Hammett sardonically. He heard Kit laugh grimly in return. A thought struck Hammett and he asked, 'When I was over in eighteen, I heard about a lord who had fought at the front. Was that you?'

'There were a few of us,' said Kit by way of non-explanation.

'So, you were there, then,' said Kit. It wasn't a question.

Hammett coughed again before saying, 'Brought this damn cough back with me.'

'We're a fine pair,' laughed Kit. 'Watch out Goodman. Although it must be said, he has us where he wants us. We should use this time to pool our knowledge. I'll start. Not sure I've much I can tell you. Perhaps when you're up to it, you can let me know everything from your side. Please don't leave anything out. Details can often be important.'

Hammett couldn't have agreed more.

The Frisco Falcon

They spent the next few minutes sharing, briefly, the events leading to their incarceration. Kit became fully acquainted with the investigation of Dain Collins, confirming Hammett's suspicion that the client was Alastair Aston. Kit, meanwhile, talked about their trip to the United States and how they had inadvertently smuggled an artefact over from Europe. He also spoke of Joel Israel's repeated failed attempts to retrieve it.

Hammett laughed harshly at this, 'He sounds pretty desperate.'

They were silent for a few moments and then Kit spoke again, on a subject that had loomed large over their conversation, like a dark cloud promising rain. Lots of it.

'These events feel as if they are related but the connection, I can barely bring myself to say.'

'Dain Collins,' said Hammett.

Kit nodded in the darkness, then remembered Hammett may not be able to see him, 'It's fantastical. I mean is it really possible that Goodman staged a meeting between Algy and Miss Collins?'

'Until you told me about the falcon, I'd been wondering the same. Initially I thought he was just out for revenge on the father. Now it looks like there's more to it,' replied Hammett. 'But it would require the boy to be a bit of a patsy.'

'Sorry?' asked Kit, mystified as to the derivation of the word, "patsy".

'A fool. In this case, a fool in love to be more precise.'

'That's Algy, alright,' replied Kit, feeling a stab of guilt almost immediately for being, at the very least, unkind and, certainly, disloyal.

'So, Galahad rescues the girl. Minutes later they're to be married, and his relatives ship over a bird stolen in

201

Constantinople,' said Hammett by way of summary. 'One thing doesn't quite fit, though.'

'What's in it for Dain Collins? I mean, she's going to enormous lengths to help Goodman. You've met the guy. He's a slug.'

Kit was beginning to pick up on the rhythm of speech now and nodded, 'Awful man. And then there's the death of your partner.'

Hammett almost sneered but stopped himself in time. Instead, he said, 'More a colleague than a partner. Where Cowan's concerned, there were a lot of people that would have been happy to see him dead.' He explained more about Cowan's background and how he came to be a Pinkerton man.

'So, we can't discount her involvement in his death, and by extension, Goodman and his gang, but nor can we accuse them either?' Kit was aware Hammett was nodding. 'What is she like? I've only heard from Algy and, as you will have gathered by now, he's not history's most objective witness.'

Hammett paused for a few moments before speaking. Exactly who Dain Collins was seemed no longer to be the central question. What was she?

A dope? Lover? Victim? Blackmailer? All of the options raced through Hammett's mind. All could be true. He sensed Kit's impatience, yet all he could do was shrug.

'She's different, that's for sure. From money, no question. Beautiful, sorry, make that strangely beautiful. She has something. I think she's vulnerable. For the right man, that can be attractive. It's not difficult to work out her hold on your cousin. Hell, for all I know, she may even love him. I still wonder about that.'

'Then why would she be working with Goodman to undermine Algy and Uncle Alastair?'

'I can think of two reasons. Both plausible. One I'm certain of, the other I can't prove.

'Which are?' asked Kit.

'She's a junkie.'

'Sorry? I only speak European languages,' pointed out Kit.

Even Hammett smiled at this, then explained what he meant.

'I see, and the other?'

'He's blackmailing her or, almost certainly, threatening her, or her boyfriend.'

'Is he so dangerous?' asked Kit.

'You've met him. What do you think?' asked Hammett.

Kit thought about this. He was dangerous, this much was evident. He'd been to jail. There was the unexplained death of Cowan. The young thug he'd recruited would probably do his master's bidding without a moment of hesitation or remorse. The silence was interrupted by the sound of a door opening.

'I think we'll find out soon enough,' said Kit.

28

Agatha followed Alastair's automobile at safe distance, although she had no reason to believe the young man would expect them to be followed. She still struggled to work the car's alien gear system, and she attracted more than a few looks from pedestrians as she screeched through the city.

Alastair, driving up ahead, could hear all that was going on behind and his heart sank. 'What's that blessed woman doing to the car?' he exclaimed, unable to contain himself after one particularly loud scraping of what was left of his gear system. Thoughts of his predicament were swiftly forgotten as he listened to the assault taking place on his pride and joy's mechanics. When all of this was over, he would have a stiff word with his sister, assuming she was able to rescue them from the young gunman.

It was with some relief that Alastair saw his sister pull over just before they reached *Bellavista*. The two men debouched from the car and walked up the path towards the mansion.

'When we go in, tell that maid of yours to make herself known. I've heard all about her,' said Cookson.

You don't know the half of it, thought Alastair. For one delicious moment, he contemplated the young man pulling the weapon on her. He almost felt sorry for him. Alastair opened the door and called out for Ella-Mae.

No answer.

Cookson took over. 'Lady get over here now or I'll shoot,' he warned.

He heard a harrumph from Alastair and looked at him questioningly.

'Now she'll definitely stay in hiding.'

Cookson put the gun to Alastair's head. He said, 'Let's put that to the test, shall we?'

For several uncomfortable seconds, Alastair looked at the gun and the young man holding it. There was certainly a wild look in his eyes, but Alastair wondered if he would actually pull the trigger. The boy was scared. Fear could drive him to do anything. This was not a time for taking undue risks. Where was that blessed woman? Finally, Ella-Mae appeared as noisily silent as ever.

'What the hell,' said Cookson, looking at the diminutive housemaid. 'Where did you come from?'

'She does that. Twenty five years and I'm still not used to it,' said Alastair.

'Sneaking up on me like that, I nearly blew his brains out,' replied Cookson.

'You must be a crack shot,' said Ella-Mae sourly, looking at Alastair.

Alastair's response was somewhere between a scowl and a grimace.

'Can you get the falcon if you would be so kind,' said Alastair, through gritted teeth.

Cookson kept the gun trained on Alastair's head to ensure nothing untoward occurred while Ella-Mae went to retrieve the artefact. 'Nice place you have here,' he said by way of conversation.

Ella-Mae returned soon. In her hand was a small black object and an envelope. The object seemed like it was made from porcelain.

205

'That's the falcon?' asked Cookson.

'No, it's a moose, you schmuck,' replied Ella-Mae.

Cookson looked at the little woman in shock. This was as nothing compared to the look Alastair gave her. Somewhere between angry and homicidal if Ella-Mae judged it correctly.

'Need I remind you; this young man is pointing a gun at my head?' he said with no little exasperation.

Cookson looked at the envelope, 'Who's that for?'

'It's for Lord Kit,' said Ella-Mae.

'Open it and read what's on it.'

Ella-Mae did as she was asked, but then patted her pockets saying, 'I haven't my glasses on me.'

'Oh, for the love of God, woman,' said Alastair, getting rather tired of the damn gun resting against his temple.

Cookson held out his hand took the telegram from Ella-Mae and stuffed it in his pocket. A he did so he lowered his gun.

'Now give me the falcon, lady.'

She held it out to him. As he reached for it, he felt something metallic at the base of his temple.

'Make no mistake, young man,' said the voice of an Englishwoman, an elderly one if Cookson was not mistaken. 'I know how to use this weapon and I certainly wouldn't miss from here. Drop your weapon to the ground and kick it over to Ella-Mae.'

Cookson hesitated a moment. His mind spun furiously on what he could do. What were his options? Then he heard Alastair say, 'I would do as she says. She was ladies shooting champion at her school three years running.'

'Five,' pointed out Agatha.

'My mistake,' said Alastair as the sound of a gun hitting the floor echoed in the entrance hall. Cookson kicked it over towards Ella-Mae. The little housemaid picked it up and trained the gun on Cookson.

'Where's Christopher?' asked Agatha stepping back from Cookson but keeping, what looked like, an umbrella trained on him. Cookson looked in shock at the old woman holding the umbrella. Agatha realised that her weapon had served its purpose and she put it down.

From the side, he heard the gun click, he turned his head. Alastair was now holding the gun.

'He's still at Goodman's.'

'What about Mary and Algernon?' asked Agatha.

'They're being held at the apartment of Dain Collins by that visitor from last night,' replied Alastair, his eyes never leaving Cookson's. 'Ella-Mae, can you go to my study and get another gun? Best be on the safe side.'

*

Sandra Robins greeted the arrival of Joel Israel with her customary delight. She seemed remarkably nonchalant about the fact that he was holding a gun on two other people, thought Mary as she entered the store. She looked around her. The contents bespoke a man who had neither a great knowledge of antiques nor, perhaps, much liking for them. If it was old, it was in. This seemed to be the guiding principle at play in the store. For a nation barely one hundred and fifty years old, not even, in fact, this probably passed muster as antiquity.

Joel Israel nodded to Sandra Robbins and she walked to Goodman's office door and knocked. A moment later she walked in and told the esteemed owner of the new arrivals.

Goodman filled the doorway. He looked at his two guests and smiled beatifically. Contrary to Mary's assumptions, he had a love of beautiful objects. It was clear to Mary a compliment was headed her way and girded herself accordingly.

'Mr Aston and Miss Cavendish. What a great pleasure.'

'The pleasure's all yours,' remarked Algy. 'What have you done with my dad and Kit?'

'They're quite safe, I assure you, and you will meet them in a moment. Miss Cavendish,' said Goodman, walking up close. Get on with it, thought Mary. She looked at him in the eye. Goodman smiled and then turned away. The intensity of hatred was such Goodman realised immediately a compliment would be redundant.

He turned back to the two young people and said to Joel Israel, 'Put them with the others.' His voice was harsh as it was hurt. Such beauty, he thought. For a moment he wondered what it was like to be loved by a woman such as this. What glimpse of heaven must the English nobleman experience every day of his life? The resentment rose in him swiftly. He had to hold onto a nearby bust of Augustus to stop himself lashing out. Who was she to look at him so? Once she would have seen him differently. A lifetime ago. And one hundred pounds, admittedly.

Algy and Mary had no choice but to do as they were told. Goodman watched them all the way out of the office. His mood had been upset by the exchange. He needed a drink. A large one.

*

Kit heard Mary's voice at the door. Relief surged through his body. Then he heard Algy make a remark to a man who was obviously the same one from last night. Kit called out to Mary.

'Kit,' exclaimed Mary. He heard her clamber down the stairs. She was in his arms before he had time to tell her to be careful. Algy arrived at the foot of the stairs soon after.

'Kit, old man, where's dad?'

Kit explained what had happened and then introduced Hammett. Algy managed to find Hammett's hand in the dark chamber.

'Pleased to meet you, Mr Hammett. What brings you here?'

'I've been shadowing your fiancée for the last week,' said Hammett calmly.

Silence.

'Sorry,' said Algy, 'What did you say?' There was an edge to his voice. Hammett wasn't stupid, he'd heard it. And he was stuck in a basement facing an uncertain future because of it. In short, he was heartily sick of the whole deal.

'You heard. We've already met if you remember.'

It was difficult to see Algy square up in the dim light, but nobody was under any illusion that this was what he was doing. 'Why you low life shamus,' said Algy, 'For good measure I'd...'

Algy felt a hand on his arm. 'Stop, Algy,' said Kit. 'He was just doing his job.'

'Not much of a job if you ask me,' said Algy, calming down a smidgen.

'No worse than writing lines like,' Hammett put on a silly voice and continued, 'wearers of Arrow shirts enjoy the pleasing distinction imparted by garments that fit.'

Algy leapt forward in the dark towards the voice that was mocking him.

209

'What are you doing, Algy?' said Kit in exasperation. 'Calm down, man. We're in a bind. Hammett's on our side.'

Even Kit found this difficult to believe following the previous exchange but calm thankfully returned, helped by Mary quizzing Hammett on how he had ended up in the basement with them. Hammett briefly covered the same ground he had with Kit.

'Have you checked if there are any doors?' asked Algy, lighting a match.

'Brilliant idea, Galahad.' said Hammett sardonically. Even Kit was somewhat irritated by Algy at this moment.

'Yes, Algy, Mr Hammett and I have already checked. There's only one way out, I'm afraid,' said Kit before adding, 'and you've just come through it.'

Algy was like a caged lion, at this stage. 'We can't just sit here and do nothing. Isn't there something we can do?'

'Will you tell him? Or shall I?' said Hammett sitting down on the ground again.

Then they heard a gunshot.

Algy bounded up the stairs and started banging on the doors, 'Let us out.'

With a gun trained on him by a man whose son was being held hostage, William Cookson realised the man before him would have no compunction about shooting him. He had no choice but to drive. The journey went with less incident than Agatha's last expedition and the young driver was at the receiving end of a number of questions from Alastair on how the automobile was handling. These were invariably accompanied by pointed glances at Agatha, who merely ignored him.

Notwithstanding the fact that Cookson was an excellent driver, Alastair was and always had been a nervous passenger. This was amplified by the fact that they were driving in broad daylight, passing policemen constantly, whilst training a pair of guns, on the driver and carrying a potentially stolen artefact from Constantinople. This did little for Alastair's peace of mind. And then there was Algy.

They had parted on bad terms. The guilt he was feeling towards Algy overwhelmed him. Yes, they had parted badly and now his life was in danger. He thought little of the girl. If anything, he found himself blaming her even more for their woes. Without her there would have been no wedding. Kit would not have come over therefore smuggling the damn falcon. Yes, Dain Collins had a lot to answer for and he, Alastair Aston, would make sure she paid the ultimate penalty if they managed to get out of this situation intact.

When they arrived at the store, Alastair's hopes were boosted by the sight of Algy's car outside. Whatever happened now, they would be together. Alastair and Cookson exited the car at the same time. On Agatha's instruction, he was to do exactly what he had done previously: walk behind Alastair with a coat over his arm. Agatha followed a few beats behind.

They arrived at the store door. It was locked.

'It's locked,' said Cookson.

'I can see that, you young fool,' replied Alastair irritably. 'What do we do now?'

'Bang the door,' ordered Agatha, stepping back out of the way. It wasn't part of the plan that she should be seen. Yet.

The banging on the door gained its reward a minute later when Sandra Robbins appeared like a ray of sunshine. She noted Alastair with his hands in his pocket and Cookson carrying the bird. The job was almost done.

She let them in.

To her surprise, an old woman followed them in. Even more surprising was the fact that she was holding a gun. When Alastair removed his hand from his coat pocket and smiled, her shock was complete.

'Bring me to Goodman,' he snarled. She suspected he meant business.

*

Goodman and Joel Israel were enjoying a celebratory drink when they heard the banging on the door. When Sandra Robins had looked outside the door and confirmed it was, indeed, Alastair Aston, returned, they clinked glasses to the successful conclusion of a project begun over four months previously in a bar in Constantinople.

The little Egyptian had received word of the existence of an unusual Caravaggio, in the hands of a rich man who had, unquestionably, stolen the object. Even if he, Joel Israel, could then steal it, and there was little doubt, certainly in his own mind, of his capability in this regard; what would he do with the object?

He and Sidney Goodman had first crossed paths two years before the War. Thanks to Goodman, Joel Israel had built up a significant export market for stolen works of art that would have difficulty finding a home in Constantinople where anybody who was anybody knew everybody who was somebody, as Joel Israel had explained to Goodman. The fat man had nodded in understanding although he found himself lost by the time Joel had arrived at 'somebody'.

Their business relationship had proved profitable for both sides, and Goodman became the market leader in the import of stolen goods from Turkey, or at least would have been had statistics on such an important area of commerce been kept. The War proved a disaster for the Goodman-Israel business. Transatlantic trade was, quite literally, torpedoed by the U-Boats of Germany.

By the end of the War, Goodman was losing money, if not much weight, and an urgent re-establishment of the lucrative trade with Turkey was as attractive to him, as much as it was for Israel. The latter had spent the War dealing in small scale contraband, mostly army supplies, with his contacts in Eastern Europe. The glut at the end of the War spelled the end of this revenue stream and made the overtures from Goodman very welcome.

The two men looked at each other as the door opened. Cookson walked in first, carrying the small black falcon. This was unusual. Alastair followed him in, and then Sandra Robins.

Goodman was the first to divine something was not quite right. Was it the scowl on his store assistant's face? Not, in itself, unusual, but still, it was a dampener on what should have

213

been a celebratory moment. Or was it the look on Cookson's face? A combination of failure and fear. It was not an attractive combination on a man sorely wanting in good looks.

Perhaps it was the semi-smile snarl of Alastair Aston. How well he recognised it. Then he knew. He knew for certain the game had changed. The young fool had messed up somehow. Alastair's gun was trained on Cookson. He could see clearly now. Joel Israel had also realised what was happening. It was confirmed when Alastair said, 'Hands up where I can see them.'

Joel Israel immediately did as he was told. Then things happened quickly at this point. Alastair pushed Cookson forward to be alongside the little Egyptian. Seeing a glimmer of a chance, Goodman reached inside an open drawer. Alastair Aston's attention was diverted by Sandra Robins moving in front of him to join Cookson and Joel Israel. Goodman looked down and reached inside the drawer, quickly extracting the gun.

Moments later a shot rang out.

*

Kit and Hammett followed Algy up the steps. Algy's best efforts to tear the door off its hinges were doomed to failure, despite a remarkable effort on the part of the young and, evidently, motivated American.

Moments later the sound of a key in the lock echoed in the dark room. The door opened. It was Sandra Robins. Beside her was Alastair Aston. He was holding a gun.

'Pops,' exclaimed Algy in delight.

'Uncle Alastair,' said Kit with one eyebrow raised. He glanced down at the gun. Mary followed through a moment later.

'Is everyone alright?' she asked. This was perhaps the obvious question to ask and Kit smiled at his fiancée for thinking of it. The group trooped through to Goodman's office. Inside they found Goodman, Cookson and Joel Israel, standing against the back wall. Agatha stood before them holding a gun. Goodman had a handkerchief wrapped around his hand, where Agatha had shot him.

'You winged him; I see.'

Agatha nodded and said, 'If anyone had it coming.'

Goodman looked very unhappy but, clearly not seriously injured. He said, 'You haven't changed, Agatha. Gad, you always were a nasty ...'

A wave of the gun from Agatha interrupted Goodman's flow. Agatha smiled, not without a degree of smugness, and said, 'You should be thankful I'm such a good shot. A few inches to the right and that would have been very painful indeed.'

The grimace from Goodman suggested it was already fairly painful. Algy strode forward toward Goodman. A molten rage erupted in his eyes and it was clear Goodman's day was about to get worse.

'Algy,' shouted Kit. 'Stop.'

Algy hesitated, looked at his cousin and stopped. He adored Kit. Hero-worshipped him. They had been close despite the ocean and continent between them. He had always looked up to Kit. The rank, his intelligence. Kit was the leader and Algy was fine with this.

Kit stepped forward and spoke directly to Goodman. Beside Kit, on the desk was the little black falcon. No one was looking at it now. There was only one subject on the minds of Kit and Algy.

'What have you done with Miss Collins?'

'Who?' said Goodman. The voice was a purr again.

Hammett walked up to Goodman. Kit let him go. He knew Hammett would handle matters differently. In the light he was able to take a good look at the detective. He was neither tall nor short. Although probably younger than himself, his hair was turning grey, at least if the tuft on top was anything to go by. The moustache and the eyebrows were dark.

Hammett put his face up to Goodman's, 'You know where she is Goodman. Out with it or we'll leave you in a room with lover boy here and see if he can get you to chat.' Hammett gestured with his thumb towards Algy.

Goodman looked at Hammett and then at Algy. It was fairly evident that the young man was a nod and two seconds away from turning him into pulp. However, Goodman had survived prison once before, he had created a business buying and selling stolen goods. He had forged a transatlantic smuggling operation. There were ways around situations like this. All it took was the one weapon he had always relied on. The weapon that had kept him safe in prison and opened up a world of relative wealth.

Words.

Just words.

Deployed in the right way they could wound as deeply as any knife. He smiled. Kit immediately felt a tingle. His senses had become attuned to danger many years ago. He sensed Goodman had another card to play. And he guessed, too late, what that card was.

'You would have me be an informant also?' asked Goodman reasonably. 'It seems to me I've done you a favour young man. Let's be honest, Algernon. Your father had enough doubt, or should I say, sense, about this young lady to hire Mr Hammett to look into her past, or should I suggest affairs? Didn't you, Alastair?'

Alastair remained grim-faced. The eyes betray anger, but the heart felt the guilt.

Goodman had his audience now, 'Yes, I think I've done you a favour young man. A man of your position. And Lord Alastair, here. What would society think if it were discovered you had married a prostitute?'

'It's not true,' screamed Algy, taking a step forward. His eyes were wild. Had Hammett not stepped in between him and Goodman, there would have been only one outcome.

'Believe what you want, young man. The plain fact of the matter is you don't know. You only have her word that she wasn't looking after Mr Lehane's customers in the bedroom as well as on the floor of his nightclub.'

'Enough, Goodman,' snarled Hammett. He'd heard enough. He didn't think much of Algy Aston, but this was like a cat playing with a mouse it intended killing. 'You've made your point. But I think you've told me all I needed to know.'

'Really?' said Goodman.

Hammett walked up to Goodman and looked him in the eye. 'Yes. I think I know who is holding Dain Collins.' He walked over to the falcon, 'I think it's the same person who wants to buy this.'

Hammett picked up the bird and looked at it. It was shiny, less than a foot high. Surprisingly light. He couldn't understand why anyone would want it, least of all kidnap or kill for it. He turned to the rest of the group and said, 'She's at a place called Lehane's, just outside town. It's a night club of sorts. Caters for a certain type of rich clientele who want to meet a certain type of young woman.'

Algy flinched at this. Hammett didn't much care. He set the bird down. Kit walked over to it. He felt it in his hand. Its heft, or lack of, in this case. He tossed it around from hand to hand. Then, a cold rage came into his eyes, without warning he smashed it on the edge of Goodman's table.

'Kit,' exclaimed Mary and Alastair in horror.

The black bird exploded into hundreds of fragments. 'Keep your gun on our friends,' warned Kit as he bent down to retrieve something that had fallen on the ground.

'What have you done?' asked Agatha, still in shock.

Kit stood up. He held a roll of paper in his hand. Inside, rolled up, was a canvas. Kit put it gently on the table and slowly revealed a painting. He held it up for the others to see.

'This, I believe, is an original Caravaggio. Created, as Mr Goodman said, on the island of Malta in 1607.'

It was a painting of a small black falcon on a perch, no more than nine inches by seven. A third of the painting was yellow ochre mixed with brown umber; the rest, aside from the falcon, was dark. The shadow cast by the falcon was enormous. A malevolent gleam of light in its dark eye.

'It's beautiful,' whispered Mary.

Alastair was less impressed, 'A bit dark for my tastes.'

'No one asked you,' pointed out Agatha.

Hammett looked at Kit and then back to the painting and shook his head. He had to know how Kit knew. So, he asked him.

'When we travelled over on the Aquitania, I found the package. At first, I ignored it. I thought it was a present from either Mary or Aunt Agatha. After someone broke into the cabin, I had another look. The wrapping paper was dreadful. I credit Mary and my aunt with more taste.'

Goodman glared at Joel Israel. The latter kept his eyes well away from the big antique dealer. '

'Idiot,' snarled Goodman, angrily.

Kit smiled at this and continued, 'I opened the package and found our friend here. I wasn't sure what to make of it, so I sent a telegram to Reggie Pilbream, an archaeologist friend of mine who's in Malta as we speak.'

'What did he say?' asked Mary, genuinely interested, and slightly put out that Kit had not said anything.

'He'd no idea. Wasn't much help if truth be told.'

'I told you he's a fathead,' responded Agatha with exaggerated patience.

'Anyway,' smiled Kit, 'I knew about the falcon long before we came to your store, Goodman. Your story made some sense even if you were clearly trying to mislead us. I mean a cheap piece of tat like this, an artefact made by the hand of Caravaggio?' Kit laughed. And then the smile left his face. While he had been speaking the door to the office opened. A man was standing in the entrance.

He was holding a gun. It was trained directly at Kit.

Kit looked at the man holding the gun. Oddly he wasn't so surprised although everyone else was. Or nearly everyone else.

'Jean-Valois,' said Kit.

'Lord Aston,' said Jean-Valois, bowing. He glanced at Mary and said, 'Mademoiselle, I am, as ever, your slave.'

Mary was somewhat perturbed not only by the Frenchman's arrival, but more pertinently, by the direction his gun was pointing. To her viewpoint, it seemed trained on Kit. This feeling of disquiet became acute when the only other person not to be surprised, spoke.

'You took your time,' said Goodman. All eyes turned to the fat man who was, once more, smiling benevolently.

It was Alastair who spoke next.

'Well, aren't reunions just lovely. Now, would someone mind telling me what the blazes is going on?'

Goodman was more than happy to fill the gaps in everyone's knowledge. 'Jean-Valois is working for me, of course. Did you think I would have Mr Israel travel across Europe and an ocean without some support? Now if you will hand over the painting and, more importantly, your guns.'

Kit looked to Agatha and Alastair and nodded. Goodman stepped forward to take the guns. He stopped suddenly as Bourbon spoke again, 'Not so fast, Sidney.'

If Goodman looked confused it was as nothing to the rest of the room.

'What do you mean?' asked Goodman but with his heart sinking fast he already knew the answer. For wasn't Jean-Valois a man like himself? A man of the world. A cultured man. An aesthete, even. A man with not a single trustworthy bone in his body.

'I think you do, Sidney. Lady Frost and Mr Aston, if you please, can you throw your weapons over to me?'

They did so and Bourbon put them in his pockets. He looked at the painting, now sitting on Goodman's desk. Kit reached down and brought it over to the Frenchman. They locked eyes for a moment. Kit tried to read the eyes of the man who had seemed such a buffoon on the ocean liner. And then not so much in New York.

Mary voiced what was on Kit's mind, 'But we saw you with the police in New York.'

Bourbon smiled and then performed a shrug so Gallic it only needed to have onions draped around its shoulders to complete the part.

'A little *trompe devil* on my part. I telegrammed the New York police in advance to warn them about my old friend. When I realised he did not have the artefact, I ensured he was released so we could follow him.'

'We?' asked Kit.

Bourbon smiled. To be fair to the Frenchman, he was an attractive man, as personable as he was dangerous. He rolled the canvas up and put it in his pocket. A thought struck him. He turned to Sandra Robins.

'Madame, could you collect the key to the office from Sidney? I need to go now, and I would prefer not to be followed.'

Moments later he saluted the group and turned towards the door.

'You won't get away with this.' Ironically, it was Goodman who spoke. Everyone else was sure, by now, he could and would get away with this theft.

'I must disagree. But for now,' and he really did salute at this point, 'I must bid you farewell. One last thing, Lord Aston.'

'Yes?' asked Kit, who was resting on the back of the sofa.

'Olly says Hello.'

Moments later the Frenchman was locking the door.

'Olly Lake?' asked Alastair.

Kit nodded before saying, 'Long story.'

Hammett walked towards the telephone on Goodman's desk. He picked up the receiver and held it to his ear. Dialling a number, he spoke and asked for Lieutenant Mulroney.

'Hello, Sean. It's Hammett. Can you come over to Goodman's Antiques? I'll tell you when you get here. On Pine, yes.' Hammett looked at Kit. He said, 'The police will be here in five minutes. Do you want to tell me about what just happened?'

*

Jean-Valois du Bourbon walked away from the office. He put his gun in his inside coat pocket. Just as he did so, a man came into the store. He was dressed in a suit with a tell-tale bulge. He was quite short and seemed to be looking for someone.

'Monsieur,' said Bourbon, 'Do you work here?'

The man looked confused and replied, 'No. Why?'

'It is strange. I arrived a few minutes ago but there is no one here.'

The man processed the information and said, 'Perhaps you should leave, sir.'

'Very well. If you see the owner, could you tell him I do not wish to part with the painting. He will understand.'

Foley nodded to the Frenchman then quickly hustled him out of the store. He looked around the store. It was, indeed, empty. He saw the door at the back. Guessing this was the office. He tried the door, but it was locked. It was then he heard the shouts from inside.

*

The door to Goodman's office was already open when Mulroney arrived with several other police officers. He looked at Hammett who came over and made the necessary introductions and briefly summarised the events of the previous few hours. All the while, Mulroney eyed Goodman. He knew of Goodman's activities, but the police had not yet been able to pin anything solid on him. The look on the fat man's face suggested they would have to wait longer.

'Excuse me, Mr Hammett,' said Goodman, his voice was almost teasing, 'you keep referring to guns and being held captive. I see no guns here.' He opened his arms expansively. 'The police have been most meticulous in their search and have uncovered nothing. It seems to me, sir, that it is your word, against mine.'

Hammett nodded and smiled. Then he pointed out, 'Not if we find your pal. He has your guns and I think we've established he can't be trusted. He'll squeal.'

This brought Goodman back to earth, but he remained composed. All of this left Mulroney in a quandary about what he should arrest Goodman for.

'What about Dain?' said Algy. There was something in his voice, though. Kit looked at his cousin. The events of the past hour, in fact twenty-four hours, had clearly affected him. The new tone seemed strained, as if he was forcing himself to care. Kit looked at Mary. Her eyes narrowed, and then a frown appeared.

Hammett explained to Mulroney about the disappearance of Dain Collins and his suspicion that she was being held at Lehane's. Kit was barely listening though. He was more worried about Algy. He walked over to his cousin.

'Algy, I haven't met Dain but from what you've told me she is not the person Goodman described.'

Algy sat down and ran his hand through his hair. He shook his head and said, 'I don't know what to believe anymore.'

Meanwhile the conversation between Mulroney and Hammett had become more heated.

'What do you mean you can't raid the place?'

'Based on what?' said Mulroney in exasperation. 'I'll be busted down to traffic duty if I turn up there with San Francisco's finest and find the state Governor and half the judges enjoying a night out without their wives.'

This point was unarguable, and Hammett let it go.

Mulroney added, 'You can't even be sure they have her.'

This was also true.

'Can't we go to this place?' asked Mary. 'We could look for her.' She pointedly ignored the contemptuous laugh from Goodman and smiled.

The policeman and Hammett looked at the beautiful, refined Englishwoman speaking. It was Mulroney who spoke, 'It's not your kind of place, lady.'

'Miss Cavendish,' said Hammett. Mulroney looked at him in confusion. 'She's going to be a real-life lady.'

Mulroney was not a man to disagree with what his eyes were telling him. Then he remembered that Kit was a lord. He shook his head and said, 'The English are coming.'

This helped lighten the mood but brought them no closer to a solution. Then Mary asked, 'Can you tell me more about what type of place this is?'

Mulroney looked at Hammett with a 'be my guest' look. Hammett explained broadly about Lehane's but drew a discreet veil over the details. When he'd finished, Mary had a look in her eye that Kit knew spelled trouble.

'In which case, I have an idea,' said Mary.

*

'This is madness,' said Kit when Mary had finished. He looked around for support.

'I agree,' said Agatha, 'It's far too dangerous.' She looked to Alastair for support. However, her brother did not meet her eye. 'Alastair?' she pressed.

Alastair shrugged and continued to look away. In fact, he was looking at Algy, sitting alone, further away from the group. As he looked at him, he realised he had succeeded. However, he felt no sense of triumph. He felt desolate. As desolate as Algy. There was only one thing to do. He turned to Mary and Hammett, who was clearly in support of Mary's idea.

'What can I do?'

Agatha glared at her brother. She turned to Kit. However, Kit was looking at Mary. It required no ability to read a mind to see who was going to win this battle.

'How do we get Miss Cavendish into Lehane's?' asked Hammett.

To everyone's surprise it was Agatha who spoke next. She looked unhappy but said, 'I should have thought that obvious.'

Hammett had the look of a man for whom the workings of the female mind had long since been territory he had considered best left unexplored. This counted double for the woman he was looking at. Agatha patiently explained her thinking.

Hammett nodded, impressed. He said, 'The singer's name is Elsa Nichols. I remember the poster outside. How do we get to her?'

'Let Saul handle it,' suggested Alastair. Hammett saw Agatha's eyes light up. He took this to be a good idea.

Mulroney had been listening with increasing incredulity to a shamus and a bunch of the English aristocracy planning a raid. He looked at Hammett, 'Count me in too. Just me. I must be mad.'

Hammett nodded, 'What about this mob?' He glanced towards Goodman, Israel and Cookson.

Goodman was looking uncomfortable, 'I hardly see what charge you can bring.'

Mulroney didn't look at Goodman, instead he turned to his men. 'Take them to the Hall,' he ordered. 'Keep them locked up until tomorrow morning. They don't speak to no one. Kidnapping and...'

'Possible murder of Dan Cowan,' said Hammett, although on this he was not so sure.

'I must protest, sir,' said Goodman.

No one was listening.

The Frisco Falcon

Eddie Lehane was in a foul mood and he took great care to ensure everyone knew it. He'd been expecting a call all afternoon from Goodman to confirm the acquisition of the painting. As he thought of this, he glanced at his walls. Aside from the Picasso, he had drawings by Luca Giordano, a Fragonard and a Renaissance piece he was hoping would prove to be a Titian. He just wasn't sure who he could bribe to prove this. He'd come a long way from the Bronx.

As it was, the only call he'd received in the afternoon was from Elsa Nichols. And this had been bad news. She was crying off due to a sore throat and a cold. It sounded genuine enough, but he was still angry. He was also angry at himself as he'd fired the only other singer. She'd proved all too resistant to his charms. This hadn't been a career-enhancing move on her part.

However, Eddie Lehane's late afternoon was about to pick up unexpectedly. One of his men knocked on the door. They entered when Lehane growled 'Come in.'

'Boss, there's a woman wants to see you. She's asking if there's a job as a singer going.'

Under any normal circumstances the coincidence would have sent Lehane's suspicious nature into a frenzy. Before he had a chance to think about the unlikelihood of such a stroke of good fortune, Mary walked in.

Lehane's brain shut off immediately. This was one of the most beautiful women he had ever seen. Then she spoke.

English.

This elevated her to the top position immediately. Listening to her speak, class oozing from every syllable, any chance of correlating this vision with the police was as far from his mind as getting to know this young woman better was front and centre.

'I was hoping you might have a job as a singer,' said Mary, accompanying this with a dazzling smile.

'When can you start?' asked Lehane.

'Any time. Mr...?'

'Call me Eddie, sweetie. Let's go out to the club. You can sing me something and maybe, if you're good, you can start tonight.'

Unless she sounded like a mating moose, and her speaking voice definitely suggested otherwise, then she had the job, thought Lehane, but he wanted an excuse to see her in action. His only disappointment was the proximity to opening time; otherwise, he would have conducted the interview along the traditional lines he reserved for the more attractive job hopefuls.

He walked with Mary through his office into the club. She saw a large room with tables and chairs sitting on top of them. A black cleaner was mopping the floor. The orchestra was slowly assembling. Lehane motioned for the band leader to come over.

'Ed, meet Mary Tanner. She's singing tonight instead of Elsa.'

Ed looked at Mary. He obviously approved because he broke into a grin, 'Good to meet you, Mary.' He had a Mexican accent.

'And you, Ed.'

'Elsa?' asked Ed to Lehane.

'Sick. Mary came asking for a job at the right time. Let's hear her.'

Mary glanced around nervously. The plan had sounded simple in theory. But she was here now and standing in front a dozen men, most of whom were professional musicians. Her qualification for singing hardly extended beyond the school choir. She was under no illusion on the criteria by which she would be selected, but all the same, she wanted to impress them professionally.

A pianist strode over and Lehane pointed to a seat by the piano. He lit a cigar. He wanted to enjoy this. The pianist was in sixties and had a kindly face.

'I'm Enrique,' he said by way of introduction. 'What would you like to sing?'

'Do you know, "*A Pretty girl is like a Melody*", Enrique?'

Enrique didn't answer, instead he played a few bars of the song and Mary smiled. Lehane looked at her smile. It said a three letter word to him. She would be f-u-n also, he thought. And then she began to sing.

Lehane along with everyone listening was immediately transported by her voice. It was crystal in its clarity. Nothing was more appropriate than hearing her sing, 'A pretty girl is like a melody, that haunts you night and day.'

She lacked the earthiness of Elsa but had something else you couldn't buy. Class. She was pure class. Lehane's mind drifted into imagining her in another outfit. This line of thinking proved as intoxicating as the cheap liquor he sold his customers.

Why bother waiting until later tonight he thought? It hadn't stopped him with the other girl. Sometimes he preferred it when they fought back. He looked directly into her blue eyes. Yes, she would be fun. And he wanted her immediately.

But this was not Lehane's day. A large man came over to him and said, 'We've had a call from our man down at the Hall.'

'So?' said Lehane irritably. He was counting the seconds until the end of the song. They hadn't much time.

'Goodman and the others. They've been arrested.'

'What?' exclaimed Lehane so loudly that Enrique stopped immediately causing Mary to stop singing. Lehane looked at Mary and apologised. He turned to a woman who was sitting watching the performance with him, 'Sweetie,' he said, unable to remember her name, 'can you take Mary down to get ready.'

'Thanks, Mary, that's great.' He meant it too.

Mary curtsied and said, 'Thank you, kind sir.'

Lehane almost cancelled the order there and then in favour of something else but business called. He followed her all the way off the stage. He and the rest of the orchestra. Then he stood up and strode towards his office.

'Who's this?' he asked on the phone.

The voice at the other end of the line, recognising Lehane's voice said, 'Frank Nelson, Mr Lehane.'

Lehane racked his memory but couldn't place him. He had so many policemen in his pocket, it was difficult to keep track of all of them.

'You say Goodman's been arrested?'

'Yes, sir, Mulroney just brought him in.'

Lehane covered the mouthpiece and asked the other man in his office, 'Do we own Mulroney?' The man shook his head. Lehane spoke again on the phone, 'Look, Frank, we need you to find out what's going on. Can you speak to Goodman?'

'They have him and the others locked up. I can't get near them,' said Nelson

'There's a hundred for you if you can. Call me back in an hour.' He hung up and cursed passionately and with no little eloquence.

*

Mary and the woman, who was called Sofia, entered a large room situated on a corridor just off the main stage. This was clearly the dressing room. Inside were lots of women, mostly Hispanic, dressing for the evening.

Sofia went to a wardrobe and handed Mary a dress. She said, 'This is for you.'

Mary held it up, then said, 'What do I wear over the top of this?'

'Honey, that's what you're wearing on stage tonight.'

Mary's eyebrows shot up. The dress was as short as it was revealing at the front. She made a mental note not to bend over too low.

'I hope it's hot out there tonight,' said Mary.

Sofia smiled and looked at Mary, 'Honey, in that dress, you're gonna raise the temperature real high.'

This was paradoxically both flattering and far from the reassurance she would have liked at that moment. She noticed that all of the other women were changing where they stood. Mary had no choice but to do likewise. She changed as quickly as she could. With the dress on, well, so far as a dress with so little material could be described as being on, she looked at herself in the mirror. Kit would have a heart attack when he saw her. She turned around to view from another angle. Oddly, she quite liked what she saw. Perhaps she would keep the dress when all of this was finished. Her chance to view what passed

231

for the dress was interrupted by a knock on the door. Sofia went to answer it. Moments later she returned to Mary.

'You should go out front and work on the songs you're going to sing with Enrique.'

Mary walked outside and joined Enrique in the corridor. They discussed a number of options for her set. Four songs were agreed on and Mary walked on stage, aware that all eyes were trained on her. She and Enrique went through the first verse of each of the songs without any problems, although Enrique hit a few bum notes when Mary forgot her best intention and bent too low on a couple of occasions.

Once the brief rehearsal was complete, Enrique suggested she return to the dressing room and wait for the call. The orchestra would play while the customers arrived. Once the room had filled up a little, she would make her entrance.

Mary walked off stage and asked a stagehand where she could find a washroom. He indicated a door at the end of the corridor. Just ahead of it she saw another door. She walked towards the bathroom; a quick check behind revealed she was alone in the corridor. She ignored the washroom door and opened the other. It was a stairwell. She skipped down the stairs.

The door at the bottom was open. She walked through into a well-lit corridor. There were three doors on her right. A man sat outside the door at the end. He stood up as she came through the door.

'Hey, what are you doing here?' was what he meant to say. He got as far as 'hey' when he took in the full view of Mary in the very short dress and the exceptionally deep cut at the front.

'Hello,' said Mary. 'I seem to be lost.'

The man had removed his hat. He said, 'What are you looking for, lady?'

Mary sized the man up immediately. He was over six feet. Possibly closer to seven feet tall. At least from where Mary was looking. Which was up. She smiled at him.

'The bathroom. But I seem to have found you. What's your name?'

'Harry, Harry Schulz,' said the giant. His voice was a bass rumble. Mary thought it better not to mention that her fiancé's manservant was also called Harry.

She pointed to the rooms, and asked, 'What's in the rooms, Harry?'

The giant looked around. He looked uncomfortable. 'I can't say.'

'And the other one, you were sitting outside?' she said looking around his shoulder. She looked up again and smiled at him.

'Say, are you new here?' He was quick. Mary also sensed he wasn't telling the full truth. He seemed uncomfortable.

'Yes, how did you guess?' replied Mary sweetly.

'People here think I'm a dope, but I'm not so stupid.'

'You're not, Harry. I wouldn't put up with it if I were you. You seem like a nice person to me.'

The giant smiled. 'You shouldn't be here, lady,' said Harry. It wasn't threatening. If anything, he seemed concerned for her. 'You should go back upstairs. The bathroom is first on the right.'

Mary stood on tip toe and pecked him on the cheek. 'Thank you, Harry, don't you let those bad men make fun of you.'

Harry floated back to his seat outside the bedroom while Mary raced up the stairs. Mission accomplished. She went through the door and ran into Sofia.

'Hey, where have you been? You're on in a few minutes.'

It was seven in the evening. Mulroney and Hammett sat facing Kit along with Alastair, Algy, Agatha and Natalie in the library at *Bellavista*. Foley was also sitting amongst the group. Kit and Alastair wore black tuxedos, but the other men remained in their suits. The atmosphere was tense. The only sound in the room when Kit was not speaking was the beating of nervous hearts on the eve of battle. No one was under any illusion as to the difficulty of the task ahead.

For once Hammett and Mulroney were glad that someone else was in command. Whether it was the accent, his bearing or just an obvious air of command, each had accepted Kit's role as the leader of the operation. He also had the most to lose, they realised.

'So, to recap,' said Kit, 'I will enter the club with Natalie and Uncle Alastair. When Mary passes on what she has found out, Natalie and I will fake a falling out. Natalie will go outside to where you will be waiting.' Kit looked at Algy, Hammett, Mulroney and Foley. 'You'll have found a way into the building, through the back, hopefully.'

Hammett nodded at Kit.

'Aunt Agatha, stays in the car in case we need to make a quick getaway.'

'Check,' said Agatha.

Alastair turned to Agatha, appalled. 'Have you been drinking?'

Agatha shrugged nonchalantly and looked up at Kit. Alastair was none too keen to have Agatha back at the wheel of his beloved car and had remained grimly silent at this part of the plan.

When Kit finished his summary, the group filed out of the house and into the several cars parked at *Bellavista*. The drive to Lehane's took around half an hour. Kit, Alastair and Natalie drove right up to the club, while the others stayed back.

After climbing out of the car, Agatha took the wheel. Alastair turned to her and said, 'For God's sake, remember what I told you.'

Agatha gave a salute which further irritated her brother. Moments later, as he was walking into the club with his nephew and Natalie, he heard the gears crunch noisily as Agatha drove the car away. Kit would have smiled had he not been in such a rush to get inside. He was desperate to see Mary and make sure she was alright.

The doorman waved the group through and they were met by another man dressed in a tuxedo. He looked at Kit and then lingered a beat longer than decorum permitted on Natalie, before saying, 'Come this way.'

Soon they were entering a large room with tables and chairs. It was still early so there were probably more people playing in the orchestra than paying customers. Kit didn't mind. He scoured the room looking for Mary.

*

Detective Frank Nelson was in his early thirties. He'd been in the force less than ten years and never risen very high. He didn't care. The pay wasn't much better at Mulroney's level, but the hours and the responsibility were greater. Who wanted that? Who wanted to spend years, like Mulroney, putting your life on the line, dealing with the very worst of humankind? All for a lousy salary and a pension that would require you to continue working until you dropped dead.

He had a better plan.

Nelson looked like a movie star. He liked their lifestyle. He liked the way they dressed. He liked the girls they had on their arms. What was not to like? His first trip to Lehane's had been with some buddies. They liked to drink, and he'd had to flash his badge to the doormen to restore a situation that had deteriorated badly. This is when he'd first met Eddie Lehane.

Lehane had the young policeman checked out. Nelson had his own racket going with a bunch of girls. The news was a gift to someone like Lehane, always on the lookout to extend his influence. He gave Nelson a choice. In fairness to Lehane, the choice had been fairly generous.

Nelson grabbed it with both hands, although he did have to give up his sideline. This was not such a great loss. He was sacrificing one income stream that combined some risk with no little hassle, for another source of revenue which, seemingly, entailed very little effort. Just information from time to time.

The detective bureau down at the Hall was the usual war zone. Nelson was counting on this. Some days, and this was one, it was anarchy. The city just went mad. They were all there: pimps, prostitutes, drug addicts, hoodlums. He ignored them and made his way along the corridor, passing a stream of policemen heading in the other direction. Soon, he found the person he wanted. He was young, one of Mulroney's men. Moore or something like that. Nelson knew some things that were career-detracting about him. He'd hinted before at the young man's secret, so they both knew where they stood.

'Hi there, good-looking,' said Nelson pointedly. The other young policeman flinched. He looked at Nelson suspiciously. Nelson nodded to the room he was standing outside of.

'Who's inside?'

The young man saw nothing in the question, so he told him.

'Can I go in?'

'Mulroney said no one could see them.'

'Come on, what's the harm, sweetie?' said Nelson. The harm in question was all too clear to the young man.

'Make it quick,' said the young man, realising he needed a change in career.

'You're cute,' said Nelson opening the door. He emerged three minutes later. Eyes ahead, he walked straight past the young man and down the corridor. The young man felt a wave of relief. It had been quick. No one had seen them. No harm done.

Nelson headed out of the Hall. Outside the sky was a mauve and orange blending into night. The sun was an orange-red. Another hot day tomorrow, he thought. The early evening traffic had thinned out and he crossed the road to a payphone.

He had no change.

'Damn,' he said. He went to a store and bought some cigarettes. He returned to the payphone. A kid was talking to his sweetheart. Nelson waited. And waited. He tapped the kid on the shoulder. The kid put his hand over the phone and told Nelson where to go. Nelson's eyes hardened. Tempting as it was to take the kid out there and then, he realised it would not look good. He showed his badge.

The kid looked at him in confusion. The Hall was just across the road. He hung up and left Nelson alone. Finally, Nelson was able to dial the number he wanted.

The Frisco Falcon

'Hello Mr Lehane. It's Frank Nelson.'

*

The first thing Mary saw was Kit sitting with Uncle Alastair and Natalie, near the front of the stage. She felt a surge of relief and confidence. All of a sudden, her dress, far from being a source of discomfort became something else entirely. A memory for the man she would spend her life with. A moment when she realised the power she had. And a realisation that she wanted only to share that power. These few moments would be theirs.

She smiled at Kit, one eyebrow raised slightly as she enjoyed his reaction, a mixture of shock and an appealing amount of undisguised desire. Her eyes never left his. Kit, alas, like any sensible chap, given the opportunity to gaze upon such a sublime manifestation of the female form, was unable to hold Mary's eyes for very long, when the rest of her person was displayed to such advantage. And to be fair to Kit, he took full advantage.

Even Alastair found himself warming to the task. He settled down to enjoy Mary's singing. No point in wasting time thinking about what lay ahead. No, it was best that he played his part as a paying customer of Lehane's, there to enjoy the entertainment provided. Less suspicious that way. As Mary only had eyes for Kit and Kit was, likewise, happily engaged, Alastair felt quite free to enjoy the show. And there was a lot on show.

Kit wasn't sure whether he should have been enjoying what he was seeing quite as much as he was. It was certainly a major distraction. The impact on the other men in the audience he didn't care about. In fact, they were the last thing on his mind. Followed closely by Dain Collins. However, the third song,

239

"*Till We Meet Again*" brought matters back to the key reason for his being there. But my god, she was beautiful. And her voice was as pure as her dress, clearly, was not.

He heard her sing, "*Smile while you kiss me sad adieu.*" Her voice swirled around his head, filled his senses and lifted him up. She smiled down at Kit as she sang, '*Till we meet again.*"

As much as he wanted to keep his eyes fixed on his fiancée, Kit managed to glance around at the audience. It was clear he wasn't the only one enjoying the show. Eddie Lehane was spellbound by the young English girl. One more number and she would be off stage for half an hour. Plenty of time, he thought. Why wait? He watched her move gracefully along the stage. Like a cat. Now she moved into the audience, along the front row. Teasing the men. She bent low over one of the front tables. Lehane cursed the head obscuring what must have been a sensational view. He was impatient for the song to end.

Finally, Mary finished her first set. At this point, she did something which sent Lehane's imagination into orbit. She leaned over to the beautiful woman in the front row and whispered in her ear. Lehane didn't care where her interests lay. In a few minutes that would be academic. Much to his amusement though, the young man who had been sitting with the young woman seemed to take offence at this. How hypocritical, thought Lehane. You were sitting with your tongue out like the rest of us a moment ago. He motioned for one of his men to come over.

'Yes, boss?'

Lehane nodded towards the departing Mary, 'Tell the girl to come to my office. Now.' Out of the corner of his eye, he could see the young woman Mary had spoken to storming away from the table. She was a looker alright. The girl had good taste. He considered calling one of his men to stop her but then thought better of it. He looked back at the table where she had been sitting. The two men seemed to be deep in conversation, remarkably unconcerned by the departure of their companion. He could hardly blame them. Lehane's specialised in providing plenty more where she came from.

The music started again. Lehane turned to go back to his office.

*

Natalie walked past the doormen, eyes staring at a point one hundred yards away. She headed directly for the automobile housing Agatha. She stopped briefly at the window and then continued walking around the corner.

She saw Algy's car up ahead.

Hammett and the other two men climbed out of the car and ran towards her. Natalie said, 'Mademoiselle Mary thinks Miss Collins is in the basement corridor to the left of the stage. The end room. It's guarded, but the man is quite nice apparently. She doesn't want him to be hurt.

Hammett rolled his eyes at Mulroney. He asked Natalie to wait in the car. At this point, Algy drove away with Natalie leaving Hammett and Mulroney by the road. The two men cut across the woods that surrounded the night club. They arrived at the back of the club. Earlier reconnaissance had established the presence of a rear fire exit. There did not appear to be any windows at the back, much like the front. They surmised, based on the layout suggested by Mary, that the doorway was at the other side of the nightclub from where it was likely Dain Collins was being held.

'What do you think?' asked Mulroney.

241

'It's unguarded, which is good, but it may be locked,' said Hammett.

Mulroney took out his gun, 'I brought a key.'

Hammett nodded. Gunfire wasn't a problem. In fact, it was a necessary part of Kit's plan. He would need a diversion to get to Dain Collins. In the meantime, he and Mulroney could keep the rest of Lehane's men busy.

*

Kit looked at the note Mary had slipped onto the table as she had whispered into Natalie's ear. He was still recovering from the sight of Mary in the dress if it could be so described. The note was clearly written in a hurry. It read:

She's in basement, possibly end room. Stairs to left of stage looking out on room. It's guarded by giant. Guard seems gentle. Don't hurt. He's called Harry.

The three of them quickly read the note. Mary had also drawn a rough map. Once again Kit's heart swelled as he thought about the young woman he was engaged to. Mary was walking back towards the side of the stage, waving to the crowd who were applauding her performance rapturously. Kit nodded to Natalie. The young French woman began to gesticulate wildly and shouted, 'You prefer her to me. I'm off.'

This was certainly true, thought Kit but Natalie had carried off her role to perfection. She stood up and turned around dramatically, before striding in the direction of the exit.

Kit motioned to Alastair to come closer. He said, 'I'm going towards the exit. Follow me as far as the stage. Don't fire unless you have to. In fact, cause a diversion if someone looks like they're following me.

The Frisco Falcon

'I'll think of something,' said Alastair.

As they were speaking, they didn't see Mary suddenly change direction from the stage and accompany a man in the direction of Lehane's office.

*

Lehane saw Mary walk towards his office. He held the door open for her as she walked in. His heart was beating like an Indian drum on the eve of battle. This was unusual, but then again, Mary was unusual. He looked at her movement, so graceful, her body, so lithe. He didn't care if she didn't sing again. He was going to enjoy this.

Mary smiled up at him as she entered the office. This sent his heartbeat racing even faster. At this rate he was going to have a stroke, he thought. He walked over and closed the door behind them. Mary turned to face him and sat against his oak table. She placed her hands behind her back. The look of submissiveness disguised the fact she had taken hold of a rather hefty paperweight.

Lehane was on the point of collapse at the sight of this barely-dressed beauty, looking up at him so compliantly.

'How do you think that went?' asked Mary with a smile that would have had a monk gleefully shouting his resignation to the Abbott.

'Swell, honey. They love you. Hey, we all love you.'

Mary's eyes narrowed. She could sense that Lehane was on edge. She wasn't so naïve as to wonder why. She walked towards him, which seemed to surprise Lehane. She put her free hand on his chest quite firmly. The other hand clutched the paperweight.

'I'm glad you liked it, Mr Lehane. I didn't want to let you down. That would have been bad.'

'Are you a bad girl, Mary?' asked Lehane. His eyes were, by now, almost in flames.

Mary wasn't quite sure where he was going with this. Her knowledge of the multifarious dimensions of human relationships extended only so far. The last time she had been a bad girl was at school.

For wont of anything better to say, Mary replied, 'Bad girls are normally chastised, aren't they?'

This seemed to have a strange impact on Lehane, who seemed on the point of collapse. He managed to croak in response, 'Yes, they should be spanked.'

'I was caned once,' admitted Mary. At school. A practical joke that went awry. The teacher was soaked. Mrs Jenkins, she remembered.

Lehane was now pawing the ground. He grabbed Mary around the waist. Mary had anticipated this.

'Is that a Picasso?'

Lehane looked to his side, 'Yes, honey. It's yours if you want.' His voice was somewhere between a growl and begging.

At this point the phone rang. He wanted to disregard it. This was too important. Then he realised his excitement had reached such an acute stage that the show might be over before it had begun.

He picked up the phone reluctantly.

'Yes,' he said, virtually panting with desire, 'who is it?'

'Mr Lehane, it's Frank Nelson.'

The man walking past Agatha in the car eyed her closely but continued on, uninterested. He was looking forward to a night with female company distinctly younger than the one he'd just seen. Still, it was an unusual sight, such an old woman at a place like this. He hurried towards the entrance. The doormen knew him and waved him through.

'What's with the broad in the car?' he asked on his way past.

'What broad?' asked one of the doormen.

The man gestured with his thumb and told them.

The two doormen shrugged at one another. Then one of them said he would take a look. He felt like stretching his legs anyway. He walked in the direction the man had said. A number of cars were parked by the road. He spotted one with a lady in the passenger seat. He walked towards it.

Agatha had seen all from her position in the car. This was, indeed, a problem they hadn't considered. Thinking quickly, she stuck her head out of the window and shouted to the approaching man.

'What do you fancy, darling? Half price for you.'

The man took one look at Agatha, 'Forget it, lady.' He waved her away and turned on his heel and walked back to the nightclub.

His fellow doorman asked him what he'd seen. The man shook his head and said, 'Some crazy old broad. Seems harmless.'

Jack Murray

Agatha put her head back inside the car, quite pleased by the outcome and not in the least bit put out by the apparent rejection.

*

Hammett looked at Mulroney. They had been by the door for a minute. Then Mulroney nodded. Hammett stepped out of the way in case of any ricochet. Mulroney aimed his weapon at the door handle and fired. The door sprang open, and they raced inside. They were now in a corridor. Up ahead they could hear the orchestra playing. They raced towards the sound of the music.

No one had heard the initial shot to open the door. They certainly heard the next two. Mulroney and Hammett each fired their guns in the air. The result was as anticipated.

Pandemonium.

Customers rose from their seats and raced towards the exit. They were joined by many of the women and bar staff. Mulroney and Hammett loosed off another shot or two before joining the throng heading for the exit. No one was any the wiser as to who had started the stampede.

Meanwhile the doormen were trying to push, without success against the rush of people coming towards the entrance. The screams and the yells drowned out their attempts to restore calm.

*

Kit was heading towards the stage when the gunfire began. All at once people were flooding from the stage, and behind him from the seats. He ignored the noise and the mayhem, heading straight for the corridor mentioned by Mary.

Behind him Alastair followed, fascinated by the impact of Hammett and Mulroney. He saw Kit duck behind the stage.

The Frisco Falcon

He stopped and waited, observing the uproar with something approaching pleasure. The orchestra he noted, unlike on the Titanic, had abandoned ship and were streaming out the rear exit. Alastair guessed this was the entrance used by Hammett and Mulroney. A few of Lehane's gunmen were heading that way also, clearly believing they were in the midst of a police raid. Alastair wasn't sure if this was to escape or to tackle the invaders directly. Seeing one of them trip up a customer by accident caused him to have a fit of giggles. He reached over to a table and picked up a cocktail which had clearly just arrived on the table. He tried a sip. Not bad. A bit strong but nonetheless it helped add to the theatre of the moment.

Behind the stage all was quiet. The corridor was empty, Kit made straight for the door at the end. Moments later he was picking his way down the stairs and finally through a door, into another corridor. A man sat at the end of the corridor. He stood up. Mary's description of him had done him no injustice, he was certainly a giant. Kit looked at him and the giant looked back.

'You shouldn't be here,' said Harry. He started to walk towards Kit menacingly.

Kit put his hand in his pocket and felt the hard metal of his gun.

*

Lehane gripped the phone tightly.

'Goodman's talked,' said Nelson to Lehane.

At the moment he heard gun shot. Then a second. 'What the?' uttered Lehane, momentarily distracted. 'Take this find out what he wants,' snarled Lehane handing the phone to Mary.

Mary took hold of the phone. She heard a voice saying 'Mr Lehane? Mr Lehane?'

'He said to tell me.'

Mary listened as Nelson revealed the plan to raid Lehane's to find Dain Collins using the new singer as a plant. Mary nodded her head. Then she said, 'Thank you Mr...?'

'Nelson. Frank Nelson,' replied the soon-to-be former copper.

Lehane was at the door. He opened it and the muffled sound of previously became all too clear. There was a stampede to get out of his club. He heard another few shots. Lehane turned back towards Mary, caught between desire and the need to do something, anything to stop people leaving.

'What did he want?'

Mary smiled up at Lehane saying, 'No news yet.'

The noise of screams grew louder.

'Honey, I have to go deal with this.' Regret was sculpted into every syllable spoken by Lehane

Mary put on a glum face. Then a thought struck her. She twisted the knife further.

'What were you saying about spanking?'

The pandemonium outside his office was as nothing compared to the chaos inside Lehane's mind at that moment. Hearing the most beautiful girl he'd ever seen utter his now favourite word in a crystal clear English accent stopped him in his tracks. A scream outside woke him up to reality. In fact, he almost howled in agony himself as he turned and went through the door.

Once he was gone, Mary picked up the phone and dialled a number.

The Frisco Falcon

'Hello, I need the police. There's been gunfire at Lehane's nightclub. Yes, that's right Lehane's. Thank you.'

She calmly put the phone down then walked over to a coat rack near the door, selected a coat and slipped it over her shoulders and walked outside to join the wave of people trying to exit the club. Somewhere in the distance she heard an explosion.

Noise levels reached a crescendo. Mary smiled at the panic-stricken faces of the old men now exiting the club. There was no chivalry. It was every man for himself. Mary found herself buffeted and her feet trod on. She lost her shoes and was almost lifted off the ground by the mass of people trying to escape.

*

Algy and Foley parked the car on the other side of the wood which separated Lehane's from a road running parallel. They heard the gunfire as they got out of the car.

'Better hurry,' said Algy.

The two men ran through the wood, hurdling logs and dodging around stumps, bushes and trees. The smaller man soon outpaced the bigger man. He reached the clearing first and fished out something from his pocket. Algy looked at it in surprise.

Lehane's was a riot of screaming. It seemed to be coming from the other side of the building. On this side, the two men could see a handful of customers and what looked like the orchestra composed entirely of Hispanic musicians. A few of Lehane's men also milled around in utter confusion. Unsurprisingly, they looked unhappy. They were just about to become unhappier.

249

'Where did you get that anyway?' asked Algy, staring down. The diminutive detective was holding stick of dynamite.

Foley looked at Algy but didn't answer. Algy had very quickly understood that the Pinkerton man was not the most communicative. Foley lit the fuse with his cigarette and waited a moment. Then he threw the stick away from where the crowd were located.

The explosion convinced the crowd that they might be safer at the front. En masse they ran in the same direction, away from the explosion, and towards the front of the nightclub.

'I guess we wait now,' said Algy.

*

'You shouldn't be here,' repeated the giant, looming over Kit. He noted that the well-dressed man before him, seemed disconcertingly unafraid. Harry rather disliked violence and was normally reluctant to use it. His size tended to mitigate the need for deploying what God had so liberally bestowed upon him.

Kit looked at the big man.

'It's Harry isn't it?'

This stopped Harry in his tracks. He was definitely Harry, no question. He nodded.

'Harry, I'm here to take the young girl.'

'Boss says she stays here.'

'You like her, don't you?'

This seemed a strange question to Harry. How did this man know? It was true. He did like her. Kit took a chance. He said, 'She's always been nice to you, hasn't she?'

The sound of the mayhem upstairs was permeating through to the basement. Harry looked up then he turned back to Kit.

'Yes, she's sweet.'

'She's not well, Harry. The boss is giving her drugs. They're making her sick.'

Harry felt his stomach tighten. This couldn't be true, yet every day she seemed to be worse. Mr Lehane would never do that. He said so.

'Then why is she so ill?' Kit didn't know if this was true, but it was worth a gamble if what Hammett said was true.

'I don't know,' replied the giant.

'Will you help me please, Harry? Will you help me help her?'

Harry couldn't remember the last time anyone had said "please" to him. The mayhem outside continued but the only sound either man made now was the sound of their breathing. Then Harry made up his mind.

*

Lehane eventually squeezed through the throng coming the other direction. He found one of his men, standing powerless, watching people go past him. He looked at his boss, dumbfounded. Lehane swore. When this was over, he would adopt a more rigorous recruitment policy for thugs. These people were imbeciles.

'Do something,' screamed Lehane in exasperation. Although even Lehane recognised there was little that could be done. He looked around wildly. What had started the stampede? He needed to find out. Grabbing the man by the arm he said, 'Come with me.'

Lehane and the other man raced into the club's main room. It was now empty save for an elderly man standing by the stage drinking a cocktail.

'Hey, you,' shouted Lehane, 'What the hell are you doing?'

Alastair glanced down at his cocktail and then back up at Lehane. He smiled and said, 'I should have thought that obvious.'

Both the answer and the accent were not what Lehane was expecting. There was something in the mocking tone of voice as well. Lehane and his man marched forward towards Alastair. Lehane didn't know why, but he felt in his bones, this man knew a lot about tonight's mayhem.

And then the reason for his insouciance became all too clear.

*

Hammett saw Lehane leave the office first. He was stuck in the middle of the throng leaving the club. Bodies surged forward towards the exit. The noise of shouting was deafening. Hammett didn't have time to enjoy his handiwork, though. He had to get to Lehane. He shouted to Mulroney.

'Lehane's going back.' Hammett pointed wildly in the direction of the club. Mulroney's heart sank. Then he nodded. Both men turned and tried to go against the torrent rushing the other way.

Inevitably this was greeted with more than dismay, and the two men had to fend off a few punches aimed their direction. I need to lose weight, thought Mulroney more than once as he struggled against the wall of bodies. He was sure he'd just rammed a state Senator a moment ago.

Finally, they broke though.

'We can't let Lehane get to Aston.'

They both ran in the direction of the dancehall. Progress was unimpeded as, by now, the majority of the customers were either in the main foyer of the club or outside.

*

Harry opened the door. The room was dimly lit. Lying on the bed was the crumpled figure of Dain Collins. Neither awake nor asleep. Kit gasped at the damage wrought by the drugs.

'My God, what have they done to her?' She seemed a shrunken, ghostly old woman compared to the photographs he'd seen.

Harry looked at her. He was shocked by the change in her appearance. The girl he had known was so full of life and had always been kind to him. This seemed like a different person. Now he understood why he had been told never to enter, never to let anyone else enter unless Lehane said-so.

'Can you lift her?' asked Kit. The giant picked her up like she was a tray of drinks, carefully but without any sense of her weight. She looked up at him and smiled. A flicker of recognition maybe. Her eyes tried to focus on Kit. She gave up and looked back at Harry.

Then Kit asked, 'Is there a way out at the back?'

Harry nodded.

Kit opened the door. The corridor was still clear. The muffled sounds of the uproar continued. They hadn't much time. Kit led the way up the stairs and into the corridor just off-stage. He turned to Harry and said, 'Which way now?'

Harry's head nodded in a certain direction, 'Follow me.'

The big man moved quickly along the corridor, so much so, Kit found keeping up difficult. Soon they were onto the main stage. Kit looked down. All at once he felt a numbness set in. It had been too good to be true. The club was empty save for Alastair, standing in front of two men. Alastair had his hands up. To his credit, one of his hands was clutching a cocktail, Kit noted. One of the two men was holding a gun. Alastair and the other two men turned to look towards the stage.

Lehane recovered from his shock and shouted to Kit and Harry, 'What the hell do you think you're doing?'

Alastair chuckled, 'My, my, sir, you're not the brightest, are you? I should have thought that obvious also.'

Both Lehane and his man looked at the Englishman in shock. Lehane was not used to being spoken to in such a high-handed manner. The situation, already out of control, was spiralling in a direction that bordered on lunacy. For a moment, Lehane actually wondered if the past five minutes were a dream turned nightmare.

If Lehane was in shock, so was his man, Bernie. He'd worked with Lehane for years. No one had ever spoken to the boss in such a manner. Given the stupefied shock of his boss, Bernie felt it was time he stepped up, or at least forward.

'You can't talk to the boss like that,' exclaimed Bernie.

'Why not? The man's obviously a cretin,' pointed out Alastair amiably.

Kit and Harry had stopped for a moment, able to hear the exchange clearly. From their viewpoint, it was clear what Alastair was up to. While it was entirely possible the glass of cheerfulness Alastair was holding up had contributed to this uncharacteristic valour, the supercilious sarcasm was all his. They watched fascinated. Lehane was on the point of blowing a fuse when he heard a voice from behind.

'Eddie, can I ask you and your man to put your hands up?'

To emphasise the point, Mulroney stepped forward and placed his gun against the base of Lehane's head. He added, 'Now.'

Hammett shouted up to Kit, 'You better get outta here. Go to the fire exit at the back. Sounds like the boys have started their show.'

Kit nodded and turned to Harry, 'Shall we?'

Harry didn't move. His eyes were on Lehane. It was true he wasn't the smartest kid on the block. Never had been. But even Harry could recognise the cold hatred in Lehane's eyes.

'If you know what's good for you, Schulz, you'll stay right where you are. Don't be a lug all your life. Put the girl down. We'll take care of her.'

Harry looked down at Dain Collins. Her eyes were open, but she seemed dead. The rage inside him wiped out the doubt, and the fear.

'You shouldn't have done this to her, boss. When this is finished, I'm gonna come find you.' He started to walk forward, slowly at first, his eyes never leaving Lehane's, their fiery intensity matching his. Lehane knew he meant it.

Soon he was hurrying towards the exit. He could barely feel the hundred pounds of Dain Collins in his arms. Kit followed him through the back corridor that led to freedom. The five men in front of the stage watched them disappear.

'What now, Mulroney?' asked Lehane. 'At some point my men are going to come. Do you plan to shoot it out with them?'

Hammett and Mulroney were acutely aware of this. They glanced at one another. There was no fear in their eyes, but they knew this was not a situation that could last indefinitely.

Alastair had, by this stage, picked up Bernie's dropped gun. He said, 'I have an idea.' He emptied the gun's chambers and handed it back to Bernie. 'There you go my man, he said. 'Now point it at Mr Hammett and Mr Mulroney.' Bernie

255

looked at Lehane in confusion. Alastair, meanwhile, took Hammett's gun and pointed it at Bernie.

'Now if you, please,' said Alastair. 'Right. Can we all walk towards the exit. One word from you Lehane and I will have no hesitation in using this. I don't like you. I don't like what you're doing here. I will spend the rest of my life making sure you and people like you don't do this again.'

They started walking towards the main entrance.

The cold air felt like a balm after the smoky, sweaty sourness of the nightclub. Mary inhaled deeply as she was pushed forward by the pressure of the people behind her. She spied Agatha further ahead and skipped over towards the car.

'Any problems?' asked Agatha.

Mary wasn't sure whether or not to bring up the topic of discussion that had Mr Lehane so excited. If Mary's suspicions about its appeal were true, it might be better discussed with Kit.

'None,' lied Mary sweetly.

'It's up to Kit and the others now,' said Agatha. 'It seems Mr Hammett and his friends have created quite a show.'

Mary climbed into the back of the automobile and watched the steady stream of people out of the nightclub. The demographic skew was towards older men, clearly wealthy. They were balanced out by the number of women, most of them young, with darker skin tones than the pink bubbling flesh of the men.

'Nice place,' said Mary. There was no mistaking the sadness in her voice. The role of these women was clear, and it appalled her. To be reduced to such circumstances chilled her. Then she felt a gathering rage inside. A desire to see the men who exploited these women punished. They had made virtual slaves of the young women, many of them younger than Mary. How could this be allowed to happen? Who were these degenerate men, clearly at the top of society who could countenance the degradation of youth?

'They should be in jail,' she said, giving voice to the thoughts of the other lady in the car. She wasn't just referring to

Lehane and his men. Her eyes hardened as she thought of what Lehane had planned. Then she remembered the phone call. What was the name of the policeman? Frank Nelson? It would start with him.

*

Foley saw the door open. He tensed. His hand went to his gun. Then he saw Kit emerge, followed by a giant of man. He was carrying a young woman. She looked as if she was dead.

'Dain,' shouted Algy running towards his fiancée. Foley swore. He hadn't wanted to make their presence so obvious in case there were any of Lehane's men nearby. Algy was already by Kit and the other man. Another oath and Foley went out to join them. There would be no time for reunions. They had to exit quickly.

'This way,' ordered Foley. Kit looked at Foley and nodded. Seconds later they were out of sight at the edge of the woods heading for the car. It was dark now. They were clear.

They stopped for a moment. 'I'm going back,' said Kit. 'This is Harry, by the way. He's working for Pinkerton's from now on.'

Foley looked up at the giant and did something he did rarely. He smiled. He looked back at Kit and said, 'He can be my partner.'

Kit turned and, with no further explanation, moved quickly back towards the club. His leg was sore as hell. But he had one more task to accomplish. It was something the giant had said to him as they'd walked out. He had to see for himself.

Back through the fire exit of the nightclub he followed the short corridor to the side of the stage. The club was now empty. He walked across the stage, rage dimming the pain in his leg. He felt metal in his pocket. A set of keys for the other doors.

On the other side of the stage he headed along the corridor, through the door and down the stairs, back into the hall from which he had recently emerged. He went to the first door and tried one of the keys, then the next. He felt the click and the door opened.

Like the room of Dain Collins, this was dimly lit. It was larger and full of beds. Lying on the beds were over a dozen young women, with several more lounging across mattresses on the floor. All had a vacant drugged look. Kit's felt tears sting his eyes. And hatred. He knelt down and spoke to the first young woman.

'Can you hear me?' he asked. She looked confused. He repeated the same in basic Spanish.

She nodded faintly.

'Are you well enough to get up?' he said, once more in Spanish.

Another faint nod. He helped her up. She seemed about Mary's age. Mexican. Kit pointed to the others. She spoke rapidly in Spanish. The others began to stir. Slowly they began to rise unsteadily to their feet.

Kit wasn't sure how far he could push his limited Spanish, so he motioned with his hand for them to follow him instead. They did. Hesitantly at first, then into the light.

*

'Do you really think my men are going to let you just walk out of the club like this?' asked Lehane in a reasonable voice. They passed the door of his office. He looked at the office with a sense of longing. If only he'd stayed. In fact, for the rest of his life, until his death in a nursing home in Albuquerque in 1953, he would replay that moment when a beautiful English woman had asked him that question. Every day.

Hammett was also wondering the same thing, but things seemed to be going swingingly well so far. What could possibly go wrong, apart from everything. The club was mostly empty, but they still had to get through the front door. At this point they were in the hands of an elderly Englishman who seemed, as he had said himself, a little squiffy. Hammett needed no Masters in original English to understand what this meant and the risk it posed to their venture. He felt like a duck entering a shooting gallery.

Alastair was certainly feeling more optimistic, bolstered as he was by the two cocktails consumed watching first Mary and then the shooting show. It had been years since he had enjoyed an evening so thoroughly. However, he was rapidly sobering up as he saw what lay ahead. Two of Lehane's men stood menacingly at the door. He moved closer to Lehane and jabbed a metallic reminder into the base of the nightclub owner's spine that this was not the time or place for anything foolhardy.

However, Eddie Lehane had not opened a nightclub, bought off a portion of the San Francisco police and a few politicians without having some, as his Mexican staff might say, *cojones*. Several of Lehane's men milled around the entrance, still stunned by what was happening. If he timed his warning right, he could be out of the way with Bernie in the line of fire. His men would soon take care of the rest.

He was just on the point of shouting to his men when he heard the first of the police sirens. More followed. The situation had worsened. He was going to have to play the game of his life. It was a tribute to the extent of his influence that he fancied his chances. The group walked through into the night air unimpeded. A crowd remained outside, standing in small groups, unsure of where to go. Lehane nodded to the senator who was clearly angry. Yes, there was still a chance to rescue the situation.

'What now, Mulroney? Look around you. Who d'you think is going down here?'

Hammett and Mulroney did, indeed, look around. A lot of important people were waiting for their drivers. The young women had melted away into the night.

The police cars pulled up to the front. Lehane turned and looked at Hammett standing with Mulroney. He put his hand in his pocket and calmly took out a cigarette box.

'Hope you don't mind if I don't offer you one. They're imported from Turkey. So, what are you going to say? It seems to me you've shot up my nightclub and ruined the night of a good many people who can see you directing traffic for the rest of your lousy career, Mulroney.'

A police sergeant walked towards the group. He was in his fifties and probably months rather than years away from retirement. The last thing he wanted was this kind of hassle. He asked, 'What's going on here Mr Lehane?'

Mister? Both Hammett and Mulroney thought the same thing at this moment. Their second thought was also identical. This ain't good.

Lehane smiled at the policemen, 'Sergeant Jefferson, good to see you again.' He indicated Hammett and Mulroney. 'These two men have just shot up my nightclub. The old guy behind them is holding a gun to my back.'

The policeman walked to the side and did, indeed, see the elderly gentleman in question and the pistol. Alastair smiled at Sergeant Jefferson and said, 'Nice evening, isn't it?'

'Put the gun down sir. On the ground.'

Alastair complied, 'If you wish.'

Lehane turned around to face the Englishman and said, 'You are in so much trouble, I actually I feel sorry for you.'

It was from this angle he got a view of something that put a ribbon on his evening. A black ribbon. Behind Alastair's shoulder, led by Kit, was a line of young women, dressed in thin slips, trooping like sleepwalkers out of the club. They were coming in the direction of Lehane and the police.

Hammett looked from Kit to the young women and back again. He was shocked by their appearance. The tell-tale vacancy in their eyes. It seemed like the *Día de Muertos*. Lehane turned to face Hammett and Mulroney. Defeat was carved into his face. This would require more than a few friends down at the Hall. Hammett pointed towards something behind Lehane. Lehane turned around he saw the senator climbing into a car. When he turned back, he was caught by a punch thrown by Hammett flush on the jaw. He collapsed like a deflated balloon.

Kit looked on with approval. A similar thought had crossed his mind. He was only vaguely aware of someone virtually jumping on him from the side. Seconds later he was holding his fiancée. She was crying with joy and sadness, fear and relief.

'What about Dain Collins?' asked Hammett,

Kit nodded to Hammett while he hugged Mary.

'Harry?' asked Mary.

The Frisco Falcon

Kit looked over at Hammett and explained the role that Harry had played in the rescue. He finished by saying, 'I trust he'll find a job with you.'

Hammett nodded. The image of Cowan lying dead in the street rose up before his eyes.

'I'll see to it. We have a vacancy.'

He glanced back at Kit. By now the Englishman was being rewarded for his bravery by his fiancée. Or perhaps he was rewarding Mary. She had pluck, and a lot else besides, much of it on show too. Lucky guy thought Hammett, but without resentment.

*

Just after midnight Alastair dropped Kit, Mary and Agatha outside *Bellavista* then drove to the hospital where Dain Collins had been taken by Algy. They walked up the path towards the house and knocked on the door.

Ella-Mae answered. She saw the three English guests and a look of anxiety came into her eyes.

Mary smiled and put a hand on her arm, 'Don't worry, everyone is safe. Even Uncle Alastair. A hero, in fact. They're with Miss Collins at the hospital.'

Ella-Mae smiled her thanks, and obvious relief. The group walked into the house. It felt wonderful to be back, thought Kit. Suddenly he felt his arm being tugged by Mary. He frowned a question.

'Something I meant to speak to you about.' She pulled his arm gently towards the library. Meanwhile Ella-Mae took Agatha's coat and asked her if she wanted anything.

'A pot of tea, I think. We've earned it.' Ella-Mae turned towards the kitchen, leaving Agatha alone in the entrance hall.

She looked around her and called out, 'Christopher? Mary? Where are you? Ella-Mae's gone to make some tea.'

Twenty seconds later Kit emerged from the library if not dishevelled, then not quite 'shevelled either. Mary followed, an enigmatic smile on her face. She looked at Agatha and said, 'Did you say tea?'

Agatha said 'Yes,' then looked at the large coat Mary was wearing. 'Where on earth did you get that coat? I don't remember you wearing it earlier.'

Kit, meanwhile, was frantically pointing at something. Mary glanced downwards. Her dress from the nightclub was hanging outside her pocket. She smiled at Agatha and quickly pushed it deep into her pocket. With her other free hand, she pulled the coat around her more tightly.

'I couldn't find my coat in the rush,' explained Mary brightly, then motioned with her head upstairs. 'I should really go and get changed.'

With a grin to Kit she turned and ran to the stairs. Agatha looked at Mary padding barefoot up the stairs, still clinging to her coat.

'Is it really that cold in here?'

Kit answered by clapping his hands together and then wrapping his arms around himself.

'Beastly draught from somewhere.'

'Really, I hadn't noticed,' said Agatha looking around, bemused.

Agatha and Alastair sat at the end of the garden in the twilight. Ella-Mae had just deposited two gin and tonics as they contemplated the sun turning the sky mauve and orange. After a busy day shuttling between the hospital, City Hall and *Bellavista*, they'd earned it.

Alastair's mood was more sombre than one might have suspected. The full picture emerging from the Lehane affair was beginning to become clear. His feelings were somewhere between anger at how Lehane had been able to run a business such as this and the ongoing guilt he felt about his treatment of his son and fiancée.

Agatha also seemed out of sorts. Or perhaps it was fatigue. Alastair looked at her. She wouldn't see seventy again and she was up to her neck in adventure and crime. He looked at the view and his spirits managed the improbable feat of rising and falling in equal measure.

'I remember how you used to sit here with Christina,' said Agatha. Alastair smiled but his eyes were clouding. He was silent for a moment.

'It's the loneliness. I never expected that. Maybe it will change with Algernon when he marries, but...' He couldn't finish the sentence. Then he looked at Agatha. Her eyes were moist. This was rare.

'Do you miss him?'

'Useless?'

'Yes, Eustace.' chuckled Alastair.

'Every day.'

He took her hand and together they gazed across the bay.

Jack Murray

*

The visitors arrived just after six. Hammett and Mulroney were led through the house and into the garden by Ella-Mae. Kit was sitting with Mary and Algy on the porch. They too seemed sombre of mood. Mary looked at Kit with concern. He had been unusually silent all day. Initially she'd assumed that it was a reaction to the desolate human beings he had rescued. As the day progressed, she wondered if something else was on his mind. He would tell her when the time came.

Algy was also quiet. His good humour and ebullient nature had deserted him. Mary wondered if doubt had set in about his impending marriage. So much had happened to Dain, so much suggested of her past. Of course, her sympathies were entirely with the young woman. She'd been exploited, drugged and made an addict. What she needed was someone to take care of her now. She hoped Algy would be that person. At that moment, Mary was unsure.

Algy stood up to greet the visitors and then went to fix them some drinks. Hammett watched him go.

'I would've thought he'd be happier,' said Hammett, looking closely at Kit.

'Give him time. Algy's a good egg,' answered Kit, trying to keep things light.

'A bit soft, isn't he?' replied Hammett.

'You're more hard-boiled, then?' said Mary with a smile.

'I guess I am.'

A silence descended on the group. Mary glanced at Kit. He and Hammett seemed to be studying one another. Something was wrong but Mary couldn't understand what. She was desperately curious. Then Algy returned with the drinks.

'Thanks,' said the two men in unison as they were handed their whiskies.

'Social call?' asked Algy, sitting down. There was a tightness in his voice. The sight of the two men was a reminder that they had all but accused Dain of murder.

'Not quite,' said Mulroney. 'We've had some news about your fiancée.'

Algy gripped the seat, 'I saw her earlier. They said she'd be alright.'

'From New York,' replied Mulroney.

'What do you mean?'

Mulroney looked uncomfortable. He glanced at Hammett then back to Algy.

'Dain Collins killed a man.'

There were gasps around the table. Even Kit looked shocked by the news. Algy was on his feet. His eyes were blazing. 'That's a damn lie,' he shouted.

Hammett eyed him closely. 'It's true. But a witness to the killing confirmed it was self-defence.'

Mulroney continued, 'She killed her step-father. Her name is Danielle Masters. We've reason to believe she'd been abused by this man. The maid in the house saw everything. She ran from the house and escaped using the car. She's been missing for six months now. She changed the colour of her hair, and with the help of Lehane, her name. In return she agreed to act as a hostess at his club. That was his hold over her. That and dope. He gave her dope to help her depression. She became hooked.'

Algy, now slumped in his chair, was listening to it all.

'How did Goodman become involved?' asked Kit.

Hammett answered, 'He wanted to embarrass the Aston family by having their son take up with a woman who was conceivably a murderer or, at the very least, a prostitute.'

Algy suddenly rose from his seat and looked like he wanted to kill Hammett. It felt like unfinished business, him and Hammett.

'Easy soldier,' said Hammett casually. 'There's no evidence to suggest that she was anything other than a hostess. But she was a plant. Her job was to make you fall in love with her. Strange thing is, I think she got into the part too well. In the end she was caught between three men, all wanting something from her. Lehane using her as a touch of class for his joint, Goodman using her for revenge against your father and you, Mr Aston.'

'I wasn't using her,' he snarled.

'Are you still going to marry her, Galahad?' asked Hammett, evenly. The look on his face suggested he didn't think so. Algy was silent but his face reddened from anger or shame. Hammett looked at Mulroney and continued the story.

'We think our man Cowan found out who she was. He worked in New York and still had some contacts. He put two and two together. He may have tried to blackmail Miss Masters. He was a swell sort of guy.'

'Does that mean it was Lehane or Goodman who had Mr Cowan murdered?' asked Mary.

There was silence for a few moments then Kit spoke. 'I don't think that's what Mr Hammett is driving at. Is it?'

They were joined at the table by Alastair and Agatha. Their arrival broke the spell for a few moments as Alastair uttered a few words of welcome to the visitors. He took a telegram out of his pocket and handed it to Kit.

The Frisco Falcon

'I almost forgot Kit, this arrived for you yesterday. In all of the excitement it had quite slipped my mind.'

Mary looked at Kit with her eyebrow raised.

Kit read the telegram and laughed sardonically. He looked up to the people gathered around him and said, 'From a contact at Scotland Yard. Apparently, our friend Jean-Valois does not work for either the French police or any other police force.'

'Bit late now,' pointed out Agatha, before draining the rest of her gin.

Alastair looked at his new guests. Noting their glasses were full he asked them, 'So what news of our friends?'

'They're in the caboose,' answered Mulroney.

Mary looked to Kit mystified. He shrugged.

Agatha shook her head and said in exasperation, 'Prison for goodness sakes. Don't you young people read anything?'

Alastair looked delighted at the news regarding Goodman. At last some good was going to come from this sordid affair. He said as much.

Mulroney explained, 'Apparently Goodman and Joel Israel stole this painting from a rich guy in Constantinople. They killed some ship's captain as well. With a harpoon if I understood correctly. Mr Goodman is going to spend a long time in a Turkish prison.'

'Well, it just gets better,' announced Alastair with a wide grin. However, he noted that neither Mulroney nor Hammett seemed quite so overjoyed by the news. But no matter, he thought.

Kit, too, had picked up on the mood of the two detectives from the moment they arrived. He felt uneasy as it chimed with his own thoughts of the last few hours.

'So, all's well that ends well,' said Alastair, hoping to raise the mood of the party. He could see it was doomed to fail.

'Not quite,' said Hammett.

'Why?' asked Alastair.

'We still have the death of Dan Cowan to consider.'

Kit noted he didn't say murder. He also noted Hammett was looking at him again. The longer the conversation went on, the heavier his heart felt. But this was something else. Alastair was asking the two detectives what they meant. He was becoming irritable. Kit recognised the signs.

'Uncle Alastair,' said Kit, which immediately silenced the elderly man. 'I think Mr Hammett and Mulroney aren't on a social call.'

Algy looked up and became aware that Kit and Hammett were both looking at him intently. He ran his hands through his hair once more. A look of desolation on his face. He looked up at his father. There were tears in his eyes.

'I killed him, father,' said Algy. 'I killed Cowan.'

'No, Algernon, stop at once,' said Alastair, a note of desperation in his voice.

'No, pops, it's true,' said Algy resignedly. 'It was an accident. You must believe me. He was blackmailing Dain. I confronted him. He said some awful things. Terrible things. Anyway, I lost my temper. He pulled a gun on me, but I was past caring. I just wanted to...'

'Kill him?' asked Hammett.

Algy glared at Hammett, 'Yes, I wanted to kill him. But that's not what happened. I swiped the gun out of the way. The gun went off. I smacked him. I smacked him hard. He fell down and hit the back of his head against the table. He was dead. I couldn't believe it.'

Algy collapsed into tears, repeating I killed him, over and over again. Alastair went over to him and put a hand on his shoulder.

'Don't worry son, I think the gentlemen can see your story is true. And we have Saul. This is a clear case of self-defence.'

'Saul Finkelstein?' asked Mulroney, his face sinking.

Alastair almost grinned at this point. He nodded and said 'Yes, Saul Finkelstein.'

A few minutes later, Algy was taken away by Mulroney to be charged. Alastair was already on the phone to his lawyer. When he came back to the group, he seemed in better spirits.

'Saul will meet them down at City Hall. Somehow, I don't think this will end so badly. It sounds as if Mr Cowan was a bigger gangster than Lehane.'

Hammett could not disagree with this assessment but felt an uneasy sense of loyalty if not to Cowan, then to the idea of what a colleague is. He said nothing to this. He looked up at Alastair Aston.

'Your son will do time, however good Finkelstein is, and I've heard he's good.'

Alastair looked away. He knew this also. There was little chance Algy could escape some form of incarceration. What was left was the hope that the justice system would see the circumstances, the individuals involved and mitigate their sentence accordingly.

'What about Dain Collins or Danielle Masters? Will the same happen to her?' asked Mary.

'No, I think that the story of the maid makes it clear that Miss Masters, and the maid also, were in danger of being killed. It's a much stronger case for self-defence.'

271

Kit looked at his uncle. His stomach tightened as he felt the guilt slowly envelop him. The overwhelming feeling that he should have done more to protect Algy. His uncle returned his gaze. Mary held her breath. Would he see Kit's actions as betrayal? She hoped not. The two men were standing a few feet apart.

Silence.

A light wind licked against Mary's face as she looked at her fiancé and his uncle.

'Uncle Alastair,' started Kit. He paused. What could he say? Sorry for helping jail your son?

But there was no hatred in his uncle's eyes, just understanding. Tears also. As much as he believed his son, as much as he trusted Saul, the future was uncertain. He shook his head and put his hand on Kit's arm.

'My boy, you did the right thing. I would ask no less from you.'

My boy thought Mary. She heard it again. My boy. A thought, an idea. An unsayable truth. Mary was aware of Aunt Agatha's eyes on her. The two ladies locked eyes for a moment.

My boy.

Families have secrets.

Mary turned to Kit. His face could not hide the despair he was feeling. There were no words of comfort, though. They would come later. For now, she held him.

'What will happen to Danielle now?' asked Mary, after a while.

It was Alastair who answered, 'She stays here until Algernon returns. The poor girl has been through enough.'

His manner had changed. Gone was the haunted gaze. He stood erect, a fire in his eyes. He turned to Hammett.

'How long do you think it will take to cure her of this terrible illness?'

'A week, no more than two,' said Hammett. He seemed satisfied by what he'd heard. He added, 'All she's known are men out to use her. She needs help.' Hammett paused for a moment and looked at Alastair. 'Will you look after her?'

The two men faced each other. Alastair nodded. Hammett exhaled then nodded also. Then Alastair turned and shouted, 'Ella-Mae.'

'Yes,' said a voice behind him.

'I do wish you wouldn't do that, anyway...'

'I've made up her bedroom,' interrupted Ella-Mae.

'Oh, well, very good,' said Alastair. He went with the housekeeper, giving instructions that, apparently, had already been carried out. At last Mary felt able to smile as the two elderly combatants' voices receded into the distance.

Hammett turned to Kit, 'At least there's one decent man in this city.'

Kit looked at Hammett and smiled.

'I think there are two, Mr Hammett.'

*

The job was finished. It was time to write it up for the company files. Time to get Geauque back on his case for writing such elaborate summaries. They were meant to be reports, he would say, not fiction.

Hammett stood up. The moment had come for him to leave. Kit and Mary rose and accompanied him through the mansion to the entrance hall.

'How did you know it was Algy, by the way?' asked Kit. Hammett smiled and shook his head.

'The hat: Cowan wasn't wearing his hat. It meant the body had been moved. I guessed someone like Algy would have had the strength to do this, certainly not Dain Collins. After this it was more of a feeling. He had the motive. He's a strong kid, so he certainly had the wherewithal. And he had the temper. How about you?'

Kit grinned, 'Normally I'm in favour of facts and evidence.'

'Me too,' said Hammett laughing.

'Rather like you, I had a bad feeling. Then when I saw how you were ragging him...'

'Sorry?' asked Hammett, smiling. 'I don't speak English so good.'

'You don't do too badly if I may say. Anyway, I could see you were goading him. I realised then that you suspected him of the killing.'

'Remind me not to play poker against you.'

Mary stepped forward and gave the Pinkerton man a peck on his cheek and thanked him. Then she asked him, 'What will you do now?'

Hammett shrugged, 'I have to write the case notes up. I think I'll call it the Case of the Maltan Falcon. Has a nice ring to it, don't you think?'

Mary made a face that indicated not. She pointed out, 'There's no such word as Maltan, Mr Hammett.'

'Really?' asked Hammett, a little perplexed and clearly disappointed. 'What should it be, then?'

So Mary told him.

The Frisco Falcon

Coda

His heart was pounding as hard as rain bouncing off the sidewalk. He was soaked. The sooner this case was over the better. He stepped off the sidewalk onto the road. Gutters were overflowing. His foot was submerged in a puddle. He swore. Ahead he could see his quarry. The man he was after had ducked into a pool hall. His heart sank. This would make it difficult. He glanced up at his partner.

Or maybe not.

Danny's Pool Hall was a dive best avoided. Situated in a semi-derelict part of town, only the most hardened of hard cases found themselves here. Even the cockroaches carried knives.

The letter 'L' was missing from the word 'Pool' resulting in child passers-by stopping and sniggering. He motioned to his partner to follow him. They were outside the pool hall now.

'Stay here. I'll go in first and see if I can reason with him. If it looks like trouble, then do what you think best.'

His partner nodded.

He pushed the door open and walked in like he was a regular. His throat felt dry and he found breathing difficult. His hand reached inside his pocket seeking something metal to reassure him. Any hope of quietly slipping into the joint was killed quicker than a stooly at a convicts' convention. Everyone looked up from their pool games. There was a hush, aside from one player who had just played a shot. It clicked against another ball.

"Lazy-Bones" Larry clapped his hands, slowly. 'Well, well, well. If it ain't my old pal Foley. What brings you here?'

275

'I need you to come with me, Larry,' said Foley. 'Now,' he added with a certainty he wasn't feeling.

"Lazy-Bones" started laughing. He was joined by half a dozen other players. Then the laughing stopped and six friends of "Lazy-Bones" picked up their cues and began to advance slowly on Foley.

The door opened behind Foley.

'This is my friend,' said Foley. 'His name's Harry. He dislikes rudeness. I mean, he really, really doesn't like rude people.'

The pool players stopped and looked at one another. Harry was around seven feet of very bad news. None of the players particularly liked "Lazy-Bones" anyway. At that moment the joint's name accurately reflected the churning stomachs of the six men who knew their next move would be one of the most important decisions of their lives.

It wasn't a difficult decision.

*

Frank Nelson put the phone down after passing the message to the woman. He felt uncomfortable, however. It hadn't felt right. A few minutes later he went back and phoned Lehane again. No answer. He tried again ten minutes later. Still no answer. He shrugged. Nothing else to be done. He went home. To bed.

He arrived at City Hall, around eight the next morning. He exited at eight fifteen minus his badge and gun. All the way out of the building he saw his former colleagues looking at him. They were shaking their heads. He suspected they were not disapproving of him being on the take so much as getting caught so stupidly. They were right.

At the exit of City Hall, he saw the young policeman, Moore, standing waiting for someone. Nelson's mood was pretty sour. One last poke at the kid would do his mood the world of good he thought. He walked over to the young man.

'Waiting for your boyfriend?' asked Nelson.

'No, you.'

Moments later Nelson was lying on the sidewalk, his nose broken and head ringing.

'Bye, sweetie,' said Moore, turning and walking back into the Hall.

*

Evening at Lake Como was breath-taking from where Comte Jean-Valois du Bourbon was standing. He was just inside the entrance to the villa, a long journey at an end. He removed his cloak and walked through the villa to the terrace. The colour of the sky was cyan blue.

A man and a woman were sitting on the terrace. A bottle of white wine was open. There were three glasses. Bourbon could think of no better way to celebrate the arrival of their prize. The two people were young, perhaps his age or younger. Both had blond hair. The woman's hair was a bubbling mass of curls, untamed, untameable. The man's hair was combed apart from a strand that descended lazily from his forehead. He had a trimmed moustache. Everything about him, his voice, his posture, his clothes suggested nobility.

Both looked up at the new arrival. They knew one another too well for formalities. The man pushed the seat out, then removed the wine bottle from the ice bucket and poured white wine into Bourbon's glass as he took his seat.

'Merci, mon ami,' said Bourbon. He kissed the young woman on both cheeks.

'Good to see you again, Jean-Valois. And congratulations. A job well done. We can't wait to hear all about it,' said the man.

'First things first, Olly,' said Bourbon. From his pocket he extracted a rolled-up piece of newspaper. He placed it on the table and unrolled it. Inside was a painting of a falcon.

'It's beautiful,' said Olly Lake. 'What do you think, Kristina?'

She smiled that enigmatic smile and nodded.

'I said hello to Lord Aston for you,' said Bourbon.

A shadow fell over Olly Lake's eyes.

Kit.

Kristina saw the change in mood in her lover. She held his hand. She said in an accent with more than hint of Russian, 'Strange how your paths keep crossing.'

Olly Lake exhaled.

'Can't you persuade him to join us?' asked Bourbon.

Lake shook his head, then stopped himself. Was it possible? Could he really do this? How? He thought about the young woman Kit was to marry. An idea occurred to him. An idea so terrible he stopped himself thinking any further about it. Kit was his friend. Had been his friend. A brother almost. But every war had casualties. Friends, enemies, sons, daughters, lovers, husbands and wives.

Could he do this to Kit?

One more?

For the greater good?

'I don't know,' said Lake. 'I do know we'll see him again, though.' He picked up his glass, it felt heavy in his hand. He forced a smile. The others held their glasses up also. They clinked.

'To the future. A new future.'

The Frisco Falcon

The courtroom was packed. On one side sat the prosecution, looking on grimly as a little lawyer strode backwards and forwards, like an amateur Hamlet, mid soliloquy. This was Saul Finkelstein's stage. It was his coliseum. He was the lion, and the pasty-faced prosecutor was a sacrificial victim.

'And so, gentlemen of the jury,' said Saul Finkelstein, 'this man, this war hero sits before you guilty only of, once more, putting the life of another before his own. He is not a murderer, he is the protector of an innocent, young girl whose life has been a testimony to the exploitative, baser instincts of men.'

Far from using this as his big finish, Saul Finkelstein, one hour into his summing up, was just beginning to warm to the task.

'Let me tell you about the type of family this man has come from.'

The opposing prosecutor nestled deep into the cushion he had brought specially. It was going to be a long afternoon.

Alastair Aston gazed out at the audience. Half a dozen pressmen and another dozen civic politicians, notaries and wives of said public officials looked on at the man and the young woman standing beside him outside the Christina Alvarez Shelter for Young Women.

To the ringing applause of all present Alastair said, 'I hereby declare this centre open.' He nodded to the young woman holding his hand. She duly cut a ribbon taped across the double doors of the building. He looked at her and grinned, whispering, 'Don't stab me.'

279

Jack Murray

The look of mischief in the grey-green eyes of the young woman suggested he was safe for the time being. She chuckled as she held his hand. Her laughter was the sound of water skipping over rocks in a brook during summer. Alastair's heart swelled and he felt tears begin to sting his eyes.

Tears of joy.

*

Sidney Goodman also felt like crying. The heat was unbearable. If that wasn't enough, the food in his new residence was unendurable. He had lost weight. A lot of weight, in fact. Not that many would have noticed.

It was just after lunch. The prison yard was full. Yet, Goodman stood alone for the very good reason he spoke not a word of Turkish. There were not many English speakers in the Constantinople jail. In fact, to his knowledge, there was only one other.

Across the prison yard he saw Joel Israel looking daggers at him. They still had not exchanged so much as a pleasantry since Goodman's mean spirited and, in hindsight, ill-judged criticism of his former partner back in San Francisco.

The thought of San Francisco was like a corked wine on the palate of this aesthete. He had to escape. This life could not continue. His mind turned over a thousand possibilities, all stumbling at the one inescapable reality. Unless he could communicate with those around him, his only weapon, his one great gift was rendered redundant.

He felt the presence of another man beside him. Asurman Yildiz was serving life for murdering, amongst others, his wife, her lover and her lover's family. He had committed the murders thirty-three years previously. Goodman looked at the old man and shuddered.

The Frisco Falcon

Yildiz looked at Goodman and smiled a shy, toothless smile. He raised his eyebrows hopefully. Gad, thought Goodman, I must find a way out of this hell-hole. Learn Turkish perhaps? Maybe there was a way of reconciling with Joel. There had to be a way out.

He felt the hand of Yildiz brush against his own.

*

He removed his wide-brimmed sable fedora and mopped his brow. Malta was cauldron-hot. This castle particularly beastly. Placing the hat back on his head he scratched his two-day stubble. He couldn't wait to shave. Damn thing itched like buggery, he thought, although he'd never actually attempted this particular pastime, unlike some others in his form. He put his hand in the pocket of his leather flying jacket and extracted a whip.

Below him was darkness. It might either be a drop of twenty feet or even one hundred feet or more. The chasm was five feet wide. Across the other side was the object of his attention. It was sitting in an alcove carved into the stone wall. A small bird, a falcon, sat on a tiny plinth. This bird didn't sing. It glistened. Hundreds of precious gems decorated its body. The reflection of light from these gems danced on the walls around them. Red, blue, green and violet shades.

The man set down his fire-lit torch. He glanced up at a beam of wood, eight feet or so overhead. He took the leather whip and cracked it in the direction of the beam.

It missed.

Reggie Pilbream wasn't a man to give up easily, unless his aunt insisted, of course. Aunts were definitely in the category of extenuating circumstances and no chap could be blamed for stopping, immediately, anything that he was enjoying.

He cracked the whip again. Success. It curled around its target like a missed three-footer. Reggie tugged at the whip. It was secure. Holding the handle in both hands he took a few steps back and swung across the chasm. He clattered into the rock across the other side, causing the falcon to topple over and down, down, down into the dark shaft below.

As he was about to pronounce this accident as beastly luck, he heard a swishing sound coming from the side. He turned to the source of the noise and saw a steel mace, with spikes protruding from, what looked like, a skull. Reggie immediately appreciated three things. The workmanship was wonderfully imaginative. It was also deadly. Worse, however, the mace's direction of travel seemed likely to arrive somewhere around his head.

'Oh bug....'

The End

If you enjoyed this book, please consider leaving a review on Amazon. It really makes a difference.

Follow me on Facebook:
https://www.facebook.com/jackmurraypublishing

The Frisco Falcon

Research Notes

This is a work of fiction. However, it references real-life individuals. Gore Vidal, in his introduction to Lincoln, writes that placing history in fiction or fiction in history has been unfashionable since Tolstoy and that the result can be accused of being neither. He defends the practice, pointing out that writers from Aeschylus to Shakespeare to Tolstoy have done so with not inconsiderable success and merit.

I have mentioned a number of key real-life individuals and events in this novel. My intention, in the following section, is to explain a little more about their connection to this period and this story.

For further reading on Dashiell Hammett I would recommend his fiction. His stories are often based on his real-life experiences as a Pinkerton Detective. Novels such as 'The Maltese Falcon' and 'The Dain Curse' are clearly major inspirations for this book. Mike Humbert also provides excellent source research material on Hammett - http://www.mikehumbert.com/Dashiell_Hammett_18_Flood_ Building.html.

Dashiell Hammett (1894 - 1961)

Dashiell Hammett was one of the originators of the 'hard-boiled' school of crime writing. His stories were based, unusually for crime writers, on personal experience. He joined the Pinkerton Detective Agency in 1915, at the age of 20. Moving to San Francisco, California, he continued his work with agency before enlisting in the U.S. Army during World War I. While he was in France he contracted tuberculosis

,which limited his direct involvement in the War. The illness was to remain with him throughout his life.

Upon his return from the War he re-joined Pinkerton's before leaving after 1922 and focusing full time on his writing. He found initial success publishing short stories with society magazine, *The Smart Set.* He began to take the detective story into new, grittier territories which found a home in pulp/crime publications of the time, including Black Mask. While still in San Francisco he began to write a series of novels that changed the face of crime writing in America.

Red Harvest and *The Dain Curse* arrived in 1929 featuring an unnamed character known as the Continental Op. *The Maltese Falcon* was published in 1930, introducing the legendary private eye, Sam Spade. *The Glass Key* arrived in 1931. Hammett's final full length novel was *The Thin Man*, published in 1934, featured Nick and Nora Charles. He was forty years old.

Within a few years, Hollywood called upon Hammett to write or co-write movie versions of The Thin Man and its follow ups.

His private life was troubled. An early marriage to a nurse he had met while in hospital for TB, fell apart within a few years. He had a long relationship with Lillian Hellman, however. His drinking and illness continued to afflict him throughout his life and probably stopped any further novels emerging. He endured a spell in jail during the McCarthy era due to his left leaning sympathies. He died of lung cancer in 1961.

The five novels he created between 1929-34 have proved to be enduring and hugely influential, not the least for this writer and the characters of Kit Aston and Mary Cavendish.

Phil Geauque (18?? - 1951)

Phil Geauque was a Pinkerton Detective in the late 1890's into the early 1900's in Chicago and San Francisco where he

The Frisco Falcon

had an office in the Flood Building as a Pinkerton Detective Agency supervisor. After Pinkerton's, Phil Geauque joined the U.S. Secret Service and served on the Franklin Delano Roosevelt's trip to Hawaii in 1934. He passed away 1951 in San Francisco.

He supervised author Dashiell Hammett in the early 1920's. He is widely believed to be the inspiration for the "Old Man" in his Continental Op books and stories.

The Maltese Falcon

The Maltese Falcon really did exist. As Sidney Goodman explains in the book, it was an annual tribute to Charles V by the Knights of St John in Malta.

More latterly the falcons created for John Huston's movie adaption of the book, starring Humphrey Bogart, have turned up. One was sold for $4.1 million at auction.

Caravaggio(1571 – 1610)

Even if he had not been one of the greatest ever artists, Michelangelo Merisi would certainly have been one of the most famous, or infamous. The dramatic use of light and dark in his paintings, *chiaroscuro*, made him an artist much in demand between the 1590's until his early death in 1610.

Although much his known about his life, his death is shrouded in mystery. Some believe it was a fever, others have written it was syphilis. More recent work on human remains uncovered in a church in Porto Ecole suggest his death could have been violent.

It is true Caravaggio's life was a reflection of the violent times in which he lived. He is known to have been involved in various violent incidents throughout his life, one of which resulted in the death of Ranuccio Tomassoni. The death, or murder, led to Caravaggio's escape to Naples followed by exile in Malta.

Jack Murray

Caravaggio is unquestionably one of the most influential artists ever. Influential art critic Bernard Berenson said, 'With the exception of Michelangelo, no other Italian painter has exercised so great an influence. Many contemporary artists, *Caravaggisti* copied his chiaroscuro style. More recently, German Expressionist film makers drew inspiration from the dramatic lighting featured in Caravaggio's paintings.

Caravaggio remains an artist for the ages.

The Frisco Falcon

About the Author

Jack Murray lives just outside London with his family. Born in Ireland he has spent most of his adult life in the England. His first novel, 'The Affair of the Christmas Card Killer' has been a global success. Five further Kit Aston novels have followed: 'The Chess Board Murders', 'The French Diplomat Affair' and 'The Phantom' and 'The Frisco Falcon' and 'The Medium Murders' is the sixth in the Kit Aston series. The next Kit Aston will be released in late 2021.

Jack has also published a spin-off series: the Agatha Aston mysteries is based on the very popular character Aunt Agatha. These are set in a period during the mid-1870's.

A new series will be published this summer based on the grandson of Chief Inspector Jellicoe.

Jack Murray

Acknowledgements

It is not possible to write a book on your own. There are contributions from so many people either directly or indirectly over many years. Listing them all would be an impossible task.

Special mention therefore should be made to my wife and family who have been patient and put up with my occasional grumpiness when working on this project.

My brother, John Convery and Charles Gray have also helped in proofing and made supportive comments that helped me tremendously.

My late father and mother both loved books. They encouraged a love of reading in me also. In particular, they liked detective books, so I must tip my hat to the two greatest writers of this genre, Sir Arthur and Dame Agatha.

Following writing, comes the business of marketing. My thanks to Mark Hodgson and Sophia Kyriacou for their advice on this important area. Also, a shout out to the wonderful folk on 20Booksto50k.

Finally, my thanks to the teachers who taught and nurtured a love of writing.